NO SAFE PLACE

DETECTIVE REBECCA ELLIS BOOK 1

ROBIN MAHLE

INKUBATOR
BOOKS

Published by Inkubator Books
www.inkubatorbooks.com

ISBN (eBook): 978-1-83756-057-8
ISBN (Paperback): 978-1-83756-058-5
ISBN (Hardback): 978-1-83756-059-2

1

The doors flew open to the night sky, and Claire cut through the swirl of snow flurries as she sprinted outside. The ground had refrozen and her balance briefly gave way on the newly formed ice. Out of breath, she hurried to the parking lot and fumbled for her keys. Her SUV was just ahead now. The lights flickered on as she pressed the remote entry and opened the driver's side door. Claire climbed inside and slammed it shut. Snowflakes clung to her blond hair, and her cheeks reddened from exertion and the bitter air.

With a trembling hand, she buckled her seatbelt and pressed the ignition. The engine turned over. "Calm down. Take a breath. You can't drive like this." Claire inhaled deeply to slow her racing pulse, and that was when it hit her. "Gas?" The odor grew stronger, and within moments, smoke billowed through the vents. "Oh God."

She quickly opened her door and reached over to unlock her seatbelt, but it wouldn't unlatch. "Come on. Come on." She pressed the button again, growing frantic as smoke filled the cabin. The open door offered her time, but the smoke turned thick and black. The plastic on the dash bubbled and warped from the rising heat. "Come on!" Claire tugged at the belt harder and harder. "Help! Help me!"

Flames ascended from the hood, small at first, but they grew and spread. When the orange glow flickered inside the air vents, Claire called out again, "Help!" Her cries appeared to go unheard as she yanked on the seatbelt over and over. She glanced at the passenger seat, where she'd left her phone. "It's gone."

The heat of the fire began to melt the plastic, and the dashboard lights flickered and sparked. Her gaze was drawn ahead toward the outdoor basketball courts several yards away, where she spotted headlights shining. Soon, a car's silhouette appeared through the smoke that still billowed inside. Her jaw dropped. "You followed me." A blast erupted and the flames rolled in like a wave. "No!" With her hands shielding her face, Claire gasped her final breath.

CARS PARKED along the street whipped into a frenzy of shrieks and flashing lights. Inside neighboring homes, dogs barked, lights flickered on, and the quiet suburb of Bangor awakened.

The weathered veteran of a forgotten war jolted awake in his recliner. He dropped his half-empty beer can onto the carpet while the familiar rumble plunged him into momentary confusion as he sought to recall the time and place.

He leaped from the chair, though his advanced age would see him suffer later for it, and threw open the blinds on his front window. With squinted eyes pressed between the slats, he gazed out. "The hell?" Tips of bright orange flames danced against a black sky and barren trees. "Oh no, the church." He snatched his phone from the side table.

"911. What is your emergency?"

"There's a fire coming from the Grace Community Church off Hickory Street. You gotta get here fast," he replied.

"Sir, do you know if anyone is injured?"

"Hell, I got no idea. I'm inside my house. I can go check..."

"No," the dispatcher cut in. "The best thing for you to do is to stay in your home. The fire department is on its way."

He ended the call and slipped on his shoes. On a hook mounted near his front door hung his coat. "Screw this. I'm going outside." He wasn't alone as curious neighbors stood in their frozen yards, wrapped in coats and untied snow boots. His next-door neighbor glanced at him, and he called out to her, "You know what the hell's going on? I called 911."

The retiree thrust her hands in her coat pockets. "It's definitely at the church. I can't see anything from here. They sending the fire department?"

"Yep." Even from where he stood, light from the fire bounced off his face. "Christ Almighty. What the hell happened?"

"Should we do something?" the woman asked. "What if someone needs help?"

"I'll go." The old man jogged into the street but stopped cold when a car's headlights captured him in its path. He pulled back as it sped by, barely missing him. "Slow down, you son of a bitch! Can't you see what's happening?" He hurried on toward the church, leading the charge as other neighbors joined him from farther down the street. They all reached the edge of the parking lot and he stopped on a dime. "Holy hell, that's a car on fire." The intense heat overpowered him a moment as he stumbled back and watched the flames consume the vehicle. "Is anyone inside?"

A younger man, likely in his forties, turned to him. "I don't know. I can hear the sirens. They're coming now. If anyone's in there, God help them."

Three fire engines roared onto the church's parking lot.

And in what appeared to have been a carefully orchestrated feat, firefighters jumped out, unleashed the hoses, spun off the hydrant cap, and doused the engulfed car. Moments later, black smoke infiltrated the grounds.

One of the firefighters waved his hands wildly and shouted at the onlookers, "I need you people to get back. Get back, now."

The old man surrendered his position. "All right. All right." He fell back alongside his neighbors, who all stood in the middle of the street.

The retired woman from next door meandered toward him. "What'd you see up there, Bill?"

He turned squarely at her. "The mouth of the devil."

BANGOR POLICE DETECTIVE Rebecca Ellis sat behind the wheel of her Chevy Tahoe and observed the fire trucks' spinning red and blue lights ahead. Several bystanders huddled in below-freezing temperatures near the end of the street. "I'm going to take a stab and say this is the right place."

Her partner, Detective Euan McCallister, returned a cock-eyed grin. "What gave it away?"

"The new guy's trying his hand at humor." Ellis pulled onto the church parking lot and stopped behind the fire chief's SUV. Her eyes crinkled at the corners. "Maybe keep trying."

McCallister opened his door to step out. "I think I'm going to like working with you, Ellis."

She grabbed her parka from the backseat and buttoned it over her slender frame. Donning a wool hat, her straight blonde hair lay just above her shoulders. And before the cold air could blunt her senses, the stench hit her. "I don't remember the last time I smelled burnt flesh."

"Probably not something you want to remember." The 38-year-old wiry Detective McCallister pushed his hand through his full head of brown hair as he focused on the charred metal. He clenched his square jaw when the smell struck him. "It'll be tough to get out whoever's inside. If it's a leather seat, the skin will have fused to it."

"Thanks for the visual." Ellis shut her door and headed toward the scene, where an ambulance waited, and the fire trucks prepared to leave. "Excuse me, Chief Gifford?"

The Bangor fire chief turned to her. "Detective Ellis, I see you drew the lucky straw. Who's this you got with you?"

"Detective Euan McCallister. He's new. I'd tell you more about him, but it's probably best to wait and see if he pans out."

McCallister offered his hand. "Chief Gifford, nice to meet you. I think this is Ellis's idea of hazing, but just so you know, I don't intend on going anywhere."

Gifford returned the greeting. "Good to hear. So, Detectives, are you ready to see what's inside?"

"What or who?" She walked on with McCallister beside her.

At 34, Rebecca Ellis had already been with the Bangor PD for over a decade. She started off in uniform and worked the streets. The department's old-timers often regaled her with stories of Retired Detective Hank Ellis, her father. Most of which, she had heard countless times. No doubt, he had been a great detective and retired from the force five years ago. That had been right around the time Ellis passed her detective's exam.

While many female officers elbowed their way into that boys' club, things here were different. It could have been because she'd practically grown up in the department. Funny thing was, Ellis never thought the other officers saw her as a woman. She was, and would always be, Hank Ellis's daughter.

The detectives advanced toward the still-smoldering remnants of what appeared to have once been an SUV. Ellis eyed the driver's door. "Glass on the ground, and the door is open."

"If it was open, why couldn't the driver get out?" McCallister asked.

"Good question." Ellis peered inside and briefly averted her eyes from the horrific scene within. Blackened chunks of flesh, scorched bones, and a slack jaw, suggestive of someone who had screamed for help that never came. Her stomach lurched, and bile climbed in her throat. The smell was overpowering. "Jesus. Do we know who this is yet?"

"No, ma'am. Female victim, but the rest is why you all are here," the chief replied. "I will say this was a fire that originated in the engine compartment."

"How can you tell?" she asked.

"Well, I've seen enough in my lifetime, but come over here. I'll show you." Gifford walked to the front of the vehicle. "See the burn patterns on the hood? You'll see a radial burn pattern on the doors too. And if you look at the dash. Come on back this way." He walked ahead. "The heat built up inside to the point that the bottom of the windshield was severely damaged. This is indicative of an engine compartment fire. The soot on the glass fragments suggests the same. If the fire had started inside the vehicle, the glass would've failed and fallen inward. Here you see some of it blown out around the exterior venting."

Ellis turned to her partner. "Euan, see if you can read the license plate. I'm going to check out the VIN." She leaned toward the windshield and pushed away the soot with her finger. "Still legible." With her phone in hand, she snapped a picture.

McCallister returned to her. "Plates are damaged, but you can still read the numbers."

Ellis rubbed the back of her neck as she walked around the vehicle. He continued beside her when she turned toward the road and into the biting wind. "We don't have some of the luxuries you had in Boston. We're a department of ten. See that unit approaching now?"

"Yeah, I see it," McCallister replied.

"That's our evidence tech. No CSI here. It's you, me, and that guy right there." She returned a measured gaze. "We miss something critical? It's on us."

"So let's not miss anything," he replied.

She waited while the unit pulled up and the officer rolled down his window.

"Detective Ellis, where would you like me to start?"

"Inside the vehicle first so we can get the body out and have a proper look," she replied.

"Yes, ma'am." The officer stepped out and grabbed his kit. He approached the vehicle and took photos of the body and everything else inside the car.

Ellis cupped her hands at her mouth for warmth and rubbed them together. "Let's take a walk while he does his thing."

"You got it," McCallister replied.

The snow on the parking lot was marred by tire tracks, and the heat from the fire had melted everything within 100 feet of the vehicle. Ellis looked out among the bystanders. "A singular vehicle in this lot catches fire with a woman inside. Her cries for help go unanswered."

McCallister nodded with a raised brow. "You're assuming she cried for help."

"The driver's side door was open. She screamed her head off, you can bet on it. And you got houses just over the street. It had to have happened quick. Before anyone could help, that SUV lit up the sky."

"She should've been able to get out," McCallister said.

"My thoughts exactly."

The evidence tech called out to them, "You two are up."

They returned to the SUV and Ellis approached him. "Well?"

The officer rocked back on his heels. "Not a hell of a lot to find, Detective. Interior's damn near melted. I documented what I could, but maybe you two will have better luck."

"We can get her out?" she asked.

"You're all clear." He returned to his unit.

Ellis caught up with the chief. "Okay, let's get her out of there."

"I'll get the equipment and my guys." The chief headed toward one of his fire trucks.

McCallister folded his arms, and cocked his head as he studied the vehicle. "What do you think? Fuel leak? Not a lot of things can make a car catch fire like that. You get vapors from the puddle of leaked gas getting sucked into the cylinders when the ignition starts, gas dripping onto components maybe, and then the spark plugs fire off. There you go."

"The engine heats up, or even faulty electrical wiring, along with the smallest leak would combust." Ellis continued to examine the SUV. "The neighbors reported hearing a bomb blast. My guess is, once the fire started in the engine, as the chief suggested, it reached the tank. No doubt it would've sounded like a bomb. Thing is, if it was a leak, the victim should've smelled the gas before getting in or, at least, soon after. Can you do me a favor and see what you can find on this VIN and the plates? We're going to be here for a while till they get her out."

"You got it." He walked away.

"Hang on a second," Ellis called out. "What I said before to the chief...I didn't mean anything by it. It was just me being a smartass."

He returned a crooked smile. "I know. They all said you were wicked funny. Personally, I don't see it."

"Hey, now, that's because you haven't seen my best stuff. I was just warming up." She grinned as he walked on.

Chief Gifford returned with his team. "Detective Ellis, we're ready when you are."

She stepped back. "Okay, do your thing. This smell's getting to me. I'll wait over here if you don't mind."

"Sure thing, and hey, be grateful you aren't used to it. I can't say the same." The chief turned to his team. "Let's get that door off first, guys."

Ellis felt a tap on her shoulder and spun around. An athletic young man with dark gelled hair stood next to her. "Sir, you need to get back behind the yellow tape."

"I work here," he replied. "I'm the youth pastor at this church. We had a service earlier this evening."

"You work here? What's your name?"

"Jeff Harwick. I forgot something and drove back and saw all this. What happened?" The man looked on in horror. "Did someone die?"

Ellis ushered him back behind the tape. "Mr. Harwick, do you recognize that SUV?"

"What's left of it? No, not really."

She peered at it again. "Right, yeah. You say the church held a service tonight? What time was that?"

"Seven pm," Harwick began. "Our Tuesday service starts at seven and ends at 8:30. Sometimes, the older kids and I stick around until nine or so, depending on what needs to be done. The younger kids go home with their parents."

Ellis jotted down the notes. "Were you here until nine tonight? Do you recall seeing any other vehicles in the parking lot when you left?"

He looked on while the firefighters pried off the driver's door. "Dear Lord."

"Mr. Harwick? I need you to look at me now, okay? Was anyone else still here when you left tonight?" She caught sight of McCallister as he approached but kept her focus on the pastor. "Jeff?"

The young man cleared his throat and returned his attention to her. "Um, I-I don't know. I wasn't paying attention. I should call Pastor Zeke. He should be here."

"Ellis?" McCallister drew her attention. "I got a hit on the SUV. You want to come take a look?" He headed back to the cordoned-off area.

"I'll be right back, Jeff, okay? Don't leave." Ellis followed her partner. "Who does it belong to?"

"Who's the kid?" he asked.

"The youth pastor. He says he couldn't recall whether anyone was still around when he left earlier tonight." She wiped her nose with the back of her hand. "Who owns the SUV?"

"Current BMV records show Maine plates registered to a Scott and Claire Allen, 1578 Oakdale Drive in Bangor."

"That's just a mile or two from here." Ellis looked back at the burned SUV. "Any reports of a stolen vehicle?"

"I'll find out right now." McCallister stepped away to make the call.

"Hey, Ellis?" Gifford called out. "You and your partner should come see this."

"Hang on." She waited while McCallister finished the call and returned. "So?"

"Nothing reported stolen. What do you think?"

"Let's see what we have here first." They headed back to the SUV when Ellis stopped, where Jeff Harwick waited. "Did you reach your pastor?"

"I did. He's on his way. Do you know who's inside yet?"

Ellis started on again. "That's what we're trying to figure out."

JEFF HARWICK HAD ONLY BEEN EMPLOYED at the church since the summer. A recent college graduate, he enjoyed working with kids in his spare time while he worked full-time at Bangor General Hospital in the pharmacy department. The baby-faced 24-year-old still couldn't believe what lay before him. The lights of the fire engines and police cars swirled. Law enforcement kept onlookers beyond the tape. He'd never seen anything like this and prayed Pastor Zeke Townsend would arrive soon and offer comfort.

"Jeff, what's going on? Have you talked to the police?"

Harwick spun around. "Pastor Zeke, thank the Lord you're here. I mean, the church is fine, but this. Look at that car."

Ezekiel Townsend was tall, over six feet to be sure. Yet while wearing a hoodie with a parka over top, the reedy man appeared poised. The 33-year-old pastor had led this congregation for the past two years. "The police haven't notified anyone from the church. Not the elders, not me. If it weren't for your call, I wouldn't even know about this yet."

Harwick returned his gaze to the scene. "The police say there's someone inside, but they don't know who, or won't say. That detective over there? The woman? She asked if I had seen that car when I left tonight."

"What did you tell her?" Townsend asked.

"That I hadn't. I truly hadn't. I left around 8:45, maybe nine o'clock, with a couple of the teens. They drove away and so did I. I promise you, Zeke, I never saw anything. I'd tell the police if I had."

Townsend placed his hand on the young man's shoulder. "Of course you would have."

"Do you recognize that car?" Harwick asked.

"In its current state? No, I'm afraid I don't. But my God,

what if it's one of our members?" He covered his mouth in dismay. "This is going to be devastating. You should go home, Jeff. I can talk to the police. I'll call the elders and let them know. Just go home and put all this out of your mind if you can. I'll have a word with the detectives and get what I can from them."

"Are you sure?" Harwick asked. "The woman detective asked me to sit tight."

"I'm sure. Go. I can handle this from here. It's my job to represent the church."

THE DETECTIVES STOOD with Fire Chief Gifford near the blackened corpse that now lay on a gurney.

The chief unzipped the bag. "Definitely female, like we thought. Here's something interesting. Once we got her out, we didn't find any ID. No purse, no phone, but we did find a wedding ring."

"How did that survive?" Ellis asked.

"Both gold and platinum have a high melting point, much higher than a car fire, which burns at about 1,500 degrees Fahrenheit. Diamonds, too. The band was probably made of either of those metals," Gifford replied.

"Car keys?" McCallister asked.

Gifford motioned to a member of his team. "Hand them over."

McCallister took the plastic evidence bag and held it up. "Okay, so we have keys. No fob. Probably melted. No identifiable markings."

"No phone or purse," Ellis added. "Are we talking a robbery or carjacking gone bad? I'd be hard-pressed to consider this an accident when the woman had no personal effects on her."

Gifford looked at the detectives. "You two pulled the VIN. Who owns this scrap metal?"

"Claire and Scott Allen, according to BMV records. Who's this person here?" Ellis shrugged. "Could be someone who borrowed the car, could be the owner, could be a thief. We can't rule out that someone other than the owner was driving. Let's get her transported to the medical examiner ASAP. And then let's do some crowd control. We're getting a lot of eyeballs over here." She spotted the youth pastor leaving and jogged to catch him. "Excuse me, Jeff? Sorry, but what's going on? I thought you were going to stick around so we could have a quick word."

"I was but..."

A lanky arm reached out for her. "I'm the head pastor here, ma'am. Pastor Zeke, Ezekiel Townsend. I told Jeff to go home and that I could help answer any questions you have. And you are?"

Ellis sized him up. "Detective Rebecca Ellis. You run the show?"

He raised his shoulders. "I wouldn't exactly say that. Our elders run the show, but yeah, I guess I do the day-to-day stuff."

She retrieved her badge. "Bangor PD. That's my partner up there, Detective Euan McCallister. Would you mind sticking around, then, for a while? I'd like to talk to you about what happened."

"Absolutely. Can you tell me anything right now? Jeff said someone died. Do you know who that is?" Townsend asked.

Ellis turned her attention to the youth pastor. "You can go home, Jeff."

"Thank you, Detective."

After he was out of earshot, Ellis looked back at Townsend. "We don't know for sure, but I was kind of hoping you might recognize the vehicle."

He pointed. "That heap of charred metal? I couldn't tell you whether that was a car or not, to be honest. I'm sorry. I realize that's not much help."

Of course, Ellis already knew the vehicle and who owned it. But it was a good idea to get a sense of what Townsend knew. It was best to let people speak up on their own rather than put any preconceived notions in their heads. "Were you here tonight, too? Mr. Harwick mentioned the church held a service earlier this evening."

"We did, and yes, I was here. Our Tuesday service isn't typically all that busy, and I try to keep things light and add a little bit of fun to the sermon."

"Sounds delightful." Ellis regretted her biting tone. "I'm sorry, I mean no disrespect."

"None taken," Townsend replied. "Not everyone sees church for what it is."

"And what's that?"

"A place for the community to come together. To share in each other's good times and bad." He looked again at the scene. "Times like this."

"Of course. May I ask when you left tonight?" Ellis pressed on.

"The usual time. Right after the service, which ends at 8:30."

"And still plenty of cars in the parking lot when you left?"

"A few, I guess. Like I said, Tuesdays aren't all that busy for us." He regarded her with a pained look in his dark brown eyes. "I have a feeling you already know who perished, Detective Ellis. It would be good to know whether it was a member of our congregation. I could prepare everyone for the news before they hear it on TV or read it on social media."

She knew he was right, but in this instance, her hands were tied. "We can't confirm anything right now, but once the family is notified, I'm sure you'll be contacted. Thank you for speaking with me." She handed him a card. "If you think of anything, give me a call."

"Will do, Detective."

Ellis returned to McCallister and Chief Gifford. "Can we take a look inside?"

Gifford nodded. "Be my guest. This is all on you folks now."

"Euan, do you have gloves handy? I have an extra pair." She pulled latex gloves from her pocket.

"I'm good." He slipped on his own.

Ellis squatted down at the driver's side and examined the interior. "I'm no car expert, but I don't see much left of anything."

McCallister leaned over her. "I'll bet she burned inside of two minutes. Look at this. The goddam steering wheel is melted."

She peered beyond the driver's seat. "Hang on."

"What are you looking at?" McCallister asked.

"This seatbelt." Ellis retrieved her phone to shine a light on it. "Can you squeeze next to me and take a look at this?"

"Yeah."

With the light trained on the seatbelt lock, she continued, "The center console is in the way a little bit, but the cover on this seatbelt is gone."

"It was plastic, so it probably melted," he replied.

"Okay, but why is there a piece of metal jammed in the locking mechanism? You see the gear wheel here?" She aimed the light closer.

"Yeah, of course. It's damaged."

"Uh-huh, but look at where that piece of metal is located. To me, it looks wedged between the teeth on the gear wheel."

McCallister moved closer for a better look. "Yeah, okay. I see it. What does that mean?"

Ellis pulled back and returned upright. "This would have

to be verified, but to me, it looks like the gear that locks the belt in place was jammed—intentionally. It makes sense now why the door was open but the driver still inside."

"And the fact that Gifford indicated the fire started in the engine," he added.

"Meaning this woman wouldn't have been able to unlock the belt to escape the fire."

McCallister held her gaze. "Are you telling me this is a homicide?"

She took a moment to consider the possibility and glanced at the thinning crowd. "It's starting to look that way to me."

2

From the age of 12 until the age of 18, Rebecca Ellis had lived in the house that her father still called home. Most nights after work, she stopped by to see him. He frowned at the idea she felt the need to check up on him, but Ellis knew that, secretly, he would have been devastated if she hadn't. It was already late, certainly by her 63-year-old father's standards, but that couldn't be helped. Not when a woman, who had burned alive in a church parking lot, appeared to have been murdered.

She pulled onto the driveway behind her dad's old Chevy truck in the tire tracks he'd carved out in the snow. It was time to get the kid from across the street to break out the shovel again.

A soft white light filtered through the front curtains, and the porch light burned above the door of the ranch-style home. "He waited up." Ellis stepped out of her white Tahoe and reached the front steps. She opened the screen and knocked on the door before turning the handle to enter. He always left it unlocked when he expected her, even when she insisted it wasn't safe to do so. Hank Ellis was a stubborn old

18

man, and what was worse, he was a stubborn former detective. A nasty combination.

"Dad?" Ellis walked inside the dimly lit foyer. She removed her coat and hat, combing her fingers through her blond hair to fix it into place again. The living room was steps away.

Hank looked at her from his chair and smiled. "Becca. There's my girl. It's late. What the hell took you so long?"

"Just working on a new case and it took a while to get the lay of the land. Figured you would've heard about it by now."

"Oh, I did. I still got friends on the force, you know," he added.

"Believe me, I know. And I'm sorry it's so late. You could've texted me if you didn't want me to stop by."

"Uh-huh. Hey, grab me another beer, would you?"

"Sure thing. Wouldn't want you to lose that belly you worked so hard to grow." Ellis retreated to the kitchen and grabbed two bottles of whatever microbrew her father felt like drinking at the moment. Hank considered himself a beer connoisseur. "Here you go. How was your day?"

"Mine? Same as yesterday and the day before. You? Car fire, huh?"

She sat down on the sofa and threw back a swig. "A woman burned to death in her car."

"Damn painful way to go. What's your first impression?" he asked.

"I'm no forensics expert, but the seatbelt appears to have been tampered with. Engine fire, according to the chief. I don't have all the facts yet. Regardless, it does push us toward homicide."

"You check the car's operating condition? Did someone fiddle with the fuel tank? The lines? Battery?"

"I don't know yet, Dad. I just left the scene and came here. The wreckage will be towed to the station for analysis.

I'll be sure to keep you posted." She took a prolonged swig of her beer to avoid any more questions she couldn't yet answer.

"Well, that is interesting." He winced and clutched at his side.

Ellis set the bottle down on the coffee table. "You okay, Dad?"

"Fine. Fine. You don't have to jump every time I twitch. Just a spasm. Good Lord."

"Have you taken all your meds today?" she asked.

"Yes, I have, young lady. You'd do well to remember I'm the parent here. Not you."

She raised her hands. "Fair enough. I'll keep my trap shut." She noticed the sports newscast on TV. "The Pats aren't doing much this season."

"Says you. I'm no fair-weather fan like you, missy. You know, I heard from your brother today." He seemed to detect a shift in her gaze. "Well, you don't have to look like I just killed your dog."

Ellis peered at her feet. "And?"

"And nothing. He just called to check in on me. Said he was worried about me. It was a nice gesture," Hank replied.

"Uh-huh. You know he's just greasing the wheels, right, Dad? Waiting until the perfect time to ask you for more money. Or maybe he'll just take it like the last time."

"That's enough, Becca. Carter doesn't have a soul on this planet besides you and me."

"And whose fault is that, Dad? He's a drug addict. You need to get it through your head we've done all we can do for him. It isn't like we haven't tried. Carter has to be the one to climb out of the hole. Helping him with money and all the rest will only allow him to dig himself in deeper."

When Hank went quiet, she regretted lecturing him on the topic. "Did you eat? You want me to throw on a grilled cheese or something for you? I wouldn't mind a bite. I didn't get dinner."

He turned to her with a rueful gaze. "I'll have heartburn all night, but sure. Why not? Thanks, kid."

THE BANGOR POLICE DEPARTMENT lay across from a community park and down a block from the fire station. The Penobscot River, where plenty of restaurants lay along the Waterfront, was a stone's throw from the stationhouse.

Ellis arrived upstairs inside the Criminal Investigation Division and headed toward the bullpen, where the detectives worked. All these guys had wide-ranging skillsets and rotated cases dependent upon need. There were no dedicated homicide or robbery units. Bangor was still a small city, even if they had big-city crime. The unit commander, Sergeant James Abbott, assigned cases as he saw fit. Abbott had been with the force for over 20 years and had worked with Ellis's father back in the day. Now, he directed his investigators and acted as a liaison between other divisions in the department.

As Ellis walked to her desk, Abbott leaned out of his office and called out to her, "Becca, come see me a minute, would you?"

She glanced at McCallister, whose desk was next to hers. "Have you talked to him yet this morning?"

"No. I was setting up our meeting with the medical examiner. Abbott hasn't so much as poked his head out," he replied.

"I'd better go see what he wants then." Ellis tugged on her suit jacket and headed to his office. "You wanted to see me, Sarge?"

"Come in." The weighty man with thinning hair, who pushed the hell out of 60, eyed her as she drew near. "I got a call early this morning from the ME's office. They got a positive ID on the victim through dental records. They want us to tell the husband and bring him in to confirm her identity."

"Claire Allen?"

He nodded.

"Okay. McCallister and I had planned on hitting up the ME this morning, so we'll relay the news to the husband and bring him with us."

Abbott removed his glasses and wiped them with a cloth while he peered at her with squinting brown eyes. "What are your instincts telling you about this case?"

Ellis gripped the back of the chair as she stood. "Well, I'd need to find out more about her, but at a glance...she was murdered. Looked to me like the driver's seatbelt had been rigged, and there was no way she would've escaped the fire once it caught."

"Rigged?" he asked.

"Yeah, to lock in place."

"Well, shit." Abbott leaned back in his chair and slipped on his glasses. "Don't need another one of those on our plates. How soon till Forensics sweeps the vehicle?"

"That's the second thing on my list this morning. I'll find out."

Abbott nodded. "You two better fully brief me this afternoon after you get more information. I want to know who this woman was, and if she was murdered, I want some idea as to why."

"You and me both, Sarge. I'll make it happen." Ellis returned to her desk.

McCallister pushed back in his desk chair and eyed her approach. "What did he want?"

"The ME called him this morning. They ID'd the body. It's Claire Allen. We have to inform the husband and get him to Augusta to confirm."

He got to his feet and snatched his suit jacket from the back of his chair. "I'm ready when you are."

———

THE SUN hardly peeked over the horizon when the detectives arrived at the home of Scott and Claire Allen in the upscale neighborhood just north of the I-95. Nestled among the now sparse trees and tucked back on a sizable plot of snow-covered land, the well-cared-for Cape Cod home was impressive.

Ellis pulled up along the edge of the pavement and peered through the windshield at the house. "We know the vehicle wasn't reported stolen. What about a missing persons' report?"

"I can find out right now." He made the call. "Hey, it's McCallister. Ellis and I are about to talk to the husband of the car fire victim from last night. Can you check to see if he reported her missing? Uh, Claire Allen. Yeah, I'll wait. Thanks." He glanced at Ellis. "Fletch is checking for us now." He returned to the line. "Yeah, I'm here. Okay, thanks Fletch." McCallister ended the call. "No reports of anyone going missing from last night."

"Really? Now, that's interesting."

"Maybe not," McCallister added. "She could've told him she was going somewhere overnight. Maybe they'd had a fight. Lots of things could've happened."

"Guess we'll have to hear it from him directly." Ellis stepped out and pulled on her coat, glancing at the dreary sky. She'd lived in Bangor since she was 12, and before that, had called nearby Augusta home. A Mainer all her life, she despised wintertime and the several feet of snow she had to shovel off her driveway every season. The frigid temperatures only added to her disdain.

She joined McCallister as he hiked up the long and narrow driveway toward the home, which was painted a light blue with white trim. She pointed to a newer model silver BMW. "Looks like someone's here."

But before they reached the front steps, the door opened. Ellis eyed the man who stood in the doorway. He knew. She'd seen that look, that pained expression, before. He knew something bad had happened to his wife. "Mr. Allen? I'm Detective Rebecca Ellis with Bangor PD. This is Detective Euan McCallister."

"You're here about Claire, aren't you? I knew you were the police. What happened to her? Is she dead?"

"Please, sir, if we could just go inside and sit down," McCallister interrupted.

"No. I have to know if she's dead. You have to tell me right now." He was a fit man, who appeared to have been in his mid-thirties, but now his sunken brown eyes were reddened and glistened with tears.

"Mr. Allen, your wife is Claire Allen, correct?" Ellis asked.

"Yes."

No matter how often she'd had to relay this type of news, it never got any easier. "She was found inside her Lexus SUV last night in a church parking lot. Unfortunately, Mr. Allen, her vehicle caught fire and she was unable to get out..."

The man collapsed in a heap on the ground and sobbed.

"Sir." Ellis shot a glance at McCallister, and the two hurried to help him to his feet. "Mr. Allen, let us get you inside." She noticed the home was beautifully decorated in grays and whites. It appeared to have been recently remodeled. They helped Scott Allen to his living room sofa. "Would you like a glass of water, sir?"

He shook his head while tears left salty trails on his face.

"I'm very sorry for your loss, Mr. Allen," Ellis began. "My partner and I were on scene last night but your wife's identity was only just confirmed early this morning. No ID was found inside the vehicle. In fact, the medical examiner's office in Augusta would like you to come down. They need a family member to confirm."

He set his tear-filled eyes on Ellis. "I don't understand. Her car caught fire at the church?"

"Yes, sir," McCallister cut in. "We don't know how it happened yet, but your wife's car is at the police compound where Forensics will do their job to determine that. She was at the Grace Community Church. Is that your place of worship?"

Grief overcame him again. "Yes. Claire volunteers there. That place was her whole life."

Ellis felt her eyes sting for just a moment. "Right now, Mr. Allen, we would like you to come with us to see your wife."

"Now? I have to do this now?"

"I'm afraid so, sir," Ellis replied. "The sooner the better. It will help us move forward with the investigation."

"But what exactly are you investigating? If her car caught fire, do you think it was intentional?"

Ellis glanced at her partner a moment before continuing, "Again, it's too early to know for sure, but we have to look at every possible scenario. Do you have reason to believe this could have been something other than an accident, Mr. Allen?"

"I-I don't know. I don't know what to think except that my wife is dead."

"Do you have children in the house, sir?" McCallister asked. "Are they at school?"

"We don't have kids. Claire wanted to have them some-day." He cast down his gaze and closed his eyes. After a few deep breaths, he looked up again. "Okay. I'll go with you now."

AT JUST OVER AN HOUR, it was a short drive to Augusta, and they'd arrived at the Chief Medical Examiner's Office at 8 am. Mr. Allen, who had been silent for the duration, stepped out of the back seat. With his palms, he smoothed the sides of his short black hair and zipped his coat.

The detectives led him inside, and Ellis reached the administration desk. "Detective Ellis. Bangor PD. We're here to see Dr. Rivera."

"One moment." The young man made the call and returned his attention to her. "The doctor will be up shortly."

"Thank you." Ellis turned to the husband. "There is something you should know, Mr. Allen. Once you confirm whether the body is that of your wife, the doctor will perform an autopsy to confirm the cause of death. I should warn you that she could only be identified through her dental records."

"What?" He hunched over and grabbed his knees. "Oh my God."

"Detectives?" The doctor appeared from the hall. "Thank you for coming down." He waited a moment. "Are you Mr. Scott Allen?"

As he returned upright, the husband pulled back his square shoulders and cleared his throat. "Yes, sir."

"Why don't you follow me back? The detectives can stay here."

After they disappeared, Ellis turned to McCallister. "What do you think about him?"

"Looks like a husband in mourning. He seems genuinely devastated."

"Yeah, that's what I thought." Ellis peered into the hall as though Scott Allen might soon reemerge. "What concerns me is that he had no idea where his wife was. Makes me think they'd had an argument, like you said, or she had something else going on."

"But why at their church?" McCallister asked.

"We'll have to talk to those there who knew her. That should be our priority, at least until Forensics has some news for us." She caught sight of the doctor and Mr. Allen's return. "Here we go."

The doctor stopped just feet from them. "Mr. Allen was able to give us a positive ID."

"Her wedding ring," Allen began. "That was the only way I knew it was her."

Dr. Rivera clasped his hands behind his back. "I did inform Mr. Allen that we would move forward with the autopsy and lab work to determine cause of death."

Ellis nodded. "Thank you, Doctor. Are you ready to go home, Mr. Allen? We'll ask you a few more questions, and then, if you could, we'd appreciate a trip down to the station for a statement. It doesn't have to be today."

Scott Allen appeared numb as he set his gaze on her. "Fine."

ELLIS AND MCCALLISTER returned the grieving husband to his home and parked in the driveway behind his BMW and another car. She glanced into the rearview mirror. "Are you expecting someone, Mr. Allen?"

He unbuckled his seatbelt and opened the rear passenger door. "I texted a friend of mine about what happened. He said he didn't want me to be alone."

Her eyes were drawn to the porch when a broad-shouldered man stepped down from it and meandered along the path toward the driveway. Wearing a wool hat, puffy coat, and sunglasses, he shoved his hands into the pockets of his jeans.

McCallister scrutinized the man who approached. "Does your friend also know your wife?"

"Yes, Claire and I are close friends with him and his wife." Allen stepped out of the car.

"Might be a good idea to introduce ourselves." Ellis stepped out and joined the two men while her partner followed. "Morning. I'm Detective Ellis. You're a friend of Mr. Allen's, I hear."

McCallister thrust out his hand. "Detective McCallister. And you are?"

"Ethan Rehnquist. Scott told me what happened. I just can't believe it." He placed his hand on Scott's back. "But I knew he shouldn't be alone."

"That's probably wise," Ellis replied. "Mr. Allen says you and your wife were close to Claire as well?"

"Were...yeah, absolutely. We spent a lot of time together. My wife, uh, she's out of town today, but we've had plenty of gatherings here over the years." Rehnquist looked back toward the house. "I brought Scott some breakfast. Should probably head inside so he can try to get something to eat."

"Of course. I'm sure we'll get an opportunity to speak again." Ellis nodded to the man and looked again at Allen. "Your friend's right; you should eat and try to get some rest. We'll be in touch."

As the detectives returned to her Tahoe, Ellis stepped behind the wheel and homed in on the men, who had returned to the porch.

McCallister closed the passenger door and fixed his gaze on the road ahead.

"We should get over to the church." She pressed the ignition and noticed his far-off stare.

Despite his occasional attempt at dry humor, Euan McCallister appeared a serious man with a heavy burden. Ellis had seen it in his eyes. Deep crow's feet from too much worry. A heavy brow that pinched together when he spoke. And he had a habit of combing his fingers through his thick dark hair as though in a constant state of concern. Still, the job could do that to anyone. And handsome though he was—after all, she wasn't blind—his looks couldn't conceal an obviously troubled past. She had one of those herself.

He glimpsed Ellis a moment. "Since I'm still new here, can I ask how many murder investigations you've worked?"

"Three," she answered. "The most recent was last year. He was a carjacking victim downtown. We caught the man who did it, but the case still hasn't gone to trial."

He groaned his displeasure. "No surprise there. Back in Boston, I worked a homicide case that took almost two years to go to trial. I'd been in Missing Persons for a while before moving to Homicide."

"Big city like Boston. Must've been pretty crazy there," she added.

"Wicked crazy."

Ellis turned right toward the church. "Since we're getting to know each other, why did you leave? Bangor's a small place, comparatively speaking."

"It's a long story. Maybe I'll tell you one day over a beer." He shot her a glance. "Unless you don't drink beer, in which case, you can stop the car right now."

"It'll do in a pinch." She drove onto the parking lot. "Looks like the crew's got everything cleaned up."

"Except for the big black mark on the pavement." McCallister opened the door and waited for her to join him as they started ahead. "You spoke to the pastor last night, right?"

"Briefly. Pastor Zeke Townsend," she replied.

"Okay, so we've established contact. Until we can get the husband to sit down with us, the people here seemed to have been Claire Allen's closest friends," he replied.

Ellis spotted the pastor at the church entrance. "Sounds

like we should focus on Mrs. Rehnquist too if they were as close as Mr. Allen suggested. I believe that's the man we're after just ahead." She approached with an outstretched hand. "Mr. Townsend, thank you for agreeing to speak with us. I can't recall if you met my partner last night, Detective Euan McCallister."

"I don't believe I had the chance," the pastor offered a greeting. "Good to meet you, Detective. Please, you both can call me Pastor Zeke. Everyone does."

"May we go inside?" Ellis asked.

"Yes, of course. Let's get out of the cold." Townsend opened the door to the lobby of the Worship Center. "My office is just this way, if you'll follow me."

Ellis noted the sleek finishes and travertine floor. "It's nice in here. Very modern."

"We do our best to keep things tidy and updated. Our volunteers clean up after each service. They're a Godsend." Townsend gestured to his office. "Right through here. Why don't you both take a seat?"

The detectives sat across from the pastor's mid-century-style walnut desk set among rows of bookshelves.

Ellis retrieved the file. "We just returned from the medical examiner's office."

Townsend pulled out his chair to join them. "So you know the identity of the victim?"

"Yes, sir. Her name was Claire Allen," McCallister cut in. "Married to Scott Allen and lives on..."

"I know who she is." He turned away a moment, blinking quickly and swallowing hard. "My God, are you sure it's Claire?"

"We're sure. Her husband ID'd her body for us first thing this morning. Dental records also confirmed it." Ellis leaned in. "I understand she attended your church."

"Oh, yes. Claire was a huge advocate for the church. A

wonderful volunteer. She usually headed up the fundraisers, and they're always a great success."

"Then I am terribly sorry for your loss, Pastor," Ellis replied. "Did she attend the Tuesday night service you mentioned? Was that why she was here?"

His gaze vacillated between the detectives. "No, she didn't, actually. That's why this comes as a tremendous shock. Forgive me." He smoothed down his blue tie and drew in a deep breath. The gangly man had been reduced to tears and retrieved a tissue.

Ellis gave him a moment to gather himself. "That does seem strange, then. Did she have business with the church last night? Was she working on something...a fundraiser, like you mentioned?"

"No," he whispered.

Ellis drew in her brow and glanced at McCallister with some misgiving. "Well, then, I have to ask, Pastor. Why do you think Claire Allen came here last night?"

3

F ield notes and crime scene photos of the scorched wreckage and burnt corpse lay scattered across Ellis's desk, and the time had come to brief Sergeant Abbott on the Claire Allen investigation. They still hadn't been able to call the case what they believed it was, a homicide. She pulled together the file and prepared for the briefing.

"I see you two are back. How're things going with the car fire victim?"

Ellis turned up her gaze to see Detective Bryce Pelletier. The slightly plump 33-year-old, with light hair and cornflower blue eyes, was one of her closest friends at the station. "Bryce, hey. We got back a few minutes ago. Sarge wants a briefing. We don't have much yet, but we're getting there. What do you have going on?"

"Working with Bevins on that department store robbery from the other night," he replied.

"That's right. Any leads?" Ellis tucked her hair behind one ear.

"Did you forget who I'm partnered with?" Pelletier

scoffed. "The guy who knows everything about investigations? Just ask him. He'll tell you all about our leads."

"Yeah, Bevins is a 25-year-old know-it-all, but he doesn't
mean anything by it. He'll mellow out with age. Like we all
have."

"Becca, the guy brings up his West Point schooling every
chance he gets. I'll say, 'Hey, what do you think about this or
that'...and he'll be like, 'West Point taught us to...blah, blah,
blah.' I mean, whatever. He's not stupid, just annoying."

"All I ask is that you cut him some slack. He's all right."
Ellis stood from her desk and straightened her gray suit
jacket. "Don't suppose you've seen McCallister? I should grab
him so we can get started."

"I think he was in the break room a minute ago," Pelletier
replied. "Hey, you want to grab dinner this weekend?"

"If we can fit it in, sure. Sounds good. I'll catch up with
you soon." Ellis headed into the corridor and spotted McCallister. "There you are."

He halted in place while holding a cup of coffee. "Are we
ready to do this, or what?"

"Unless you have another case you're working," she
replied.

"Nope. Just one murder today. I'll swing by my desk to
grab my things and meet you inside."

Along the way to the sergeant's office, Ellis ran into Detective Connor Bevins. It was no wonder the guy behaved the
way he did. With short black hair styled on trend, an athletic
build, and a face that belonged on a men's fashion magazine,
he had probably never heard the word "no." Add to that a
coveted education and it would be enough to give anyone a
big head. They all knew he'd graduated West Point, but then
for reasons he kept close to his chest, he'd joined Bangor PD
instead of the military or some cushy government job. So
some of the guys upstairs were a little jealous of him. Throw

that in with the fact he'd only been with the department for two years and made detective, and it was easy to understand their response. Unfair, but easy. She was one of Bevins's few defenders.

"Morning, I hear you and Bryce are making headway on the department store case," Ellis said.

"Not enough, but we're getting there. You got the mother-lode, though, huh?" Bevins asked.

"The fire?"

"Yeah, I'd kill to be on that case. Guess you have to be the daughter of a legend to get that gig."

As he walked away, Ellis pondered why she defended him to pretty much everyone in the station. Times like these, he made that damn difficult. She reached Abbott's office and stood in his doorway. He sat at an old oak desk scarred with water rings, dents, and a worn finish. The department hadn't much in the way of a budget, and his office made that all the more obvious. He appeared riveted by whatever was on his computer screen until he finally caught sight of her and removed his reading glasses. "Becca, there you are."

"Sarge, if you're ready?" she asked.

McCallister turned up a moment later with his files in hand. "Morning, Sarge."

"I see Becca is keeping you on your toes. You got your hands full."

"Yes, sir. A case like this tends to do that," he replied.

Abbott waved his meaty hand. "Both of you, come on in."

The detectives took their seats while Ellis retrieved her notes.

Abbott gave them a once-over. "All right. Let's talk about where you're at right now. So, are we looking at murder?"

SCOTT ALLEN CONSIDERED himself a successful man. In his late thirties, he was the vice president in charge of new accounts at the Eastern Union and Trust Bank in Downtown Bangor. His beautiful wife, Claire, had been a respected member of the church, where she'd burned to death in her SUV last night.

Scott slumped forward, laying his head down on the kitchen table, where he'd sat for the last hour since insisting to Ethan he would be fine on his own. "Yeah, right." It hadn't seemed real. How could she be dead? In his mind's eye, he saw her on the metal table, her flesh blackened, most of it melted off her bones. They'd let him take her wedding ring, and he twisted the intricate band of gold between his fingers now.

Why she had been at the church confounded him. She'd claimed to be going out to see a friend who'd been ill. When she hadn't returned by eleven o'clock, he grew a little worried and called her, but the call went to voicemail. He hadn't thought much of it, believing she'd probably lost track of time. There was nothing to worry about. Why would there be?

Eventually, he'd fallen asleep. It wasn't until he'd awakened this morning and her side of the bed remained empty that it hit him. His wife was gone. An hour later, the police turned up at his door. Scott closed his eyes and the tears fell again. "What the hell were you doing at the church?"

It occurred to him, at that moment, to log onto her computer. Her phone was synched to her laptop. Maybe she'd received an email, a text message. Something that would hint at her actions. Maybe he would find answers there. It was best to do this now because soon enough, the police would take her things. The detective wanted to call it murder, but she'd held back. He could see it in her eyes. It was best if he got ahead of this, whatever *this* was.

Scott walked upstairs to their bedroom and stared at the unmade bed. Her pillow still bore the indentation from where she always lay her head. He did his best to remain poised and walked to Claire's laptop on the writing desk near the window. She mostly used it for her church work. The church was her life and she volunteered to do everything for them. It was her only job, even though the church hadn't paid her. It never bothered Scott because he earned enough to take care of her. Mostly. Maybe they were old-fashioned that way, but it worked for them. They'd been married for ten years and now he was a widower.

He sat down at her desk and opened her laptop. For a moment, he stared at the password-protected screen and then keyed in the code. *Incorrect Password* flashed at him. "What the hell?" He tried again and was again refused access. "Did you change your password?"

His phone rang in his pocket, and he answered the call. "Hello?"

"I'm so sorry about what happened."

"How do you know already?" he asked.

"The police came by to talk to me at the church. Scott, if there's anything I can do, or the church can do, please just ask."

"Do you know why she was there, Zeke?"

"I'm sorry, but I don't. If you'd like to talk..."

"I'm fine. I just need some time to figure this out. Thank you for the call, Pastor." He hung up.

INSIDE THE POLICE station's garage were two other vehicles known to have been involved in armed robberies, and then there was the burned-out SUV. The detectives needed an update on that SUV if they hoped to keep momentum on their investigation.

Ellis approached one of the officers on the Forensics team. "Seavers, are you working on that charred piece of metal over there?" she asked the stocky man with a crew cut.

"Hey, Ellis. That's your case?"

"Yes, it is. McCallister's, too. I don't know if you've had the chance to work with him yet." She turned to her partner. "Have you met Seavers?"

"I don't believe I have." He offered his hand. "Euan McCallister."

"Where you from, McCallister?" Seavers asked.

"I was a detective in Boston. Came here about a month ago. I'll be working alongside Ellis on this case."

"All right then. Good to meet you." Seavers pivoted to the vehicle. "I can tell you what I know right now. Still working on it, of course, so don't take this as gospel, but Ellis, you mentioned in your report you thought the driver's side seatbelt had been jammed?"

"That's right," she replied.

"You were on the nose. We had to remove the driver's seat for a better view, but take a look here." He pointed to the wheel. "This is where you saw that scrap of metal jammed in between the teeth on the latching mechanism?"

"Yep," Ellis confirmed.

"So, yeah, that's how it looks to me and my team agrees. Someone got into this SUV, pulled off the plastic panel covering the seatbelt, and wedged in this piece of metal that's smaller than a dime. The belt latched, but when the wheel turned, it clamped down on that metal. Nothing would've pried it open." Seavers walked to the engine compartment. "There's something else too. Come down here with me if you don't mind messing up your suit."

Ellis joined him on the concrete floor, which was finished

in a polished resin, and she lay on her back next to him, both with their sights set on the vehicle's undercarriage.

"You see that line right there?" Seavers pointed to the metal pipe that ran from the tank to the fuel pump. "Most of the lines and belts are rubber, so they would've melted soon after the fire started. But here is the fuel line. It's metal."

Ellis peered up. "I see it."

McCallister leaned over the engine and aimed his phone's light through the compartment. "Is that the fuel line?"

"It is," Seavers added. "And there's no mistaking that someone cut that line. Used a hacksaw, or hell, I don't know, a good set of bolt cutters would do the trick, too. But this looks fairly precise, so right now, I'm saying some kind of hand saw was used. Now, the line was cut only a short distance to the tank. Easier access, I guess. Point being, it would've dumped a lot of gas onto the ground. The vapors alone would've ignited as soon as the victim started the engine, thanks to the spark plugs. But you also got the high-pressure fuel pump. Gas would've still been in the line, so when the engine started, fuel would've been pushed through and leaked out onto other components. And again, the spark plugs, the electric pump...all that would be enough to ignite the fuel." He pushed off the ground and offered Ellis his hand. "Come on up."

"Thanks." She grabbed it and stood again. "No sign of any electrical systems malfunctioning?"

"Not that I've seen. Course, most everything in here's shot to hell. Regardless, the line was intentionally cut, and that was all it took. Now, had the seatbelt not been jammed, the victim would've likely smelled the gas, seen the smoke billow from the engine compartment, realized something was wrong, and unlocked the belt to get out," Seavers continued.

"But she couldn't," Ellis cut in. "Someone made sure she couldn't get out."

"That's how it appears at the moment. We still have a lot to sift through. Protocols and such, but that's what we know right now." Seavers crossed his beefy arms. "Again, I don't want to speak out of turn, but preliminary findings suggest you two have a homicide on your hands."

THE MUSIC inside the Lucky Oyster Bar and Grill near the Waterfront reminded Ellis of college. Well, the short time she'd spent in college. Her roommate had listened to this very song over and over and refused to wear headphones. Could've been that her roommate was the real reason Ellis quit in her freshman year. "Aren't you hungry?"

McCallister scratched his head and mussed his hair, which was styled long and wavy on the top. "Yeah, it's just..."

"The case. I know. But you have to eat. We didn't get lunch, and I'm not one of those women who pretends she doesn't eat. To hell with that."

"You don't strike me as a woman who cares, at all, what other people think," he said.

"Not particularly. There's not much room for that in this line of work."

"Is that why you always defend Bevins? I've only been here a month, and I can see the kid's arrogant as hell."

"Like I told Bryce, he's young. He'll figure it out, especially when he realizes he has no friends left in the department." She plunked a French fry into her mouth. "It's obvious he's been handed everything on a silver platter. You don't get into West Point otherwise."

McCallister took a bite of his burger and dabbed his mouth with a napkin. "Which I find wicked strange that he wanted to work for this department. No offense, but a West

Point grad working here? Those guys usually get a nice comfortable job at the Pentagon, you know?"

"Yeah, well, I think there's more to that than we know. I've never asked him, but thought if he wanted to talk about it, he would," she replied. "But what about you, huh?"

"What about me?"

Ellis narrowed her gaze and raised her chin. "What's your story? You left Boston. Who leaves a department of that size to come to Bangor? Usually, it's the other way around. You said you'd tell me over a beer. Here's your chance."

He shrugged and took a drink.

"Oh, you're just going to drink your pop? It's not beer, but come on. Okay, you don't want to answer that. I get it. Makes no difference to me. You seem all right—so far."

"Thanks. I'll take that as a compliment," he replied. "So what's next? We start talking to the friends and extended family?"

"Sounds about right. Mrs. Rehnquist tops that list." Ellis took a bite of her Philly cheesesteak. "Now that we have the Forensics' opinion that this was an intentional act, it's time we push the husband to come in and give us his statement. The more time that passes..."

"The more likely he'll forget something," McCallister replied. "Yeah. Okay."

Ellis reached for her wallet. "Listen, I hate to eat and run, but I have family I need to stop by and see."

"Your dad? I heard he was a detective for a lot of years at the department," he replied.

"Yes, he was, 23 years to be exact. Retired five years ago. And yes, I stop by his house to check in on him."

"You must be a good daughter." He paused a moment while she retrieved cash from her wallet. "I also heard you went through some stuff when you were a kid."

Ellis had hazel eyes that appeared green on some days

and brown on others. Now, however, they turned dark as she regarded her partner.

He held up his hands. "Hey, I'm sorry. It's none of my business. Forget I said anything. And please, let me pick up the tab. It's the least I can do since you've been showing me the ropes."

Ellis studied him a moment, trying to work out his angle. "No, it's okay. Hey, I asked you what your deal was. Turnabout's fair play. But that's definitely a story for another time, and several beers. And thanks, but I can pay my own way." She dropped a twenty onto the table and stood to pull on her coat. "I'll see you in the morning."

THE MORBID CURIOSITY of others had followed Ellis around for most of her life. Nevertheless, she felt mildly guilty about brushing off McCallister like that. He was only asking what she knew her co-workers were telling him. It wasn't their fault. Didn't mean it didn't bug the hell out of her sometimes. Most everyone knew to leave it alone, and they respected that. But new blood in the department meant a new round of, "Hey, do you know what happened to Ellis?"

She tried to shake it off and remember that McCallister seemed like a decent guy, even if he was from Boston and put the word "wicked" in front of just about everything he said. Big city cops were all the same. Big-headed, always looking down their noses at the small city operations like hers. They passed through her department on occasion and never lasted long. It was sort of their last hurrah before retirement. But something else was going on with McCallister. Maybe when he was ready to tell her what that was, she would tell him about her past.

Ellis hopped out of her Tahoe and walked to her dad's

front door to open it. "Dad? I'm back. Earlier this time." She closed the door behind her and headed into the living room. "What the hell?"

"Hey, sis." Carter stood to greet her. "Long time no see."

Hank stood from his chair. "Carter just stopped by to bring me some dinner. Wasn't that nice of him?"

Ellis continued inside and set down her carrier bag. "I could've made you something, Dad."

"Well, I know, but now you don't have to."

She eyed her half-brother. Carter was 23 but looked at least ten years older. Drugs tended to age people like that. He stood a hair's breadth taller than their father, who was six feet even in his old age. His face appeared sallow, and he had sores on his cheeks. What hair he had left had thinned even more. Carter was a poster boy for opioid addicts. "Thanks for bringing him food. Where you staying? I didn't see a car outside."

"A friend dropped me off. I'm crashing with him." Carter shoved his hands into the pockets of his baggy jeans. "Thought I'd stop by since I hadn't seen Pop in a while."

"You need money?" she asked.

"Jesus, Becca," Hank cut in.

"What? You think he's here for any other reason, Dad? For God's sake, he stole from your wallet the last time he was here."

"I was in bad shape then, Becca, okay? Christ, can't you cut me some slack once in a while? Like you're so perfect," Carter replied.

She scoffed. "Okay, whatever. Well, I guess you don't need me here tonight since you already have company. I should go. I have plenty to do for work."

"Wait, Becca, don't leave." Hank approached her. "Stay and eat with us. When was the last time the three of us broke bread together, huh?"

"Probably not since Mom died," Carter replied.

"Your mom." Ellis turned on her heel. "You didn't know my mom."

"Becca, stop. Don't you come into my house and disrespect my dead wife, you hear me? That woman loved you like you were her own."

"This isn't about her." She spun around. "You'll never learn, Dad. Carter uses you and you continually let him. I'm sorry, but I'll see you tomorrow." She looked back at her half-brother. "Unless you're planning on sticking around a while?"

"No, uh, I gotta be getting back to…"

"Don't bother. I really don't give a shit." She walked out and slammed the door.

THE DOWNTOWN BAR was still packed after the Thursday night football game between the Patriots and the Packers. The Pats won and everyone celebrated, including Ellis and her best friend, Piper Dixon. The two had gone to high school together and remained as close as sisters. Piper was a Realtor and lived in a luxury condo Downtown. Ellis made the last-minute call to her while driving home from her father's house. Carter had a way of getting under Ellis's skin and she needed to blow off steam.

"I'm so happy you wanted to go out tonight. Look at you, enjoying your life." Piper sipped on her gin and tonic.

"I didn't feel like going home. Thanks for indulging me. Where's Matt tonight?"

"Matt?" Piper asked.

"Yeah, your boyfriend, Matt."

Piper swatted at the idea. "Oh, yeah. We broke up a few days ago. I forgot to mention that to you." She flicked away the long dark hair that hung in soft curls down her back. Dressed in a black silk top, dark jeans, and stilettos, Piper was anything but a shrinking violet. The money she made was evidenced by her designer labels and her looks drew lots of attention from the opposite sex. She never minded that attention until they got too needy, which somehow, they always did.

"I'm jealous." Ellis sighed as she took a drink from her whiskey and Coke.

"Of what, me? Why the hell is that?"

"You have the perfect life, plenty of money, a great place with a view of the river. A job that doesn't require you to notify next of kin. I don't know, maybe I'm just feeling sorry for myself."

"That's not like you, Becca." Piper regarded her. "What happened tonight?"

She rubbed her dimpled chin. "Carter."

"Ah. Well, that makes sense now. I figured it was Andrew or something."

"No. We haven't spoken in months. As far as I know, he's made himself at home in Connecticut, just like he always wanted."

"Well, good for him. And good riddance for you. I did warn you about marrying him."

"And I didn't listen." Ellis took another drink. "It feels good to be out, actually. I had an early dinner with a coworker, and I had just planned on seeing Dad before calling in an early night. Then Carter screwed up everything."

"No surprise there. So are you working on something big?" Piper asked.

"Pretty big, yeah. Homicide investigation."

Piper rested her fingertips on her cheek. "I don't know how you do it. After everything that happened, you went ahead and followed in your dad's footsteps. But are you happy?"

Ellis nodded. "I'm happy."

"Good. Then how about we try to get you laid tonight, huh?"

"Piper!"

"What?" She waved over the server. "Another round over here, please. I'm trying to get my friend drunk."

"Coming right up," she replied.

Piper returned her attention to Ellis. "So tell me about your partner. Male? More importantly, is he single?"

"His name is Euan McCallister, and he was a detective back in Boston. I think he's single, yes. He's all right."

Piper nudged her as a young man approached the table. Ellis drew her eyes to him.

He shoved a hand in the pocket of his jeans and smoothed down his untucked J. Crew oxford shirt. "Evening, ladies. My friend and I wanted to know if you'd like to join us for a drink?"

Piper raised a single brow at Ellis. "Well?"

She shrugged. "Sure."

"Great." He waved over his friend and slid into the booth. "I'm Jayden; this is my friend Brandon."

Ellis assumed these guys were in their early twenties, especially with names like that. Too young and far too much effort for her. Not to mention, Piper would eat them alive. It had been a few months, maybe longer, since Ellis had been on a date. But right now, she wasn't interested in these kids, even if it was just for the night.

"So, what do you do?" Jayden placed his arm over Ellis's shoulder.

"I'm a cop."

"Seriously?" He laughed.

"Yeah. Is that funny?"

"Becca, he's just asking," Piper cut in.

She bit her lower lip. "Sorry about that, Jayden. It's been a long day. What do you do?"

He answered, but Ellis tuned out everything around her. She couldn't shake the idea that Claire Allen had been trapped in her car while she burned. Who would do that to a church volunteer, no less? More importantly, why? She nodded and pretended to listen, but quickly came to the realization that it was time to call it a night. "You know, I've got a really early day tomorrow. I think I'm just going to head out. Piper, you ready?"

"You don't have to go yet, do you?" Jayden placed his hand on Ellis's thigh.

"I do, so if you'd be so kind as to remove your hand." She glanced back at Piper. "Let's go, yeah?"

"Fine." Piper reached for her purse when the other kid grabbed her wrist.

"Come on, don't go," Brandon said.

Piper looked at Ellis with some apprehension.

"Hey now, there's no need for that. We really do have to go," Ellis said.

Piper tried to pull away from his grasp, but he refused to let go. "Becca?"

"Dude? What are you doing?" Jayden asked. "This one's a cop."

Ellis pushed him out of the booth and stepped over to Brandon. "Let her go. Now."

The guy rolled his eyes and laughed.

Ellis yanked on his arm and pulled him up, twisting it fast behind his back. The move forced him to let Piper go. She pressed him against the table. "Next time, when a woman tells you to let her go, you better fucking let her go." She released him and waited for Piper. "Come on. Let's get out of here."

ZEKE TOWNSEND OPENED his desk drawer and retrieved a miniature bottle of vodka—the kind the airlines offered. Several more rolled around inside as he pushed the drawer shut again. He twisted off the tiny cap and wrapped his lips around the bottle, throwing back the liquid within like it was medicine. Maybe it was. Claire Allen was dead, and the congregation would look to him now more than ever. But he had more pressing concerns than his pastoral duties.

A gentle knock sounded on his door and it opened. A head poked inside. "Oh, excuse me, Pastor. I didn't know you were still here." A petite woman with dark hair pulled back in a tight bun appeared to notice the empty liquor bottle on his desk. "Should I come back later to empty your trash?"

Townsend glanced at the bottle and then back to her. "I'll take care of it, Mary. Thank you. I was just finishing up for the night."

"Okay. Goodnight, Pastor." She made a hasty retreat, closing the door behind her.

He snatched the bottle and tucked it inside his carrier bag, waiting a moment to be sure the footfalls outside had faded. Townsend pushed away from his desk and walked to his door, turning the handle to open it. The hall was dark except for the emergency lights above. He craned left and then right. All clear. After what had happened yesterday, shock spread through the church and he was one of only a select skeleton crew who came in today. And apparently, he would be the last to leave.

When he returned to his desk, he felt how the single bottle hadn't been nearly enough to smooth out the edges. After all, he was a big man, it took a lot more than one shot, so he pulled out three more bottles. "That ought to do it." He lined them up and downed each one.

Townsend closed his eyes while the booze slid down his throat, burning as it reached his gut. He'd taken it too far this time. Taken too many risks. He'd gotten away with it before but he'd recruited another and that was his mistake, one that couldn't be fixed. "I'm not going to prison." He opened a messaging app on his phone and typed:

Move it all. Delete everything. We'll meet up soon to discuss.

4

E uan McCallister had been an astute observer for most of his adult life. A quality any good detective should possess. He excelled at picking up on the nuances of colleagues and criminals alike. So when he arrived at the station this morning before Ellis, his senses heightened. He hadn't believed the word "tardy" existed in her vocabulary. The thought that she might have held onto some animosity toward him after his probing question at dinner yesterday seemed trivial. Nevertheless, she was still an unknown entity, and anything was possible.

McCallister's curiosity was short-lived when, from around the corner, Ellis appeared. "Burning the midnight oil, Ellis?"

She arrived at her desk and set down her bag. "Something like that. Sorry I'm late."

"Don't worry about it. I managed to hold down the fort in your absence." He checked the time. "The whole fifteen minutes of it."

"Thanks."

Her abrupt responses raised his interest once again. "Hey, are you okay? Did something happen last night?"

"No, sorry. It's nothing." She logged into her computer. "I got a file last night from Fletch. She pulled Claire Allen's phone records from this month. I only briefly glanced at it because it was pretty late, but I'll print off a copy for you and we'll go through it."

"Sure." He watched her walk to the printer and snatch the papers before returning to hand over a copy. "Thanks. Listen, if you're pissed off about what I said at dinner..."

"What? No, it's not a problem. I promise you. We're good. I found a phone number on here that Claire had called multiple times, including just hours before the fire. I think we should focus on that first."

McCallister was by no means a timid man, but he felt Ellis kept him at arm's length now, a shift in her behavior since working together on this case. The last thing he needed was another Boston on his hands. There were only so many places he could go to outrun his mistakes. Bangor was his last shot and he'd better not blow it. "This must be the number you're talking about. Several calls to it, you're right. Do we have a list of Claire's friends yet?"

"No. I'll make a call to Scott Allen and get it from him. Whoever this is had to have been a close confidant given the number of calls and texts."

"On the other hand, if she was being blackmailed or targeted in some other way, that number could belong to her killer."

"Wouldn't that make our lives easier?" Ellis picked up her phone and made the call. "Good morning, Mr. Allen. It's Detective Ellis. Yes, I'm fine and how are you doing?" She nodded. "Of course, yes, it will take time. Listen, the reason I'm calling, and I hate to bother you again, but it would be helpful if you could provide us with the names of Claire's friends and associates. As many as you know. Also, we really would like for you to come down and give us a statement.

Momentum is building and your statement will go a long way to helping us move forward." She listened to him speak. "Today at 2 pm, that would work well for us. Yes, Mr. Allen, thank you so much. Thank you, bye." She turned to McCallister. "He'll be in at two today."

INSIDE THE ALLEN HOME, Scott slumped back on his sofa with a raging headache. A nearly empty bottle of Jack Daniel's sat on the coffee table, with which he'd attempted to spend the night drowning his pain. It hadn't worked. He'd put off making the call to Claire's family. Most of her friends already knew, thanks to the church's rumor mill. Some had stopped by with cheese-laden casserole dishes, enough to last him a month. He fucking hated cheese. Others had called to ask if he needed help with the arrangements. And now the police wanted him to make a statement. About what? What the hell did he know about what happened to his wife?

"Goddam it." He rubbed his temples to soothe the throbbing and then heard the knock on the door. "Christ. Please don't be another casserole." With all the effort he could muster, Scott rose to his feet and shuffled to the door. Two people stood on the other side, and they were the only two people he felt relieved to see.

Maxine Rehnquist rushed inside and threw her arms around him. "I'm so sorry. She was my best friend. I can't believe she's gone." The dainty woman, who couldn't have weighed more than a buck ten, burrowed her head in his chest.

Ethan Rehnquist laid his hand on her back. Sorrow imbued his light brown eyes. He pulled off his hat and revealed a disheveled heap of dark blond hair. "Max, let the man breathe."

She pulled away and wiped the tears from her cheeks. Her short brunette locks clung to her face. "I'm sorry, Scott."

"It's okay. Come in."

Maxine stepped into the living room and immediately spied the booze on the coffee table. Scott picked up on her observation and hurried to grab it. "It was a rough night. Have a seat. Can I get you two anything?"

Ethan toyed with his keys. "No, I'm good, man. Why don't you sit down?"

Maxine joined him on the sofa. "Scott, what happened? I don't understand. Ethan said Claire's car caught fire? How? How could this have happened?"

"Cops don't know anything yet except she was at the goddam church, of course. Where the hell else would she have been? She told me she was going to see friends." He clenched his fists. "Why would she lie to me, Max?"

Ethan took a seat on the side chair. "Take it easy, Scott. Like you said, the cops don't know anything. You know Claire. She probably had to drop off something and swung by afterwards." He glanced into the hall. "You mind if I use the restroom?"

Scott waved his approval while keeping his gaze fixed to the floor.

Maxine grabbed a tissue from the coffee table and dabbed at her eyes. "I've never seen Ethan like this before. He's worried about you, Scott. We both are. What can we do to help? Please don't shut us out, okay? Let us help you."

He studied her a moment. "Where were you when it happened, Max? You two are best friends—were. Did Claire call you?"

Her chin quivered under her full lips. "I was out of town for work. She did call but it went to voicemail. She texted me too, but I was busy. I didn't reply." With a watery gaze, she continued, "I ignored her messages, Scott. I'm so sorry.

She said she wanted to meet and I didn't think anything of it."

Ethan returned to the living room, his thick wavy hair now tucked behind his ears. "Listen, you want to come stay with us for a while? I don't think you should be alone, man."

"That's a kind offer, but I want to be here." He let his eyes roam. "Everything in this house reminds me of her. I don't want to forget her smell. I can still hear her voice. No, I'm not leaving. This is our home."

A TEXT ARRIVED on Ellis's phone while she sat at her desk. She read it, then glanced at McCallister. "I got it. It's a text, but I got the list of her friends with numbers from Allen. It's almost noon now, and we asked him to come down at two to make his statement."

"Gives us a couple hours. You want to track down the Rehnquist woman first? Seems she might have some insight," McCallister replied. "We can make it happen."

"Yep. I'll call her now. I'm going to assume Allen gave her the news, but if we have to deliver it, then that's just the way it has to be. We can't afford to lose any more time." Ellis picked up the phone and made the call.

"Hello?"

Ellis perked up at the unexpectedly quick answer. "Good afternoon, I'm Detective Rebecca Ellis, Bangor PD. Is this Maxine Rehnquist?"

"Yes, it is. Oh, God. This is about Claire, isn't it? Scott said the police would want to talk to me."

"So you know about Claire Allen?" Ellis asked.

"Yes, my husband and I visited Scott earlier. He's our friend. We're all just devastated. I loved Claire like a sister."

"Of course. I met your husband briefly when we drove

Mr. Allen home yesterday morning. Mrs. Rehnquist, since Claire was your friend, my partner and I would like to ask you a few questions. I realize you're still processing this loss, and for that I'm truly sorry, but we'd really like to speak with you just as soon as possible."

"Um, yeah, of course. I'm at home. My address is 1465 Cherry Tree Lane."

"Thank you. We'll be there in about 20 minutes. And I have to ask, Mrs. Rehnquist, are you aware we're investigating Claire's death as a homicide?"

She paused a moment. "I'm not entirely sure that comes as a surprise to me."

AMID THE TREE-LINED street lay a modest cottage home not far from the Allens. The older neighborhood, while buried in several feet of snow, appeared well kept. Ellis shifted her Tahoe into Park in front of the house. "They're practically neighbors. The Allen house is only a couple of blocks away. I don't think this couple has the kind of money their friends do, though. Still, this congregation looks to be pretty tight. That could work for or against us, depending on how far back we pull this curtain." She opened the passenger door and stepped out. The salted sidewalk had turned the snow to slush in the bright light of the day and her boot sank into a puddle. "Damn it. The one day I don't wear waterproof shoes."

McCallister joined her and peered down at her feet with his hands in his coat pockets. "You did grow up in Maine, right?"

"Yes. Yes, I did. You lived in Boston. You like the snow?"

He turned down his mouth before starting along the path

to the front door. "Doesn't bother me that much. Watch your step. It's a mess up here."

"Thanks for the heads-up." Ellis followed him to the front steps and noticed the door open. A petite woman in an oversized sweater and leggings stood on the other side. She appeared to be around the same age as the victim. Her brunette hair was pulled back in a short ponytail, and her eyes looked like they could cry no more. "Good afternoon. I'm Detective Rebecca Ellis. We spoke on the phone."

"Nice to meet you." She sized up McCallister. "Are you with her?"

"Yes, ma'am. Detective Euan McCallister."

"Well, come in." She stepped aside while the detectives entered. "Can I get you a cup of coffee? I might have some tea."

"No, thank you, but I appreciate the offer," Ellis replied.

McCallister raised a pre-emptive hand. "All good here, but thanks."

"Suit yourself." Maxine folded her arms as though a chill had suddenly struck her as she led the way to her kitchen table. "We can sit here if you'd like."

"Sure." Ellis pulled out a heavy wooden chair that screeched on top of the laminate floor. "As I said before, I'm very sorry for your loss. Can I ask how long you knew Claire?"

McCallister took a seat while Maxine lowered herself with some effort onto the chair. "Oh, I guess about five years, give or take. We met at the church and hit it off well. Became fast friends after that."

Ellis retrieved her notebook. "You said earlier that Mr. Allen informed you about Claire just this morning?"

"As I mentioned on our call, my husband and I visited him at his house this morning. It was the first I'd seen him after Ethan told me what happened. I had been out of town for work."

"So you're aware the incident happened at the church?" McCallister asked.

"That's what I heard." Maxine peered through the window of her breakfast room at the snow-covered trees outside.

"Where is your husband now?" Ellis asked.

"He had to tie up some loose ends at work, but he'll be taking off a few days to help Scott." She turned back to Ellis. "You think this was intentional? I don't get it. How could she not manage to get out in time?" Her eyes welled and her chin trembled as she appeared to consider the horror. "I just can't believe she's gone."

"I know how difficult this must be, but there is reason to believe this was an intentional act. As my partner and I analyzed the phone records, it seemed like you and Claire had spoken and texted a lot in the days and hours leading up to the incident. In fact, it seemed that you anticipated it when I mentioned this was a homicide."

"Like I said, I had been out of town for work, and we do— did, talk a lot. Including the other day, but her call went to voicemail."

"What kind of work do you do, Mrs. Rehnquist?" McCallister asked.

"Please call me Maxine. I work for an advertising firm. I went with my boss to close on a new client. I don't travel much, so it's nice when I get the chance, even if it's for work. Anyway"—she drew in a deep breath—"over the past few weeks, Claire seemed off."

"How so?" Ellis asked.

Maxine scratched the polish from her nails. "There's something you should know about Claire. She volunteered at the church more than any of us combined. It was her life. She didn't have another job outside of that. No kids. But she—and I hate to even say this—but she liked drama. I'm sure you must know people like that."

Ellis nodded. "I do. So she was texting and calling, and you think she just had some drama going on? Maybe with her husband?"

"No, it wasn't her husband." Maxine reached for her phone. "Maybe it's best if I show you." She opened her phone to the text messages. "Claire sent me these messages Tuesday morning."

Ellis pulled the phone closer and read aloud. "'I know you're out of town for work. Can we meet as soon as you return? Will Vanessa stay with your mom while you're away? Maybe I can pick her up and she can stay with me?'" She looked at Maxine. "Who's Vanessa?"

"My daughter."

"With your husband here, why would she ask for your daughter to stay with her?" Ellis continued.

"She loved Vanessa," Maxine replied. "Ethan's usually busy with work. She probably thought she'd be doing him a favor by keeping her while I was gone. That's the only thing I can think of."

"Okay, so he was here with your daughter on Tuesday night?"

"Yes."

"I'm picking up on a slightly urgent tone here," McCallister said. "But there must be another reason you believe she was murdered."

Maxine held out her hand. "May I?"

Ellis returned the phone. "Of course."

She opened her voicemail and pressed play. "There was this too."

"Max, I was hoping to reach you. Listen, I thought we could grab lunch when you get back into town. I think we should talk. I

know I've been distant with you lately and I'm sorry for that. I haven't been myself. So much has happened. I don't want to lose you. You're my best friend. So, please, call me back. Let's meet soon and talk. A lot needs to be said. Love you, my friend. Bye."

Maxine ended the message. "The thing was, I just thought it was Claire being Claire. She kind of always thought other people at the church were jealous of her. But this was unusual."

"Unusual, how?" Ellis asked. "And why would she think people were jealous of her?"

"Claire liked to give people the impression she had a perfect life. Her husband took care of her. They had money. I mean, not real money, but money. She drove a nice car, wore nice clothes, bought expensive handbags."

"But you knew better?" Ellis pressed on.

"She did have all those things, but I think she was over-compensating. For what, I don't know. Maybe because she didn't have kids. She'd wanted them, but I don't think Scott did." She paused for a long moment, looking down at her now-chipped nails. "My husband and I spent a lot of time with the Allens. We'd have dinner at each other's houses. Go out for drinks." She swallowed hard. "The four of us were close. But you have to know, I never thought Claire was in danger. Given what's happened, after what you said, I look at that call and those messages differently. I swear I would've done something to help. And now I'm going to have to live with the fact that I didn't."

Ellis nodded briefly as she continued to read through the messages. "And these others, you thought it was Claire being paranoid? Because the way I read these, she sounds like she's concerned about someone or something she found out. Doesn't say what. Like this one here." She read again. "'I thought the church was a safe place. A good place. Now I'm not so sure.' And that was just before her phone call on Tuesday. It seemed a catalyst, of sorts."

"Right. Again, I sort of blew it off, thinking she thought one of the other volunteers was getting on her about something." Maxine wiped away a tear. "And now she's dead."

"Claire's phone wasn't recovered from the scene, so we have no way of knowing if she was communicating with someone else about all of this," McCallister added. "Of course, we obtained her phone records and that will reveal some further details; however, a lot of people use encrypted apps to send messages. That could be the case here. Right now, we need clues."

Ellis spotted a small child emerge from the hall and peek into the kitchen. "Your daughter?"

Maxine glanced back. "Vanessa, you can come say hello." She waved over the child. "These nice people are with the police."

The girl shook away rogue strands of wispy blonde hair. "Did you do something wrong, Mommy?"

"No. No, sweetheart, I didn't. They're here to help Mommy with something for a friend." She turned to Ellis. "She's five and goes to kindergarten for half-days."

Vanessa tucked her head behind Maxine's arm.

"She's a little shy. Once she gets to know you, honestly, you can't shut her up."

"Hi there, Vanessa." Ellis gave the little girl a wave. "Do you just have the one child?" she asked Maxine.

"Yes. For now. We're kicking around the idea of another. Do either of you have kids?"

"No," the detectives replied in unison.

"Oh, okay." Maxine turned to her daughter. "Why don't you go back upstairs, sweetheart? Mommy will be finished soon."

The child looked at Ellis, held her gaze for what seemed a long time, and finally darted away.

Maxine waited for Vanessa to fall out of earshot. "What else do you know, Detective? If this was a murder, how are you certain?"

"We know that Claire's SUV had been tampered with," McCallister replied.

"Tampered with?" Her eyes sharpened. "In what way?"

McCallister looked at Ellis for apparent consensus before he continued, "Preliminary reports show that her fuel line had been cut and her seatbelt jammed. These are the reasons why we're certain Claire was murdered. Can you think of anyone who would want to hurt your friend? Anyone at all."

Maxine straightened her back, and in a resolute, but fractured tone, she continued, "Rumors have gone around recently at the church. I don't like to entertain them because more often than not, they're nothing. But given what's happened." She teared up again. "I never asked Claire directly about this because, again, I don't like to give these things any air, but some people thought that maybe Scott was having an affair."

"Uh-huh. You said you were close to the Allens," Ellis began. "Do you think the rumor could have been true?"

Maxine shrugged. "I don't know."

"Were names mentioned?" McCallister cut in.

She pressed her lips together, appearing to hold her tongue a moment. "You'll want to talk to Ann Kemper."

5

Great detectives aren't born, they are built. Hank's words. Ellis agreed with them to an extent, but she believed, unlike Hank, that there had to be an inherent attribute that allowed an investigator to wade through the bullshit to get to the truth. Reading body language, fluctuations in tone, nervous tics; picking up on those clues could be taught. But recognizing a lie as it was being spun took an innate quality, and Ellis possessed it. This was what made her a great detective, who would one day rival her legendary father.

Questioning Scott Allen had, so far, gone as expected. As Ellis and her partner probed him inside the station's only interview room, indications that he had played a part in his wife's murder had substantially diminished. His remorse over the loss had not only appeared genuine, but the facts spoke for themselves. Good for the husband, not good for the investigation.

Ellis flipped through her notes. "You say that you were working from home that evening, and then went to bed even though Claire hadn't responded to your text asking where she was?"

"That's correct. I had no reason to think anything was wrong," he replied.

"Maxine Rehnquist suggested Claire hadn't been herself over the past several days or even weeks leading up to the incident. Had you noticed that as well?" Ellis observed Allen while he twirled a pen between his fingers and averted his gaze. This didn't exactly scream guilt, but it gave her pause.

"No, I hadn't noticed anything. I guess I should have." Allen cast occasional glances at the detectives while he answered. "I've been busy with work and I took a lot of it home. Claire didn't like that."

"There is one last thing we'd like to ask you, Mr. Allen." Ellis eyed McCallister a moment before continuing, "Apparently, rumors at the church swirled with the idea you were having an affair. You won't get any judgment from us. We're here for the truth. Is there any truth to the rumor?"

Allen raised his chin. "Who told you that?"

"Does it matter?" McCallister cut in. "It would explain Mrs. Rehnquist's notion that Claire hadn't behaved as usual if she had heard this rumor."

"It matters when my reputation is being tarnished," he shot back.

"Like I said, Mr. Allen, we don't give a damn about what you were doing unless it impacts our investigation. That rumor does. Please just tell us the truth. No one outside this room needs to know," Ellis said.

"Of course I wasn't having an affair. I love my wife. Those gossips at the church were all jealous of her. She told me as much."

"Why?" Ellis asked.

"Because she wore expensive things. Shoes, handbags. In case you weren't aware, our community isn't exactly upper middle class. But I gave Claire everything I could to make her happy."

McCallister raised a single brow. "To make her happy, or keep her happy?"

Ellis stood from the table. "Okay, thank you for coming down, Mr. Allen. We appreciate your cooperation. As you know, we are treating this as a homicide investigation. As such, we will proceed with interviewing Claire's friends, associates, and arrange to speak with her family."

McCallister took to his feet. "We will also come by first thing in the morning to collect Claire's laptop, tablet, and any other of her electronic devices from your home. It might be a good idea for you to offer your personal devices as part of that, just to convey your total cooperation. We'll just need you to sign the release authorizing us to collect it as evidence."

"I already told you that I tried to get into her computer. She changed her password, although I have no idea why she wouldn't have mentioned that to me. As far as my phone and laptop go, they belong to my company. I'm not sure if I can authorize their release."

"That sounds like something we'll want to work on," McCallister replied.

Ellis opened the door. "Will you be okay to drive yourself home? I'm happy to have someone..."

"I'll manage." He started out into the hall and stopped a moment. "You know, maybe you should look at the so-called 'friends' who were jealous of Claire. You'd be surprised at the lengths people will go to take others down."

"I don't think I would, Mr. Allen. We'll be in touch." Ellis waited until he disappeared beyond the corridor. "Gonna need to peel back some layers there. I'm not sure if he's pointing us to her friends as a diversion or to suggest someone knew of his alleged affair and was blackmailing him for it. Why else would he have tried to get access to his wife's computer if he didn't suspect someone had called him out?"

"Fair point. As far as his phone and laptop, we'll need cause to get a search warrant from his company if that's the angle we want to pursue."

"Hey, Gabby, what's going on?" Ellis called out as she noticed Detective Lewis's approach.

"Hey." Lewis peered over her shoulder a moment. "Was that the husband?"

"Yep."

"So, Becca, listen, one of the guys who works the south-side came up here looking for you a while ago. I told him you were interviewing someone." She pushed away her long, dark braids and chewed on her lower lip. Forty-year-old single mother, Lewis worked mostly on computer crimes and money laundering. Worked the same thing at her precinct back in Chicago until about three years ago when she moved to Bangor with her teenage sons.

"What is it?" Ellis asked.

"He got a call about a disturbance at a pawnshop. The owner was trying to get a guy out, and he wouldn't leave, so the cops were called. Becca, I'm sorry, but they arrested your brother. He's downstairs."

"For God's sake." She turned on her heel and started down the hall but stopped and turned back. "Euan, can you confirm Scott Allen's alibi, starting with his work history."

"On it." As she walked away, he called out, "Hey, you need a hand with this, or..."

Ellis spun around. "Thanks, but no. My brother is my problem."

THE HOLDING cells were located on the station's ground floor in addition to the bullpen that housed the patrol officers. Ellis made her way to the booking area and stopped at the desk.

"Hey, Liz, I was told you guys have my brother."

"Yeah, sorry about that, Becca." The officer pointed down the hall. "He's down there with Triggs."

"Thanks." Ellis headed into the corridor and found Officer Triggs at his desk with her brother sitting in the chair next to him.

Carter looked up at her. "Look who's here. My loving sister."

"Detective Ellis—" Triggs began.

"That's my father," Carter cut in. "Becca tries to be like him, but she can't hold a candle."

"That's enough from you," Triggs replied. "Detective, Mr. Ellis was attempting to sell a gold watch and when the pawnshop owner wanted him to verify ownership, this man here got irate. The owner found an inscription on the watch."

"Can I see it?" Ellis asked.

Triggs opened his desk drawer and retrieved the watch from inside an evidence bag. "Here you go."

Ellis examined it. "Are you kidding me, Carter? You took the watch given to Dad when he retired?"

"He never wore the damn thing," Carter snapped in reply. "I was going to get it back. I'm just waiting on a friend to pay me what he owes."

"Uh-huh." She peered at the officer. "Can I return this to its rightful owner?"

"Yes, ma'am, but we are going to have to charge Mr. Ellis with disorderly conduct and trafficking of stolen property."

"What?" Carter shot him a look. "No way. Are you shitting me right now? They'll give me two years, minimum."

"Officer, I'll speak to my father, who I'm certain won't press charges. The disorderly charge is fine. Let him spend a few nights here. At least he won't be sleeping on the streets and freezing to death." She started away.

"Gee, thanks, sis," he called out. "It's nice to see how much you care."

Triggs turned to him. "Dude, your sister just saved your ass. You should be grateful."

Carter scoffed. "Whatever. Becca kills a guy when she was twelve, and everyone thinks she's some kind of fucking hero or something."

Ellis said nothing and returned upstairs to her desk, where McCallister looked on. "Everything okay?"

She sat down. "Fine. I'm sorry about that. My brother's a handful."

"They say you can't choose your family," he replied. "I went ahead and pulled up the employment records on Scott Allen. He works for a bank. Some paper-pusher. Well, the head paper-pusher by the look of it. He's the vice president of New Accounts at Eastern Union Bank. Their Downtown location. Looks to be their main branch."

"New accounts?" Ellis asked. "How would that translate to bringing home work? What could he have to bring home?"

"Good question. He indicated he worked a lot from home at night and sometimes on the weekends. I mean, look, I'm no business major, but it seems reasonable to assume a man in that position might work more than your average bank teller."

"Okay, I'll bite. That would also suggest he had access to the bank's computer systems from his house," she added.

"Most likely."

Ellis peered through the second-floor window as she considered a notion. "I'll bet we could reach out to the bank and ask if he'd logged into their system that night. That would go a long way to corroborating his alibi."

"They won't do that voluntarily, but that doesn't mean we

can't take a run at them and get a feel for their reaction. Their office isn't far from here," McCallister replied. "Let's test the waters and see if we get the runaround."

"Then we can decide how hard to push on asking them to release Allen's phone and laptop. I'll leave that in your capable hands. I'm going to talk to Claire's church friends." Ellis grabbed her coat.

CLAIRE ALLEN'S life appeared to have revolved around the church, according to her husband and closest friend. Everyone in her circle still needed to be vetted. If an affair had taken place between one of those friends and Scott Allen, it was time to root out the betrayer.

According to Townsend, Claire hadn't attended the Tuesday night service, but she'd gone to the church for a reason. And if she suspected her husband was having an affair, it was a motive in the making.

Maxine had mentioned that the ladies met at the church in the afternoons to plan weekend events. She'd opted out of today's gathering, still reeling from the murder of her best friend, but what struck Ellis as odd was that the meeting was still scheduled to take place despite what had happened.

She arrived at the church's administrative office and displayed her badge to the hefty middle-aged woman behind the desk. "Good afternoon. I'm Detective Rebecca Ellis. I understand there's a volunteer meeting taking place. I'd like to pop in and speak to them, please."

"Oh my." The woman appeared flustered as she looked at the badge. "This is about Claire, isn't it? Lord, you have no idea how devastated we all are here. It's just awful what happened to her. You're the one who's looking into all that?"

"Yes, ma'am. And since Mrs. Allen was here when it... Well, it's best to get a full picture."

"Yes, of course. The ladies are meeting down the hall there in room 110. It's my understanding they're working to put together a candlelight vigil for Claire soon."

"I'm sure that will be helpful to the community and the church that Claire seemed to love so much. Thank you for your help." Ellis headed down the hall and glimpsed pictures, looking to have been drawn by children, pinned to the wall. A few short Bible verses written in script, and a framed photo of Townsend. His bright white smile and square jaw. His perfect dark hair, combed neatly to one side. Hardly a line on his face. He looked ready-made for television.

She reached room 110 and gently knocked before opening the door. "Excuse the interruption."

"May we help you?" A woman in her late twenties stood at the head of the table. She pushed back her long red hair without disturbing the black headband that kept it neatly in place.

A tray of coffee and cookies lay in the middle of the table. Notepads and pens had been placed in front of the other volunteers, who appeared somber. Mostly younger women, which caught Ellis off guard. She'd expected retirees. The walls were adorned with more children's artwork alongside several photos of various church events. Not a single window in the room, only artificial light from the fluorescents above.

"I hope so. I'm Detective Rebecca Ellis. Bangor PD. I'd like to talk to you ladies about a friend of yours. Claire Allen? I'm sorry, I know this must be an incredibly difficult time for all of you. I understand you were her friends."

The redheaded woman offered her hand. "Yes, Claire was a wonderful friend and a highly valued member of this church. Please come in. My name's Callie. We were just discussing plans for a vigil in her honor."

"Thank you, Callie." Ellis returned the greeting. "First of all, I want to say how sorry I am for your loss."

"It was a tragedy. A shameful tragedy, Detective Ellis," Callie replied.

She continued inside. "I've spoken with Maxine Rehnquist, and she mentioned you all would be here today. I'd like to ask you a few questions."

"It's a shame she couldn't make it. I guess she doesn't realize we're all grieving for Claire, too, yet here we are. Sorry, I'm Ann Kemper." The woman, in her early thirties with dark wavy hair and full cheeks, held her chin high. "None of us can believe it. What a horrific accident."

This was the Ann Kemper Maxine had mentioned. Ellis noted her hard stance. "Yes, it's a terrible situation. I understand all of you were here on Tuesday for the evening service, but Claire wasn't. Did she usually attend?"

The ladies traded glances before Ann spoke up. "Sometimes. She worked really hard for the church and could be counted on to attend the Sunday service, but she wasn't always available for Tuesdays. We were all here, though, yes, well, except for Maxine."

"I understand she was out of town. It seems to me all of you work hard for the church," Ellis said.

"Yes, well, Claire didn't work a regular job, so the church was a big part of her life. I, myself, only work part-time, but I also have children," Ann continued. "In fact, even Claire's husband volunteered his services to help with the church finances. He's a genius with numbers."

Ellis cocked her head. "I didn't realize he volunteered too. Very impressive couple."

At the other end of the table, a young brunette dressed in a plaid shirt and fleece vest cleared her throat to garner attention. "I'm pretty sure he got paid for it. My name's Hailey Barnes. My children aren't in school yet, so I can only make myself available at certain times. Right now, they're with their grandma. I do what I can, though."

"I'm sure you do," Ellis replied. "And when you say Scott Allen was probably paid, was he considered a part-time employee?"

"Well, I don't know, really. I'm just making assumptions," Hailey replied. "It's just that I saw him a lot with Pastor Zeke, and I assumed it was all about the church's books. He'd be a saint to volunteer that much in the way of professional services and not be paid for it."

"You could be right." This was where that inherent ability to call bullshit kicked in. Ellis not only felt the tension in the room, but it seemed these women were aware of quite a lot that went on in this church, so it was up to her to extract that knowledge from them. "May I ask how you ladies found out what happened to Claire? I understand that everyone had pretty much gone home for the night and for whatever reason, Claire was here at nine or ten o'clock, then of course..." She trailed off. "We're still putting together a time-line of events."

"Word gets around quickly, Detective," Ann cut in. "I mean, everyone thought the church was on fire at first. Our youth pastor, Jeff Harwick, he only left a while before it all happened, and came back for something. He called Pastor Zeke and then it went down the chain. Of course, we all believed this to have been a horrific accident, so I'm left wondering what it is you're doing here. Is there more to the story, Detective?"

"This is all standard procedure, Mrs. Kemper. We're still in the very early stages of learning what exactly happened, which is why I came to see you all. As Claire's friends, it's important for me to understand her support system."

"She had a great deal of support from all of us," Callie added. "We loved Claire very much."

"I can see that." Ellis flipped through her notes. "Going back to Tuesday evening, what time had you all left for the night?"

"I had to hurry home to help my son get ready for bed," Ann started. "So I left a little before the rest of the group. I'd say around nine."

Callie glanced around the room. "I think the rest of us left shortly after. Maybe 9:15 or 9:30. No later than that."

Ellis nodded. "And was anyone else still here?"

"Oh, Pastor Zeke was. In fact, I ran into him in the hall and asked why he was hanging around," Hailey replied. "And I thought I saw Pastor Jeff leave around nine, but I think that was it."

"Did Pastor Zeke tell you why he was still here?" Ellis asked.

"Honestly, I wasn't really paying attention. I was just making chitchat and trying to get out of here."

"Sure, of course." Ellis glanced at the other women. "Does anyone else recall seeing Pastor Zeke after the service?"

"I don't," Callie replied. "We all just jumped in and started cleaning so we could get out of there. Gosh, does this help you at all, Detective?"

"You know what? It does." She returned her notebook to her bag. "Well, I should get going. I want to thank you all for helping to clear up a few things for me. I'll be calling on each of you, individually, in the next day or so for an official statement. Again, I'm so sorry for your loss. Claire Allen was clearly beloved around here. I appreciate your time." Ellis tossed her bag over her shoulder. "Actually, Mrs. Kemper, do you have time to sit with me for a few more minutes?"

6

Torrid love affairs made fodder for good television, but, in real life, they hurt real people. Sometimes enough that a person would consider murder their only solution. It was time to get a glimpse inside the life of Ann Kemper to determine whether she'd been pushed to the brink and selected to take out her competition, assuming the rumors were true. First impressions? She seemed polite enough, if not a little abrupt. A church volunteer, married with children. The question remained, if an affair had occurred between Ann Kemper and Scott Allen, had Claire discovered it, and had it resulted in her murder?

Mrs. Kemper stood tall at about five feet ten. Hands clasped at her front. Her formal appearance was punctuated by a beige silk blouse and black dress pants. "Of course I can spare some time." She offered a curt nod and turned on her heel. "We can talk back here."

Down the hall lay one of the church's many classrooms. "Right through here. Take a seat wherever you like." She closed the door behind them and continued in. "I'm left to assume you're not very close to finding out who killed my friend."

If the rumors were to be believed, then it seemed Kemper played fast and loose with the term "friend." Ellis sat down at one of the tables. "We are continuing to follow up on leads, but this relates specifically to your relationship with Claire Allen."

Kemper sat down on a hard plastic chair next to Ellis, crossing her legs and placing her hands over her knees. "I've already told you we were friends."

"Yes, of course. However, it's important that I clarify a few things about your relationship."

When it came to interviewing suspects or witnesses, Ellis had an eye for their behavior, their tells. And, right now, just by her facial expressions, Ann Kemper might as well have screamed out that she'd murdered her so-called friend.

"I'm sorry, am I a suspect?" she asked.

"As I said in the other room, I'm questioning everyone who was at this church on the night of," Ellis replied. "Please don't take offense. I'm just doing my job."

"Well, as I said, Claire was well respected here. She put in more hours than any of us. Of course, she didn't have children or a job, so she had plenty of time on her hands."

Ellis scratched down more notes. "Did the two of you spend time together outside the church? And, I mean to say, outside of any church events as well. You know, were you two close friends?"

"Did we go out for brunch or drinks or anything like that?" Kemper turned up her chin. "Not really. Claire didn't do much at all outside the church. This place was her whole life. I often gathered with some of the other ladies outside the church. So, in that respect, Claire and I weren't close friends, no."

"And Scott Allen?" Ellis asked. "Were you two friends?"

Kemper shifted in the chair a moment. "He did the books for the church sometimes. I'm in charge of the money for the fundraisers, so yes, I do contact Scott often to discuss deposits and things of that nature."

"Sure, that makes sense." Ellis nodded.

Kemper pressed her lips together. "I'm beginning to get the feeling that you think Scott Allen and I are involved in something we're not. Frankly, I don't appreciate the implication. I'm a married woman with a family. I don't need to be made to feel as though I've done something wrong for speaking to the husband of my dead friend."

Ellis rubbed the back of her neck. "You are absolutely right, Mrs. Kemper. You can speak to whomever you want, whenever you want. My purpose here is to understand your relationship with the Allens. That's all this is, and if I've given you any other impression, then I certainly apologize."

"Thank you."

"And what about your husband? Does he do much for the church?" she continued.

"No, not particularly. He travels a lot for work. I'm left taking care of the kids, so the three of us spend a lot of time here. They like to play with the other kids."

Ellis put down her pen and placed her hands on the table, setting her sights on the woman. "Part of my job, Mrs. Kemper, is to read people. Often, when someone is asked to talk to the cops, innocent or not, they change their behavior. It's just a part of human nature, I think. Does that make sense?"

"I suppose so," she concurred.

"I don't think the person you're showing me now is who you really are."

"Excuse me?"

Ellis peered down at her feet a moment. "You're an intelligent woman, so I won't treat you as if you aren't. I'm sure you've heard the rumors."

Kemper's lips turned down and quivered just a little as she averted her gaze.

"If you and Scott Allen were having an affair, that shines a spotlight directly on you, Mrs. Kemper. So the questions I'm going to ask you now, please know that it is critical you tell me the truth. Do you understand?"

Kemper blinked hard and nodded.

"Good. You were here on the night. You said in the other room that you all left around nine o'clock. Claire was dead by 10:15 pm." Ellis fixed her sights on her. "Where exactly were you between nine and ten last Tuesday night, Ann? Think carefully before you answer."

Kemper swallowed hard and her breaths appeared labored. "I stopped by to see Scott on my way home. Just for a little while."

"Do you have proof you were at the Allen home?" Ellis pressed on.

Kemper's brow knitted. "What kind of proof?"

"Text messages between you two arranging for the meeting would be a good start," she replied.

Kemper hesitated for a long moment, then retrieved her phone and opened the screen. "Here. It's all right here."

Ellis examined the exchange. The woman was telling the truth. She and Scott Allen had traded messages discussing meeting up after the service because Claire was out for the evening. She handed back the phone. "Thank you. I'll need you to come in and make an official statement as soon as possible."

Ellis stepped outside the room and pressed her back against the wall in the corridor. Ann Kemper had not only given herself an alibi, but she'd reinforced Scott Allen's as well. The rumors were true, but it hadn't seemed to make a damn bit of difference to her investigation.

She continued along the corridor and spotted Townsend's office. This wasn't finished yet. If Allen helped out with the church's books, why hadn't he mentioned that in his interview? Seemed relevant considering his wife had spent the majority of her days at that same church. She reached his office and peered inside. "Afternoon, Pastor."

He jolted in his seat and caught her gaze. "Detective? I didn't know you were here. Come in, come in." After she stepped inside, he continued, "Is everything going all right? Did you need to see me?"

"I was just speaking to some of Claire's friends, the other volunteers, and Ann Kemper. Just trying to get a full picture of her life," she replied.

"Well, yes, of course. I hope they offered helpful information."

"I think so. They seem like a very nice group of women." Ellis adjusted her bag on her shoulder and meandered farther into his office.

"That they are. We're lucky to have them. Just as we were lucky to have Claire. How is the investigation going? Have you determined what happened?"

"Working on it. I would like to ask you about something that the women mentioned. I guess Scott Allen also helps out at the church?"

"Yes, he does. He's an expert with numbers, being a banker and all that. Helps us out with our bookkeeping sometimes. Not often, but when we're shorthanded, he'll jump right in."

"That must save the church a decent amount of money, not paying an accountant," Ellis observed.

"Oh, we still have a firm we use. Scott just does the odds and ends every so often."

"I see. Well, I won't take up any more of your time." She turned to leave.

The pastor stood from his desk. "Detective Ellis?"

"Yes?" She returned her attention to him.

"I've heard rumors that Claire's death wasn't an accident. Rest assured, I've not spread any such rumors, but is there anything you can tell me about that?"

She took notice of how his dark brown eyes seemed to smile at her, strange, considering the question he posed, yet he licked his lips with nervous expectancy. "The rumor is true, I'm sorry to say. Claire was, in fact, murdered, Pastor. So you'll be seeing a lot of me for a while."

PASTOR ZEKE TOWNSEND exuded the sort of narcissism Ellis had only seen in those who'd committed fraud and scams that relied upon gaining the trust of others. Even the volunteers she'd spoken to, Claire's own friends, appeared self-serving yet claimed to be for the betterment of the church. Maybe, she thought, it was her own utter disinterest in the church as a concept, or in religion as a whole.

Cynical by nature, Ellis came by it honestly. A cop for a father, a mother who had no sense of self-worth, a drug-addicted brother. It was no wonder. And it seemed her victim's entire life revolved around the giving of herself to others. Time, money, maybe even love. Selfless or selfish, Claire had been killed for it.

The afternoon had surrendered to evening by the time Ellis returned to the station. She noticed McCallister at his desk and approached him. "Still here, huh? Thought you might've gotten fed up and called it quits."

"What, and leave you to take all the credit? We'll see how this case goes." He raised his index finger. "I did find something interesting while you were out. First of all, Scott Allen was, in fact, logged into the bank's computer system on Tuesday night, like he said. The bank was very helpful and provided me with the server logs. They didn't even ask for a warrant. Why? I don't want to pull at that thread right now." He tossed the files onto his desk. "Here they are, in black and white."

She picked up the papers to examine them. "What about the IP address? Did it come from the Allen household?"

"I put a call in to the service provider. It'll likely be morning before they get back to me. Pending those results, it appears Mr. Allen was telling the truth."

She tossed them back onto his desk. "Well, that squares up with what Ann Kemper said."

"How so?"

Ellis sat down. "She admitted to the affair. And she was with Scott Allen roughly from the time the church service ended until about ten o'clock when she returned to her house."

"Shit. Can we confirm that?"

"She showed me text messages they exchanged that night setting up the rendezvous." Ellis retrieved her notes. "Something else that was interesting, Allen sometimes helps out with the church's books. Funny how he never said a thing about that. I later asked Townsend about it. He said Allen lends a hand on occasion, but that they use an accounting firm."

"Why the hell would he do that?" McCallister asked.

"Don't know, but it raised the hairs on my neck when he told me. Thing is, all the volunteers seemed to have left at roughly the same time. But now that we're about to get hold of Claire's computer and other devices, I think that could open things up for us. We should also go back to the bank and see how far their cooperation extends by asking them to release Allen's phone and laptop. We'll need to make it look like it's strictly for the purposes of eliminating him as a suspect. I'm not ready to cross Scott Allen off our list yet. Right now, it doesn't look like he killed his wife, but he's still hiding something. Why else keep that detail from us? But if we get the service provider involved, they'll insist on a warrant being issued to the bank to release them."

"The bank's information contained on those devices would be substantially more sensitive than server logs. Unless we're ready to pull the trigger and call Scott Allen a suspect, I'm not sure the bank will be that cooperative," McCallister observed. "And it doesn't sound like we're anywhere near that point."

She mulled over his concern. "No, I don't think we are. For now, Allen's alibi appears solid. Let's hit this from another angle. I'll bet if I call the church office and play nice, someone will offer up the name of their accounting firm."

McCallister raised a single brow. "And the endgame? What are we talking about here, Ellis?"

"Our initial motives for whoever killed Claire Allen were sex and money. We know about the affair. Hard to say whether Claire knew, but it doesn't appear she was murdered because of it. And do you remember what Allen said about the women at the church? Some seemed to have been jealous of the nice things she owned. The Allens have a nice car, nice house. Sure, Scott Allen has a middle-management job, but Claire enjoyed designer things. Those things cost money, maybe more than they had. And now we know that Allen helped out with the church's books. There's our other motive —money. Still valid and our best option at this point."

"It always comes down to sex or money," he said with a shrug.

"Sometimes both. So we have an affair that Claire might've discovered. Or, and I'm just throwing this out there, she learned that her husband was cooking the books and decided to tell the pastor. Why the hell else would he help out with their day-to-day accounting when they already employ an accounting firm? And then, more significantly, he chose not to disclose that?"

McCallister returned a curious gaze. "I don't know. Cooking the books would point back to her husband, though. Meaning why would he go to the effort of killing his wife at the church if she was going to rat him out to the pastor? Why not do it at home or anywhere else?"

Ellis raised a brow. "To put us through what we're talking about right now. Diverting our resources away from him and pointing the finger elsewhere."

"It'll take some legwork, but hell, if money's the motive, it's one of the strongest ones."

She pulled back in her chair and crossed her legs. "And usually the most reliable."

7

The Waterfront Bar, or as the locals called it, the Cop Joint, was located within spitting distance of the police station. Ellis was the last of her team to arrive, and she spied Pelletier and the others at a large hightop table. He waved her over.

Out of all the detectives, she was closest to him. The two shared a common bond, having both lost a parent. And while neither of them discussed it much, if at all, it was an unspoken understanding of a shared experience. Pelletier's mother had died of cancer a few years ago. Ellis's mother had been murdered, so not a totally shared experience.

"Hey, you made it. I was starting to worry." Pelletier wore a tender smile that made his blue eyes sparkle. A little full around the waist and softer than some, he had a look about him that still turned heads.

"I had a few things to take care of." Ellis eyed the bartender. "Bottle of Peroni. Thanks." She looked beyond the table, where Bevins appeared to have struck up a conversation with a young woman. "Looks like Connor's having fun already."

"That guy." Pelletier picked up his glass of beer.

"I know, I know. You think he's an arrogant ass," Ellis added. "He is, but that's beside the point." She noticed McCallister make his way toward them. "Hey there."

"Back at you. Did you get a drink yet?" he asked.

"I did."

"Here you go, ma'am." The bartender set down the bottle. "That'll be eight fifty. You want to start a tab?"

Ellis grabbed her wallet.

"Let me get that for you." McCallister turned to the barman. "Put it on my tab, would you?"

"Yes, sir, Detective McCallister."

"You don't have to do that," Ellis replied.

"I know I don't have to. I want to. Hey, you've been stuck with me all week. It's the least I can do and coming here saved me a trip to the packie."

"Uh, what's that now?" Ellis asked.

McCallister laughed. "Sorry, the liquor store. What's that saying about how you can take the kid out of Boston?"

"Wicked," Pelletier shot back.

"You from Beantown, man?" McCallister asked.

"No. Portland. And, you know, Mainers say that a lot too. It's not just a Boston thing." He tipped back his glass before setting his sights on Ellis. "So, Becca, how's the investigation going?"

"It's going. Not as quickly as I'd like, but when does it ever?" She nudged McCallister. "Right?"

"Yep."

"I'm sure it'll break loose in no time." Pelletier glanced over at Fletcher, who hadn't taken her eyes off her phone. "I think Fletch would prefer to stay behind a desk instead of working a case."

Everyone called Detective Lori Fletcher "Fletch." She was

the girl next door, only smarter and maybe a little more devious.

"She's one of the brightest we have here. She'd be happy working up the ranks, but everyone has to put in their time doing the grunt work."

"What's that about grunts, Becca?" Bevins walked toward them. "Glad you decided to join in on the fun."

"Strike out with the girl, there, Conn?" she asked.

"Ha, as if." He held out his phone. "Got her number right here. Don't be jealous; you're still my girl."

Ellis slugged him in the arm.

"Ouch." He laughed. "Shit, you been working out, Becca, or what?"

"Maybe." She surveyed the bar. "Where's Gabby? I thought she was coming."

"She was," McCallister cut in. "I guess she got a call from one of her kids and had to leave. She asked that we send her best to you. So, do you dance, Becca? Is it okay that I call you that?"

She choked on her drink and laughed. "First of all, yeah, Becca's fine. Everyone calls me that. And, hell no, I don't dance. By the way, you might want to work on honing your icebreaker topics."

"Hey, you can tell a lot from a person by how they answer that question," he shot back.

"Oh yeah? And what does it tell you about me?"

"That you have a hard time letting down your guard. Letting people in."

Ellis wasn't going down this road. Not now, and not with him. She eyed Pelletier, who'd gone quiet. "This one here, now he's a hell of a dancer. You remember that event last year? What was it?"

Pelletier closed his eyes. "Don't. Don't you dare."

McCallister noted the direction the exchange was taking. "Oh, now what's this all about?"

"It's fine. It's fine. Let me tell him. Please?" Ellis asked. "Last year, at some event Lieutenant Serrano made us all go to."

"Becca, come on," Pelletier pleaded.

"No, it's funny. Okay, not funny, but geez, Bryce, you shouldn't be embarrassed. This man right here pulled off moves like I've never seen before. The man can dance his ass off." She leaned in and kissed his cheek. "Aw, you know I love you."

Pelletier's full cheeks flushed while he raised his beer to his lips.

"Seriously. He could show up any one of us, I guarantee it," Ellis added.

McCallister patted him on the back. "Hey, man. It's all good. Your secret's safe with me."

Bevins turned back to them. "What secret? What'd I miss? Another chance at working a murder case? Damn it."

"Trust me, Connor, you'll get your shot." Ellis cocked her head. "You know, that's got me thinking about tomorrow." She turned to McCallister. "The sooner we get those devices out of Allen's home, the less opportunity he'll have to dump whatever he can from them."

"You think he wouldn't have done that already?" he asked. "It's the first thing I would've done if I killed my wife. And I would've done it before the cops showed up at my door to tell me she was dead. The only thing we have on our side is that he said he couldn't access her computer. There could be something there; we'll just have to wait and see."

Ellis glanced at her phone as a call arrived. "You guys excuse me a second? I gotta take this." She stepped into the hall that led to the restrooms and answered. "Hey, Dad, thanks for calling me back."

"What's going on? You can't make it over tonight, kiddo?"

"Not at the moment. I can swing by later in the evening. I'm having a drink with the guys right now."

"Ah, I see. That explains the racket I'm hearing. Don't worry about it. I think Carter's planning on dropping by."

"Actually, Dad, that's why I called earlier. He, uh, he was arrested today."

"What?" Hank asked. "Is he at the station?"

Ellis closed her eyes. "Dad, he was trying to pawn your retirement watch. Did you give it to him?"

"No. No, I didn't give him my watch. I love that watch, you know that," he replied.

"That's what I thought. He was high and put up a fight with the owner of the pawnshop. The guy called the cops. Out of courtesy, Officer Triggs called me in. I got them to drop down the charges to disorderly conduct. I knew you'd never press charges for theft, so you should expect a call soon asking about this. I'm surprised you haven't already."

"I saw a missed call from the station, but I haven't checked the voicemail. Goddam it, Carter."

"He'll be spending at least one night there. I'm sorry, Dad. I did the best I could."

"I know you did, kiddo. Look, you don't think I know Carter, but I do. I know he's not going to change. He's been in rehab more times than I can count, and it never took. I know that. And I'm sorry you had to get involved today. I'm sure stepping in like that wasn't what you wanted to do, and especially with the guys you work with."

"To be honest, most of them know all about Carter," she cut in.

"Fair point. Listen, go enjoy your drink. I love you, Becca."

"I love you, too, Dad. Goodnight." Ellis returned to the team and caught the bartender's attention. "Hey, another round for my friends. This one's on me, guys." She waited until they were served before she leaned into McCallister's ear. "And just for future reference, I hate owing anybody anything."

WHEN ELLIS STEPPED outside the bar, her eyes were drawn to the delicate flurry of snow that fell from the night sky. The winds that came off the river sent them swirling in all directions and the faint clatter of metal drifted in from the docks behind her. "As much as I hate the winter, I guess it can be a sight to behold sometimes."

Bevins peered over his shoulder at the rest of the team who followed. "Okay, who's taking Becca's keys from her?"

"Yeah, you're hilarious." She flipped up the hood of her coat while they carried on into the parking lot next to the bar. McCallister caught up to her, and she gave him a sideways glance. "Seriously, I had one drink an hour ago. I'm fine."

"I didn't think you weren't. Just wanted to say thanks."

"For what?"

"For making sure to include me in this kind of stuff. It's not easy being the new guy, and I'm pretty sure Pelletier doesn't like me much. I'll have to work my charms to get him to feel otherwise."

Ellis glanced back at Pelletier, who was in conversation with Fletch. "He's a little protective of me. Don't take it personally."

"If you say so."

She stopped near her Tahoe and turned back to the team. "I'll see you guys tomorrow. Goodnight. And I'll see you in the morning, Euan. Drive safe."

"You too, Becca. Night."

The team carried onward to their respective vehicles while Ellis retrieved her keys. She stopped a moment when her eye caught the footprints that patterned the light snow and led straight to her car. "Hey, Euan?"

"Yeah?" He turned to her. "Everything okay? You got your keys?"

"It's not that."

He started toward her when Pelletier also took notice. "Becca, everything okay?"

"Fine. Don't worry about me. We'll talk tomorrow." She remained fixed in place until McCallister reached her and she quickly thrust out her hand to stop him. "Wait." The team drove ahead out of the lot.

A deep frown and pinched brow revealed his concern. "What is going on?"

Ellis set her eyes on him. "Footprints. They lead straight to my car."

McCallister looked down to examine them. "Holy shit. Did someone try to break in?"

"I don't know." She sidestepped the prints and reached the driver's door. "Doesn't look like anyone tried to jimmy the lock."

McCallister gave a wide berth, stepping with caution around the vehicle. "More prints back here, Becca."

"Shit." She headed toward him and reached for her phone. "They're the same ones. I'm taking pictures of these."

He planted his hands on his hips. "No one knew we were here tonight. You're not thinking this is somehow related to our investigation?"

"Maybe. Did you notice prints at your car?"

"No," he replied.

"That's because I usually drive and everyone we've spoken to knows my vehicle." She turned around to face the street ahead. "Too many prints in all directions out that way, and they're getting covered with this flurry. I know how this sounds, but thieves don't usually just wander around vehicles, not bothering to so much as try the handle to see if it's unlocked. And any regular person isn't going to be walking around cars for no reason. I got a weird vibe from the pastor today. You weren't there, you didn't..."

Their attention was drawn to headlights that flipped on from a car parked curbside several feet away. It pulled out onto the road. Ellis narrowed her gaze. "Can you make out that car?" She slapped the side of her leg. "Shit. It turned the corner."

McCallister raised his hands. "Look, we might be getting ahead of ourselves here. There's no reason to think someone's trying to get to you or intimidate you."

Ellis returned to her SUV and examined it top to bottom. She unlocked the doors and checked the seatbelts while he stood aside with his arms across his chest. "Maybe I am being paranoid, but we still have a killer on the loose. Someone who let a woman burn to death at her church. If that's not symbolic of something, I don't know what the hell is."

"That's true. You want a unit at your house?" he asked.

"No, but I sure as hell won't be driving home the same way twice till this case is over."

ELLIS THREW her gearshift into Park and squinted through the windshield at the Allen home cast in the bright morning light. "He said he'd be here. It's almost nine o'clock and I don't see his car."

McCallister canvassed the neighborhood street. "Give him a minute. We're a little early." He was quiet a moment and placed his hands in front of the vent to warm them. "Before you came in this morning, I thought about something."

"Oh yeah? What's that?" she asked.

"We know the church didn't have security cameras, which is strange, but the youth pastor claimed not to have noticed anyone in the church parking lot when he went home on Tuesday, so I looked up the records with the city and pulled up the schematics." He glanced at Ellis. "The building, where they hold the youth activities, Bible school, and all the rest, it has a direct view of the parking lot."

"Really?" She peered ahead. "Let's put a pin in that. There he is."

Allen turned onto the freshly snowplowed driveway and parked his BMW near the garage.

Ellis followed and stopped a few feet behind him. "I wonder what he's been doing this morning?"

"Hopefully not scoping out your house." McCallister opened the passenger door and hopped out.

"We'll see." She joined him as they walked along the driveway. "Good morning, Mr. Allen. I have the paperwork we talked about for Claire's things."

"Right. Come in." He unlocked his door and stepped inside, holding it open for them. "I took the liberty of putting it all in a box. It's over there in the living room. Feel free to look around. I just thought there wasn't much point in you wasting time hunting down her things."

"Thank you. Did you find her phone?" Ellis asked.

"No. I tried to track it, but it says the phone isn't on," he replied. "She had to have had it with her. Claire never went anywhere without it."

"Forensics is still going through the car. Maybe it'll turn up somewhere. Not that I expect it to work if that was the case." Ellis surveyed the room. "It'd probably be a good idea for us to just have a quick run-through."

"Whatever you need to do, Detective. I'll be in the kitchen. Can I get either of you a cup of coffee?"

"No, thank you," she replied.

"I'm good." McCallister thumbed toward the staircase. "I can check upstairs if you want to have a look around down here."

"Sure." Ellis meandered through the living room. "You have a beautiful home, Mr. Allen."

"It was all Claire," he replied. "She loved it here."

Ellis moved on through the downstairs, not really finding anything of interest, and certainly nothing that wasn't already stated on the authorization. As she reached the back of the hall, beyond the utility room, she came upon what looked like a home office.

Inside was a desk with a computer on it. A printer on a credenza at the back. More computer equipment she wasn't familiar with. CPUs, maybe? Whatever they were, they ran a little loud. Otherwise, nothing appeared out of the ordinary, and nothing was inside that they had been authorized to remove.

Nevertheless, she wanted to know exactly what Allen had done for the church regarding their books. Why had he been involved when they had a firm dedicated to their accounts? Lending a helping hand seemed a vague answer. Ellis returned to the kitchen. "Mr. Allen, I noticed some computer equipment in your office. Can you tell me what all of that is?"

"Oh, just some software I'm testing. I need heavy-duty servers to run it. It's something I'm working on for the bank."

"I see. So it has nothing to do with Claire?"

"No, ma'am," he replied. "Are you finished? I don't mean to be rude, but I have a lot to deal with right now."

"Actually, I did learn something that I wanted to ask you about. I understand you help the church with their books on occasion."

"Yeah, sure. Zeke will ask me to help him review statements, double-check his accountant's entries."

"Are you a CPA?" she asked.

"Oh, no. But I do work for a bank and have been around numbers for most of my career. I don't certify anything if that's what you're getting at."

"No, I wasn't getting at anything at all, really. Just trying to put together the pieces. So that's pretty much the extent of your involvement in the church's finances?"

"Yep. That's about all."

Ellis's attention was drawn to the stairs, where McCallister descended. "Are we good?"

"Yeah, all set. I think we have what we need." He peered into the kitchen. "Thank you for your cooperation, Mr. Allen. We'll continue to keep you posted on any new evidence that presents itself."

"Before we go, Mr. Allen." Ellis approached him. "You may already be aware of this, but we've spoken to Ann Kemper." She noticed his expression fall. *Oh, that struck a nerve.* "She said she met you here after she left Tuesday's service."

Allen clasped his hands in front of his body and widened his stance. "I don't know what she's talking about."

Ellis pursed her lips. "It's really not in your best interest to lie to us, Mr. Allen. Look, we just want answers. And withholding relevant information like that doesn't make you look good. You already failed to mention your assistance with the church finances, and now this."

"What am I supposed to say right now, Detective?" he asked. "That I was fucking my wife's friend on the night she died? Well, I wasn't, okay? And what the hell difference does it make if I helped the church? Claire did that all day long."

"But you and Mrs. Kemper were together when it happened? When your wife died?" she continued.

Before he had a chance to reply, McCallister focused on Allen. "Seems to me like she backed up your alibi. You should thank her."

Ellis started toward the door. "We're done here."

As Allen stood from the chair, she raised her hand. "We're happy to show ourselves out. Thank you again."

ONE MACBOOK and an old iPod that probably no longer functioned. That was the extent of what had been removed from the Allen home that had once belonged to the victim. The items were logged into Evidence, where the computer forensics team would proceed to remove the hard drive from the laptop. Accessing data directly from it was the only way to ensure any reboots of the laptop wouldn't destroy existing or deleted files. Passwords made no difference. Even encryption keys could be found on a hard drive with little effort. Still, the process would take time, but Ellis could use that time to look into the Grace Community Church's finances and what exactly Scott Allen's role had been with regard to those.

From her desk, she made the call to the accounting firm. "Hi, yes, I'd like to speak with the person in charge of the Grace Community Church account. I'm Detective Ellis, Bangor police." She nodded. "Thank you."

A moment later, the line picked up again. "Hello, this is Josh Hunt. How may I help you?"

"Mr. Hunt, I'm with Bangor PD. I have a few questions regarding Grace Community Church and was given your contact from their office staff."

"Of course. I heard what happened. Terrible tragedy. I'm happy to answer what I can," he replied.

"I appreciate that. I'd like to know who are shown as the signatories on the church's accounts," Ellis said.

"Sure. Hold on just a moment. Let me pull up that information for you. Ah, here it is. I show Mr. Scott Allen and

Pastor Ezekiel Townsend as the signatories for banking and account management."

At this information, her face revealed a knowing smile. "And do you contact Mr. Allen on a regular basis for accounting inquiries?"

"Any questions are generally directed to Mr. Townsend," Hunt replied.

"I see. Thank you. Listen, if you're available, I wouldn't mind sitting down with you for a few minutes so I can get a full understanding of the arrangement."

"Absolutely. How about this afternoon. Say at one?"

Ellis jotted down the appointment. "That'll work. I'll see you then. Thank you again." She ended the call and turned her attention to McCallister. "Guess what? Scott Allen is a signatory on the church's accounts. Sounds like he was a little more involved than he admitted."

He regarded her a moment. "Meaning he had access to the money or just the books?"

Ellis raised her brow. "Both."

8

With momentum waning and the meeting with the accountant who handled the church's books set for this afternoon, Ellis hoped that the parameters of Scott Allen's access and involvement would be quickly defined. She needed a solid lead to home in on the husband. Anything that would provide a judge with enough proof to sign a warrant for the phone and laptop that belonged to his employer. He had a solid alibi, but in no way did that mean he was innocent. Of course, according to McCallister, if Scott Allen had murdered his wife, he wouldn't have left evidence of it on his devices, least of all, his company devices. Nevertheless, motive still existed and its role would become more apparent with a greater understanding of Allen's so-called volunteer work.

With a swift stride, Ellis headed to her desk when a call rang through. She answered the line. "Detective Ellis."

"Detective, my name is Nate Caulder. I understand you're looking into certain accounting aspects of Grace Community Church."

She slowed her pace. "Yes, I am. And how would you know that?"

It seemed McCallister took note of her arrival at this point and drew his attention away from his computer.

"I work for the church's accounting firm and I have some information you might find useful. Information regarding Pastor Ezekiel Townsend," he added.

"This information, can you back it up?" She returned to her chair, keeping an eye on her partner.

"I can," Caulder confirmed. "When would you like to meet to discuss it?"

"Now, if you can spare the time. I have another meeting soon. Text me the address, and I'll see you soon." She ended the call.

McCallister pulled back his shoulders. "Who was that?"

Ellis wore skepticism in her gaze. "Someone from the accounting firm who claims to know all about Zeke Townsend."

"The pastor?" he asked.

"He wants to meet now." Ellis opened her desk drawer to retrieve her bag.

"You're going to meet with this guy now? Do you want me to be there? After what happened outside the bar, maybe some caution is in order," he said.

"You were the one who thought I was being paranoid. No. I'd better meet him alone. He could be skittish. And it's probably best to divide our resources. It's been days and we still don't have a suspect."

"I can light a fire under Forensics. See how close they are to wrapping things up," McCallister offered. "Hey, how did this person know to call you?"

"You got me. But if this man has something to say on the matter of the Grace Community Church, I'm going to listen," she replied.

"Good luck. Keep me posted. I'll see what I can get on my end."

ELLIS TURNED into the parking lot of the coffee shop situated on the north end of the Waterfront. She stepped out of her Tahoe and pulled on her coat before making her way to the door.

Inside the small café, her gaze wandered over the bistro tables and ahead to the display case that exhibited decadent baked goods. It wasn't until a man approached that she realized he must've been the mysterious caller.

"Detective Ellis?" he asked.

"That's me. How'd you know?"

He shrugged. "You look like a cop. I'm Nate Caulder."

"Nice to meet you." She shook his hand. "Guess I should reconsider my wardrobe then, huh?"

"It's not that. You just looked a little lost, so I thought I had the right person." He started on toward a table that overlooked the river. "Thank you for seeing me. Please, sit down."

Ellis pulled out a chair and kept her eyes fixed on him a moment. Tailored suit. Nice tie. If she had to judge, she'd consider him average looking. "I have to say, I was a little surprised to get your call. I spoke to your firm only this morning. How did you..."

"I know. I was at the front desk when your call came in. I heard the receptionist say your name before she transferred your call to Hunt. To be honest, I guess I've been expecting it." He sat down across from her. "Can I get you a coffee or tea?"

"I'm fine, thank you. So, Mr. Caulder, you work for Cooper & Myers Accounting."

"I do, and please call me Nate."

He was nervous. Ellis noted how he chewed on his lip and glanced through the window, hardly able to make eye contact with her. "Okay, Nate. I'm here, so what's on your mind? And, just so you know, this will stay between you and me, if that's what you're worried about."

He shot her a glance. "I look worried?"

"I've seen cows headed to slaughter looking less worried," she quipped.

"Duly noted," he replied with a closed-lip grin. "All right, here's the deal. I used to handle Grace Community Church. They were my client. I'm a CPA and specialize in tax-exempt organizations like churches. There's a lot that goes into the filings and regulations and such." He took a drink from his mug. "My firm's handled that church for a few years now. Five years, I guess."

"And you say it was your account, but not anymore?" she asked.

"At first, yes. I handled it, but I was kicked off about a year ago. Now, one of my coworkers, Hunt, who you spoke to, handles their bookkeeping and filings."

"So what happened? Why'd they pull it from you?"

"Because I opened my mouth." He stopped to take another sip of coffee. "I was doing what I do, going through the filings for their annual reports, and something caught my eye. I noticed an inconsistency that led me to run through their accounts again before I authorized the filing. Obviously, the church gets a lot of cash, right? That cash is deposited into the bank account. And I noticed on one quarterly statement that the cash deposits dropped over the course of a few months. Nothing too dramatic, but it was odd because, according to the church elders, their congregation had grown."

"Meaning they should've been taking in more cash donations, not fewer," Ellis cut in.

"Exactly. And this is where things got a little hairy." He darted his gaze, as though someone watched him. "I started looking into Pastor Ezekiel Townsend. At that point, he'd only been with the church maybe a little over a year. Funny timing, right?"

"What did you find?" she asked.

"I stumbled across a police report."

"Stumbled?"

"Well, maybe I intentionally dug around," Caulder admitted. "The pastor's name was attached to another church's filing from years prior. I don't know, maybe two or three years earlier. The filing had been flagged, so I started digging into it, thinking what the heck was going on, you know?"

"Sure," she replied, wanting him to continue.

"Detective Ellis, the police report had been filed for an investigation into Ezekiel Townsend. He'd been suspected of embezzlement at a former church, where he was an associate pastor. No charges were ever filed, and the case was dropped."

Ellis's interest was very much piqued by now. "Where was this church?"

"In another state, New Hampshire, if I recall."

She'd considered that Claire's murder was likely tied to either money, sex, or both. It was starting to look like money could have been the main player if Townsend was involved. "What did you do with this information?"

"That was where my big mouth got me into some trouble. Like I said, I started talking. My boss didn't like it."

"Do you suspect he was in on it, assuming what we're talking about here is embezzlement at Grace Community?"

"No, I don't think so," Caulder added. "I don't know who would've wanted to keep this hidden. It puts our firm at risk of losing its business license. And, of course, the suspected crime of embezzlement, itself, isn't something we should conceal in any way. The only thing I can think of was that maybe the elders of the church, maybe they hadn't wanted the bad publicity. I just don't know."

"And you say that the original investigation had been dropped?" she pressed on.

"That's the thing. It appeared to go nowhere. I only found the one report and it wasn't that easy to find. I may have asked for a few favors I've yet to repay. But no charges, nothing. The whole thing just up and disappeared. Next thing you know, Grace Community Church is no longer my client."

Ellis rubbed her chin. "When I spoke to Hunt this morning, I asked him who the signatories were on the account."

Caulder grunted. "Shortly after the account was handed off, I kept my eye on it for a little while. I just felt like this guy might be doing the same thing. If my boss found out I'd done that, I would've been fired on the spot. And so you're talking about signatories. Back about six months ago, I noticed they added someone who wasn't employed by the church, which I thought was strange."

Ellis eyed him. "Scott Allen?"

"Yeah, that's right. You know him?"

"He's the husband of my homicide victim."

McCALLISTER LEANED back in his chair as Ellis filled him in on the findings. "What are the odds Scott Allen's working with the pastor skimming money from the church? And, if so, had Claire found out?"

"Like we talked about before, if this was about money, then I'm not sure she thought her husband played a role. She showed up at the church. Maybe she was going to confront Townsend."

"True. But how much money could we be talking about here?" McCallister asked. "It's not a big church. I can't believe they'd take in that much in cash donations. So skimming what, a few thousand. Ten, at most? Is that worth killing someone for?"

"Are you kidding? The way things are now, you'd be killed for five bucks. No, that's a fair question. Depends on the extent of it. Townsend was the target of an embezzlement investigation already. And that's just what we know of." Ellis considered their next steps. "We should learn all we can about that investigation and why it was dropped. Caulder said it happened in New Hampshire. Shouldn't be too hard to find. In the meantime, given what we now know about Allen's involvement in the church's finances, maybe we have enough to get a warrant on his tech. His office was home to a lot more than a company laptop."

McCallister appeared deep in thought when he continued, "Just so we're prepared. If we pull the trigger on Scott Allen by naming him a suspect, which is what we'd be doing, things are going to move real fast. And we'll have to act quickly before he has a chance to get rid of any evidence, assuming he hasn't already."

"What I saw in his home office looked like whatever he was doing was active and ongoing. I agree his company laptop and phone would probably already be compromised, but he has no reason to suspect we know a damn thing about Townsend. This could be our shot at the first solid lead we've gotten." A text arrived on Ellis's phone and caught her attention. "Damn it. I have to run downstairs. Hang tight a minute." She jogged down to the first floor and found Officer Triggs. "I got your message."

"He's being released now," Triggs replied. "I guess your dad still has some pull around here."

"He likes to think so. Thanks for the heads-up." Ellis

made her way to the booking area. "Dad, what the hell are you doing?"

"He can't stay another night, Becca. He called me this morning and sounded terrible. He'll rip off his own skin if he has to stay here."

Ellis lowered her gaze a moment. "So you're bailing him out after what he did? He should feel some pain over this, Dad, or else he'll do it again."

"What choice do I have? He's my son, Becca."

"And I'm your daughter," she bristled, "or did you forget you were married to my mom first?"

"I don't want to fight with you, Becca, and especially not here. I'm sorry, but I'm taking Carter home." He turned away from her.

"You won't be happy until he takes everything from you, is that it?" she called out, too incensed to be discreet.

Hank spun around and marched back to her. "Now, you listen here. I'd do the same goddam thing for you if I had to. I won't let my kids suffer, you understand me?"

"Is that right?" Her expression hardened. "Then why did you leave Mom and me?"

"I can't change what happened with your mom." Regret masked his face. "God knows I would if I could. I can't change what happened to you either and I've done everything in my power to make up for that. I'm sorry if it wasn't enough." Hank didn't wait for a reply; he just walked away.

Ellis closed her eyes. "Goddam it." A few moments later, she spotted her dad with Carter. She could admit that her brother looked like hell, like he waited on death's door this very moment. Still, his private agonies wouldn't absolve him of what he had done to their father, even if Hank had already forgiven him.

She locked eyes with Hank while he led Carter through the hall. Her brother said nothing, instead kept his eyes straight ahead. It took every ounce of energy for her to get back a semblance of cool. Anger seethed in her gut, but she knew it was a lost cause. Ellis loved her father more than anything in this world, but he was blind, and she knew he would never see the truth about his son.

———

SCOTT ALLEN WAITED in the parking lot of the strip mall as late afternoon arrived. The frozen rain that had fallen earlier now lay in icy patches on the asphalt. "Come on, man. Where the hell are you?" Allen pulled up at attention when he spotted the approaching truck. "Finally." He rolled down the window of his BMW and waved until the truck stopped beside him. "Where the hell have you been, and why didn't you answer my call last night?"

Townsend peered at him from behind the wheel of his F-150. "I'm sorry. I didn't hear my phone. Look, Scott, I know you're hurting right now."

"Do you, Zeke? Do you know? Because it seems like you've gone out of your way to avoid me the past few days. I got your text and then you went dark. I've been dealing with the cops, my wife's funeral arrangements, and my own pastor is avoiding me."

"I wasn't avoiding you, I promise. I was just trying to clean up the books. Do you really think the cops won't make the connection?"

"They won't find shit. You told me to clean up the mess, and I did. Look, none of this had anything to do with Claire, anyway." It was then he paused, noticing a subtle shift in Townsend's gaze. "This has nothing to do with my wife, isn't that right, Zeke?"

9

In the dead of winter, the sun had already begun to set, and the dusky light emitted a blue glow atop the snow-covered yard. The backup units had arrived at the Allen home, and Ellis stepped out of the car as McCallister joined her. It had been her call to push the warrant through, so whatever the fallout, this was on her.

She and her partner peered up at the driveway. Ellis surveyed the grounds. "I'll get this lined out and meet you at the front." She headed toward one of the officers, wrapping her scarf securely around her neck. "I don't expect any trouble, but you know the drill."

"We're ready for whatever happens," he replied.

"The warrant covers all electronic devices, phones, tablets, PCs, and laptops. We want to get in and get out before the neighbors come home from work."

"Yes, ma'am," the officer replied.

Ellis quickly caught up to McCallister, who waited at the door. "Okay, we're ready."

He knocked, and only a moment later, Scott Allen

appeared on the other side. "Mr. Allen, we have a search warrant for your property."

He darted his gaze between the detectives. "What the hell are you talking about? What the hell's going on? Am I a suspect now?" He scoffed. "Are you shitting me? I want to know who killed my wife more than you do. You come up here after my wife was murdered and..."

"This is just standard procedure, Mr. Allen," Ellis cut in. "We have to be thorough, and that includes ruling out any potential involvement you might have had in your wife's murder."

"Jesus, you cannot be serious." Allen returned a look of derision. "I can't believe this."

"I'm afraid you don't have a choice," McCallister replied.

He stared at them a moment until relenting. "Fine. Come in."

Ellis walked inside. "We'll need to take all electronic devices in the house, Mr. Allen. That includes your company phone and laptop. They have a copy of the warrant already. I'll point the officers in the right direction so they don't have to turn your home inside out. But this will include everything in your home office."

"Oh my God," he groaned with obvious hostility. "I can't believe you're doing this. And here I thought the police were on my side."

"We're on Claire's side, Mr. Allen." Ellis waved in the officers. "The office is at the back. Start there."

They walked in and fanned out.

She turned back to Allen. "You should've told me you not only worked on the church's books, but that you had authorization on their financial records and accounts."

"Why would I? How is that even remotely relevant to my wife's murder?"

McCallister stepped in. "The fact you didn't mention it is the relevant part."

Allen held Ellis's gaze. "You're only doing this because you have no idea who killed Claire, do you? Do you even know what you're doing, Detective?"

McCallister thrust his hands between them. "That's enough."

"It's fine," Ellis said. "I'm not concerned whether you think I'm doing a good job, Mr. Allen. In fact, I don't give a shit what you think about me. The only person who matters to me right now is your wife, Claire. Frankly, it surprises me that you've taken her death as well as you have."

"Fuck you." He took a step closer. "You don't know me. You don't know what I'm going through."

"Step back, Mr. Allen," McCallister warned. "It doesn't need to go this way. We're here to do a job. If you have nothing to hide, then you have nothing to be upset about."

"You guys are real pieces of work, you know that?" He marched into his kitchen and leaned against the granite counter.

Ellis turned to McCallister. "Well, that could've gone better."

"What do you expect? The guy thinks we're after him," McCallister replied. "Hell, maybe we are."

One of the officers returned with a box full of items. "Detective Ellis? This is everything from the office. You want me to tag it?"

Ellis peered into the box. "This is everything?"

"Yes, ma'am."

She whipped back around to Allen. "Where are the large pieces of equipment you had in there? You said they were servers."

Allen raised his brow and turned down his lips. "I'm

sorry, Detective, I'm not sure what you're talking about. If that's everything in my office, then that's everything."

THE EVIDENCE ROOM inside the Bangor police station rivaled that of any big-city operation. File boxes labeled with case numbers lined the metal shelves. Procedure was followed to a T. Nothing was going to get past the officer in charge of the facility. He turned to see the detectives who'd brought in the evidence from the home of Scott and Claire Allen. "Ellis, McCallister, everything's logged and in the system."

"Then we'd better head to the lab and let them know," Ellis replied. "Thanks for knocking that out. I know it's getting late."

"Not a problem, Detective. Anything I can do to help."

She and McCallister walked into the hall, working their way to the rear of the building, where the computer forensics department was housed. Ellis pushed in through the double glass doors and spotted two technicians. "Hey, guys."

"Detective Ellis, what brings you by tonight?" Officer Elliot Harding was all of about 27. Most of the people in this department were young; they had been raised holding a screen in their hands.

"McCallister and I are working the Claire Allen homicide. I wanted to let you know that we just brought in computer equipment owned by the husband, Scott Allen. I know you've got the victim's laptop you're working on already, but what are the odds you can move this to the top of your pile?"

Harding regarded her. "Look, Detective, if I do it for you, I have to do it for everyone else too. There's only so many hours in a day."

She cocked her head and placed her hands on her narrow hips. "When was the last time I asked you for a favor?"

"Let me think, last week?" he shot back.

"Okay, but before that?" She smiled warmly. "I know you guys are slammed, okay? But we've got a guy on the line, and we need to know whether it's time to reel him in."

Harding regarded them with mild contempt. "I'll do the best I can."

"That's all we ask." Ellis started back toward the door while McCallister caught up to her. As they reached the corridor again, she continued, "Now we've got this situation with Townsend, I say we put in a request for the church's financial records..."

"On what grounds?" he asked.

"On the grounds that Townsend had once been under investigation for embezzlement. Scott Allen was recently authorized to access the church accounts. Do we have to spell it out for them?"

"Yes. Yes, we do," he said. "We need more than that. The lab will get what they can, but in the meantime, let's put together a history on Townsend. That starts with details on the previous allegation. I have a friend up in Concord. Works for the state police. I can have him look into it. We find something worthwhile there, we might have enough to obtain the church's records."

INSIDE ELLIS'S three-bedroom house in the south part of the city, she curled up on her sofa and turned on the news. She and her ex-husband, Andrew, had bought the place about a year into their five-year marriage. She'd tried to live the life he wanted. One that saw her home for dinner every night. One that allowed her to lavish attention onto her husband no matter the kind of day she'd had. Kids playing in the background.

Andrew had worked Downtown at a commercial investment firm. His job was a real snooze-fest compared to hers, but he liked it that way. Another two years had gone by, and she was forced to admit that kids would never be in their future. His relentless prodding over the course of their relationship had become a sore spot. And when it came to her past, well, he refused to let her talk about it, even though she rarely had. He always told her it was best to move on. As if she hadn't.

A glass of red wine sat on the side table, and Ellis drew it to her lips. The bold notes of blackberry and currant lingered on her tongue a moment while she recalled what Townsend had said on the night of the car fire. He'd been speaking to the youth pastor, and she'd happened upon them in conversation. Ellis glanced up in realization. "You couldn't have known when Harwick left. You said you were already gone." And as her mind homed in on the night of, she distinctly remembered Hailey, one of the volunteers, had mentioned she'd spoken to Townsend at around nine or 9:15. The only explanation she could conjure was that Hailey had been mistaken about the time. She shook her head. "But Harwick couldn't have been wrong too."

Ellis checked the time on her phone. "I have to call him." The line rang, and Hank picked up. "Dad, did I wake you?"

He cleared his throat. "No, I'm awake. Are you okay? What's wrong?"

"Nothing's wrong. Dad, look, I'm sorry about earlier, back at the station. I hate it when Carter comes between us."

"He'll never come between us, Becca. I just need you to understand that I'll never abandon my son."

She cast down her gaze and rubbed her forehead. "I know that, Dad. I'm just—I'm sorry. I'm not Carter's parent, you are, and I'll respect your decisions regarding him."

"Thank you. But, somehow, I don't think that's the reason for the call at almost midnight."

"No." She turned off the television and perched on the edge of the sofa. "I'm calling about the Allen murder."

"Okay. What's going on with it?"

She gave him a brief rundown of where they currently stood in the investigation, including the evening's warrant and seizure of the husband's electronic devices. "I was just sitting here, staring at the TV, and then I remembered something the church's head pastor said. Well, he said it to one of his staff, but I was walking toward them and caught about half of it. I hadn't thought much of it at the time, and it wasn't until just now that I remembered the pastor's statement to me didn't match what he'd said to his own staffer. And then another person again recalled something different from that."

"Has this pastor come into the station to make a statement?" Hank asked.

"No. I haven't had reason to bring him down. Although, we're digging into a situation in his past about an embezzlement charge that got dropped a few years ago. Dad, I think that he and the victim's husband might've been skimming from the church."

"And the victim found out and was killed for it. That's a possibility." Hank pulled in a deep breath and coughed.

"We seized the husband's property today. He already knows we're looking at him hard," Ellis added.

"Okay, so you want to be careful not to show these fellas your cards, understand? You overheard a conversation. You got some discrepancies from witnesses. You even got a prior, regardless of whether the man was charged. But what you don't have is real evidence. Not yet. But I'll tell you how you can get this over home plate."

"Sports analogies aside, Dad, I need to put to paper the names of suspects for the sarge. I know Lieutenant Serrano is going to start hounding him. And then I'll get hounded. What can I do to scratch up enough on this pastor to bring him in for questioning? Like you say, I don't want to show him my cards just yet." There was a slight pause, and Ellis could picture her dad lining up his thoughts for her, just like he always did.

"This previous case of embezzlement you say was dropped. Root around in there and find the reason why. And put in a request to search the church's finances. They can always reject it, but my gut tells me the church will want to fully cooperate in this investigation. In fact, the request shouldn't go through the pastor. Take it up the chain, all the way to the top. And make sure they keep a lid on it. If the good pastor is falling back on his old habits, you'll see it 'cause you'll know to be looking for it."

"We've got the ball rolling on some of that already. So you think I should hold off bringing in the pastor until we better understand the situation?" she asked.

"Hell yes. He'll run as sure as I'm alive, that man will run. So be damn sure before you raise his alarm bells. Also, have you found any weak links inside the church? Someone who turns the other way when you're around. Someone who clams up the moment they see you."

Ellis thought for a moment. "We discovered the husband was having an affair. Unfortunately, both have solid alibis."

"That won't help you with the pastor," Hank pointed out. "Those are two separate leads."

"I might be able to pry open the youth pastor. He's young, inexperienced," Ellis added. "He could be the weak link."

"Now you're talking. Exploit the hell out of that, all right?"

"Yeah, I will." Her lips rose into a half-smile. "Thanks, Dad. I don't know what I'd do if I didn't have you to talk to about stuff like this." A flash of light passed slowly in front of her living room window. Ellis stood from the sofa and pulled back the curtain just enough to scope the street.

"You'd do just fine, Becca. You don't need me. You only think you do." After a too-long pause, he added, "Becca, you with me?"

"Uh, yeah." She dropped the curtain. "Sorry, Dad. I thought I saw a car in front of the house. It's gone now."

"You sure?" Hank asked. "You got your gun nearby?"

"It's fine, Dad. Hey, I'll let you go. Love you and thanks for the help." Ellis ended the call, then snatched her gun, which lay on the side table. In socked feet, she walked to the front door and turned off the switch to the exterior porch light. With a turn of the handle, she stepped outside.

Dressed in a T-shirt and sweatpants, goosebumps rose on her skin as she held her gun at her side and carried along the path to the front sidewalk. Ellis glimpsed the end of the street.

Brake lights flashed several feet from the intersection ahead. Her mind flashed back to the glimpse of the car from the other night when she was at the bar with the team. "No way." She raised her weapon. "Hey!" The lights flashed again. Ellis sprinted. "Stop!" The damp street drenched her socks and it felt like she ran on ice, but she pushed on. "Who the fuck are you?" Her voice was drowned out by the squeal of tires when the car reached the intersection.

She nearly closed the gap and had almost reached the car before it made a right turn. Ellis slowed to a stop at the intersection, out of breath and with her hands on her knees, she watched the car disappear into the distance. "Shit!"

10

From behind the wheel of her Chevy Tahoe, Ellis stared ahead where the white sky met the salted road in a seamless stretch of dull late morning horizon. But in her mind's eye, all she could see was the back end of a large, dark-colored sedan. Rectangle brake lights. Newer car. It was insane to think that whoever killed Claire was coming after her too. Intimidation seemed an archaic and risky notion, unless it was the mob. That was sort of their thing, but unlikely in this case. If someone was coming after her, then there was a hell of a lot more to this investigation than how it appeared on the surface. Meaning, the time had come to push back—hard.

Ellis parked in front of the church and grabbed her coat from the passenger seat.

She walked inside the main entrance, then headed down the breezeway toward the building where they held the youth gatherings. The proximity to the parking lot made it clear that anyone inside that particular building had a direct line of sight to the cars outside. "Strike one," she whispered and opened the door. "Hello?"

A perky teenager donned a smile and approached the door. "Hi there. Which one is yours?" She looked back at the kids, who all sat at tables, eating snacks.

Ellis glanced at the children inside. "Oh, none of them. I'm here to talk to Pastor Jeff. Is he around?"

The girl blinked quickly with the smile still plastered on her lips. "I'm sorry, and you are?"

"Detective Rebecca Ellis. Bangor police." She presented her badge.

"Oh, gosh. I'm so sorry. I just—never mind. We had a Bible class this morning and I thought you were a parent picking up someone. I'll go get Pastor Jeff for you. Come in."

Ellis walked inside while the young volunteer disappeared beyond the corridor. She surveyed the groups of kids, who appeared to have been separated by age. The older ones, maybe preteens, were tucked into a corner of the room and stared at their phones as though no one else existed. Ahead of her, she spotted the younger ones. They were four, maybe five years old. That was when she noticed Vanessa—Maxine's daughter. The girl looked at Ellis, and she returned a gentle smile and a slight wave.

Vanessa jumped from her chair and ran to her. She wrapped her arms around Ellis's hips and held on tightly.

"Hi, Vanessa. You remember me?"

She looked up with big brown eyes and nodded. "Police officer." Only she couldn't pronounce it correctly and the words came out, "Powice osifer."

"That's right. Are you having fun?" Ellis asked.

Vanessa shrugged and looked away.

"Oh, well, I'm sure your mom and dad will be by soon to take you home. You know, I was always kind of shy, like you."

"You have a way with kids, Detective."

Ellis whipped around. "Pastor Jeff. Good morning."

"Same to you. You must have little ones, huh?" he asked.

"Actually, no, I don't."

"Oh. You could've fooled me. I'm surprised to see you here on a weekend. Do you work seven days a week?"

"If I have to, yes." Ellis looked around. "Can we talk somewhere private?"

"Yeah, sure. My office is back here." Harwick started back. "Is everything all right? Did something happen with the case?"

Ellis followed him, glancing over her shoulder at Vanessa as she went. The girl stood frozen and stared at her as she walked away. "Uh, we're still following up on some leads, which is why I stopped by."

"Come on in. Can I get you a cup of coffee?" he asked.

"No, thanks." Ellis walked in and surveyed the office. Posters were pinned to the wall displaying various Bible verses written across a beautiful sunrise or mountain terrain. Children's books were lined along the several shelves behind the pastor's desk.

"Take a seat, please." Harwick walked around his desk and sat down. "What can I help you with, Detective?"

"I wanted to go over that night with you again." Ellis pressed the record button on her phone and set it on his desk. "You don't mind if I record our conversation, do you?"

He glanced at the phone. "Is that necessary?"

"I just want to be sure I don't misunderstand anything you say. I'm happy to turn it off." She reached for it.

"No, it's fine. I suppose it doesn't really matter. I'm here to help however I can."

"I'm glad to hear that. So, going back to that night. You mentioned you'd left around thirty minutes or so before it all happened."

"Something like that, yes. I can't remember the exact time," he replied.

"And that you'd come back because you forgot some-thing," she continued.

"And I saw all of it, then, yes." He looked away a moment. "Sorry, it's still hard to go back to that night. Picturing all of it. Honestly, I'm so grateful Claire and Scott didn't have chil-dren. I can't imagine a child losing their mother at such a young age."

"Yes, I'm sure that would have been tragic." Ellis wondered whether her eyes betrayed her pedestrian response. She'd worked hard to master indifference in matters of death and pain, even her own. "So you came back and saw what had happened. And then what?"

"I noticed several people from the neighborhood across the street draw close. One of them, I believe, had called the fire department. I don't recall who. To be honest, I was so shocked, I couldn't believe my eyes." He swallowed hard. "I should've tried to help get her out. I didn't know..."

"No one could've helped her, Jeff. It happened quickly; she didn't suffer long. So, soon after, Pastor Zeke turned up."

"Yes, I called him straight away, and he was there in no time. He said he would contact the elders," Harwick replied.

"I remember seeing you two talking for a moment before I came up to you," she added.

"Sure, I remember that."

Ellis turned away in thought. "I wonder if he was mistaken about his timing, then."

"What do you mean?" Harwick asked. "Who?"

"Pastor Zeke. It kind of seems like he arrived quickly from the time you called him. I'm thinking that maybe he hadn't made it home by that point and just turned around and came back to the church."

Harwick appeared to search his thoughts. "Well, I can't really say. I wasn't paying much attention to the time."

Ellis peered at him with friendly curiosity. "And I think he said something like, he'd seen you leave, or something to that effect? You'll have to forgive my somewhat vague questions. I'm just trying to make sure I have the right timeline of events. It's important we know exactly when Mrs. Allen's car caught fire."

"Um, I don't really know. Have you spoken about this directly to Pastor Zeke? I'm sure he could clear this up for you."

"To a degree, yes, but it's important that I cover all the bases. It's best to get the story from every angle, and somewhere in there is where the truth rests." She raised her hands in defense. "I'm not suggesting you're lying, nor am I suggesting Pastor Zeke is either. Far from it. I'm just looking for the closest timeline I can develop in order to draw the most accurate conclusion regarding Claire's murder."

"Yes, I heard you all believe it was murder," he said.

"That's right, Jeff, Claire Allen was murdered. Someone tampered with her vehicle." Ellis studied Harwick's expression. He wore fear and trepidation on his face, and she thought she detected a hint of remorse. Maybe this weak link was about to break.

"Well, come to think of it," Harwick began. "Pastor Zeke did turn up pretty fast after I called. Gosh, maybe you're right. The more I think about it, it is likely that he hadn't made it home by that point. I guess I kind of remember him telling me that he'd seen me earlier that night after the service. Now, that could've only happened if he'd been there later than he said because I remember jogging back to the sanctuary to grab the candles and put them back in the cabinet. That would've been around 8:45 or so, just before I left. So, yeah, I guess Pastor Zeke was there longer than he thought he was."

It wasn't a confession or some great revelation, but it was something Ellis could work with. Casting Townsend in a new light meant the focus could shift toward a different approach and possibly open new leads aside from Scott Allen. However, Hank had often warned Ellis about letting herself fall for the low-hanging fruit.

"Jeff, I can't thank you enough for your help this morning. I know what a toll this has taken on you and the other members of the church. But your help is really appreciated." Ellis stood. "We will find the person responsible for taking Claire's life, please know that."

"And God will judge that person harshly," he declared.

"God and the great state of Maine." Ellis grabbed her phone. "Thank you." She headed back into the hall and reached the front room again, where it appeared that some of the children had been picked up by their parents.

Vanessa now sat alone at one of the tables, and Ellis approached her. "I wanted to say goodbye, Vanessa. It sure was nice to see you again." The girl didn't look back at her and instead continued to draw on a piece of paper. Ellis looked at the drawing. "What you got there?" Her gaze narrowed with concern. "Vanessa, what is this?"

She shrugged in response.

Ellis kneeled beside her. "Did you see something like this happening, and you decided to draw a picture of it?"

Vanessa nodded.

"Where did this happen?" Ellis continued in a gentle tone.

"Here."

"I'd like to take a picture, okay, Vanessa?" Ellis pulled out her phone and snapped a photo of the drawing. "Where was your mom when you saw this?"

"With the other moms."

Vanessa pulled the drawing toward her again and continued to color it. "Am I in trouble?"

"Oh no, of course not. Look at me, Vanessa. You've done

nothing wrong. I'm sorry you saw fighting like that. People aren't supposed to fight, are they?"

"Boys don't hurt girls," she replied.

"No, they aren't supposed to. Is your picture of a boy and girl, or a man and woman?"

Vanessa shrugged her reply.

Ellis stood again and turned to the door when she noticed Maxine walk in.

"Detective Ellis, what are you doing here?" she asked.

Ellis walked over and pulled her back a moment. "I was talking to the pastor, asking some questions. When I came back out, I saw Vanessa drawing. I thought I'd say goodbye to her and then I looked at what she drew." Ellis opened her phone and held up the photo. "What does that look like to you?"

"Well, it's the church. There's a big cross on the roof. And..." She paused a moment. "I don't know, but I guess it looks like two stick people in a fight."

"Vanessa said boys don't hurt girls, and when I asked if they were kids or adults, she didn't answer," Ellis said.

Maxine glanced at her daughter, then turned back to Ellis. "You know, she's been acting differently about coming here. I thought she'd picked up on all that's been happening, but I'm wondering if this is why. Question is, what *is* this, exactly?"

"I don't know, and she said it happened here. I don't know when, or if Vanessa has a concept of days or weeks."

"Some understanding, yes." Maxine walked to the table. "Hi, sweetheart. I see you've been drawing. Did you see people fighting here at the church?"

"Yeah," she replied.

"Do you remember when this was?" Maxine asked. "Was it just a few days ago, or longer?"

Vanessa shrugged.

"You don't remember?" Maxine continued.

"I don't know."

"That's fine, sweetheart. But can you tell me who you saw? Who are those people in the drawing?"

Vanessa looked back at Ellis a moment before returning to her mother. "I don't know."

"Okay, honey. It's okay. Why don't you get your stuff, and we'll go home?"

Vanessa jumped from the chair and ran to get her backpack.

Maxine returned to Ellis. "She doesn't remember or won't say who she saw. I don't want to press her. Not here."

"I understand," Ellis reassured. "You just let me know if she comes around and feels like talking about it. It could be nothing, but under the circumstances, I'm keeping everything on the table."

11

Kids were nothing if not observant, and Ellis suspected the drawing meant something to Vanessa Rehnquist. But what? From the table where she sat inside the coffee shop, her faraway gaze landed on the cars parked out front. Fresh snow blanketed them.

"The life of a detective, huh?"

The voice pulled her back into the moment and she turned to find McCallister at the table. "Hey. Sit down."

"Thanks." He pulled out a chair. "Did I interrupt something? You looked deep in thought."

"No. Well, yes, sort of." Ellis stirred her cup of coffee. "I went to the church this morning and talked to Jeff Harwick, the youth pastor. He confirmed that the timeline Townsend offered wasn't as he recalled it, though he fell short of saying Townsend was wrong. But that isn't what's got me thinking. When I was there, well, I guess they'd had a Bible class earlier in the morning. Bunch of kids were there and I saw Vanessa Rehnquist, Maxine's daughter. Euan, she drew this picture of what appeared to be two people in a fight. Here, take a look for yourself." Ellis opened her phone to display the image.

McCallister studied it for a moment. "Okay. So what does that mean? How is it relevant?"

"I'm not sure it is. But what she drew, apparently, had happened at the church. What if she saw something that night? A struggle between Claire and her killer?"

He raised his index finger. "It couldn't have been that night. When we talked to Maxine, she'd indicated her husband took care of the girl while she was out of town. She wasn't there that night. Must've happened on another occasion. Did you ask her if the drawing was of people she knew?"

"I did. The girl clammed up. Maxine arrived and she tried to get more details, but, see..." Ellis pursed her lips. "That's what got me thinking. It looked like the girl was scared to say anything more. Why would that be? You're right about it not being that night. Vanessa did say her mom was with the other moms, and we know Maxine was out of town. So when did it happen? Was it a precursor to Claire's murder? A catalyst?"

"Something we need to dive deeper into, I'd say."

She glanced at him and opened her mouth to speak, but stopped short.

"What? What are you not telling me, Becca?"

Resigned, she continued, "I saw that car again last night. Well, I can't be sure it was the same one from the bar since I didn't get a good look, but I'm going to assume it was. It was at my house."

His brow rose high. "And you're just now telling me this? Jesus. Last night? When?"

"I don't know. Late. I was on the phone with my dad." She hesitated a moment longer. "I chased after it, hoping to identify it..."

"I'm guessing you didn't because you probably would've led with that."

"I didn't. It's a dark sedan. Full-size car. If I'm on someone's hit list, we have a problem. But I don't think that's what this is about. It's either a way to send us on a wild-goose chase to distract us long enough for our killer to cover his tracks, or it is the killer and he thinks I scare easily," Ellis replied. "I'm not ready to entertain the idea I'm next in line for my car to go up in flames."

"Don't dismiss it that easily, Becca, I'm telling you. People are emboldened. We all got targets on our backs right now whether we're investigating a crime or just turn up somewhere in uniform. And we're already talking about a killer."

"Maybe in Boston..."

"No. Everywhere," he insisted.

"Regardless, whoever it was wasn't expecting me to go after him. I'm sure I looked crazy as hell running in the street at midnight waving around my gun. That said, Townsend's on my radar. You'd better believe that. I'm going to find out what he drives. What his friends drive. I'll figure out it if was him. And I know how to watch my back." Ellis wrapped her hands around the coffee mug and took a sip. "So, tell me what you found out about the allegation. Maybe that'll put this issue of Townsend to bed."

McCallister pulled out a file from his bag and laid it on the table. "Take a look here."

Ellis pulled the file close and examined the police report. "I have to say, I'm a little impressed that you found all this. Did your guy say why the hell this case was dropped? This looks pretty damn cut and dry, doesn't it? Townsend was accused of stealing from his last church. His bank records indicated unusual deposits. What more did they want?"

"Here's the thing." McCallister pointed to the file. "None of this stuff ever stained his record, but I think that's because he has friends in high places."

"What makes you say that?" Ellis asked.

"Because this case just vanished. Like that." He snapped his fingers. "That doesn't happen unless you know some powerful people, or you were partnered with them. I don't know how the accountant here found out any of this because my friend had to dive deep to pull this up. Anyway, as far as we can tell, the guy's clean apart from that."

She considered the notion. "Maybe these powerful friends are the ones following me."

"I'll ask my buddy in Concord what else he scratched up on that front. Hard to say, but it's a door worth stepping through."

Ellis drank the last of her coffee, which had already turned cold. "We're dealing with a man who's been down this road before, only this time, he might've recruited a partner and now that partner's wife is dead. If nothing else, we understand Zeke Townsend isn't the sparkling-clean, made-for-TV pastor his congregation thinks he is."

Now that they knew who they were dealing with in Zeke Townsend, it was time to understand whether Scott Allen was playing the same game. Evidence of embezzlement from the Grace Community Church existed, or, at least, looked damn suspicious, according to Nate Caulder, their former accountant. And access to the church's finances wouldn't likely be granted until Monday morning. So the detectives had but one angle to run on at the moment—Mr. Allen's computers.

They returned to the station and headed straight for Forensics in hope there had been news on the seized equipment. Ellis opened the door to the white coats inside who'd drawn the lucky straw and got a Saturday shift. "Hey, guys. Anyone see Brown today?"

"He's in the back," Harding replied.

"And good morning to you, too, Harding. Nice to see your smiling face." Ellis patted his shoulder.

They retreated into the long corridor that led to the ballistics lab, where Officer Leo Brown worked on another investigation.

Brown, a thickset millennial with a heavy beard and full cheeks, looked up from the table. "Detective Ellis, Detective McCallister, didn't think I'd be seeing you today."

"I had planned for a quiet day alone, reading a good book. But we both know that wasn't going to happen," she said.

"Since when does it ever?" Brown rolled his chair away from the table to face them. "Hey, I'm still working your case. Got my team accessing the files on the hard drive of the victim's laptop. We recovered several emails..."

"Can I see them?" Ellis cut in.

"Yeah. There could be more, but I can send you what we have right now." He peered beyond her shoulder into the hall. "Harding? Send Ellis the emails you recovered from the Claire Allen laptop."

"On it," Harding called out.

"And we're only now getting into the new evidence you brought in belonging to the husband. It takes time, you know that."

"Yeah, but we need an opening here. What do you have right now you can share?" McCallister asked.

Brown walked back to his desk and sat at his computer. "Let me see where we're at. Okay, says here...Oh, we've just plugged into the husband's laptop hard drive. The personal one, not the bank's. I thought you would want our focus on that one first."

"Phone?" McCallister pressed.

"It's clean. If he was into some bad shit, he used an encrypted app to communicate and then deleted it, because we found nothing. And given that it was a company phone, that doesn't surprise me. But hang on, let me run some analytics first and see what pops out." He keyed in commands. "What are you hoping we'll find exactly?"

"Hold up, before you get too far, did you gather GPS information from the phone?" Ellis asked. "Confirming his whereabouts is critical to flushing out his alibi."

"I did think of that," Brown continued. "Location services on the phone were turned off. I reached out to the service provider. They have all the GPS details, but I'll tell you this. Your guy is smart."

"How so?" Ellis asked.

"According to the provider, the phone was turned off several times over the past few weeks. Mostly at night. Can't track a phone that's off." Brown yanked a sheet of paper from the printer. "This is their report. See for yourself."

Ellis grabbed it. "On the night of, his phone was on. He was home."

"Well, shit." McCallister flung his hand in the air. "He was logged into his company's server from his home IP address. Kemper confirmed she was with him there. The man's got no cracks in his alibi. He didn't kill his wife."

She eyed him. "Doesn't mean he didn't plan it."

"Okay. Hang on. The screen's populating." Brown examined the data and narrowed his gaze. "What? Oh shit."

"What is it?" Ellis stepped closer.

He turned the screen toward her. "The personal laptop's hard drive was scrubbed. Big red flag. But I see there appear to have been several files he attempted to delete. Some URLs pointing to websites. You know, people have no idea that it's nearly impossible to delete anything for good."

Ellis scrutinized the screen. "What am I looking at?"

"Wait a minute. Is this?" Brown fixed his gaze on the data before him. "Yeah, uh, not sure how to say this, but it looks like your guy was into child porn. At least, he accessed some websites containing explicit images."

"What? Are you sure?" She took a step back. "You just said his hard drive was scrubbed."

"It was, but like I said, crumbs always get left behind," Brown replied.

McCallister crossed his arms over his chest. "Maybe we were wrong thinking this was about skimming off the church or some extramarital affair. What if Scott Allen was doing more than looking at this stuff? Maybe he was acquiring it, and Claire found out. You want to look for motive? Facing heavy prison time for possessing child porn would be it if your wife found it and tried to turn you in. Say she caught wind of this, saw it, or whatever, and drove to the church to beg Townsend for help." He peered at the screen. "This is what we needed to find. Something tangible. Something we can use. This, right here, Becca...this is actual proof of wrongdoing."

"No. I don't buy it. A woman who learns her husband is involved in something like that doesn't drive to her church for help. She goes straight to the police. And let's not forget that Scott Allen was at home while Claire burned to death. That's now a fact. No, this still links back to Townsend and money. Somehow, it all ties together. I don't know what these websites have to do with it, but I know both men were doing something criminal, and Claire died because of it." Ellis turned back to Brown. "Can you print a detailed report of what you recovered? Dates and file names, those are going to be important."

"Yeah, I'll run it now. You should know that I'm still performing the analysis. Can you wait a day for me to finish? There could be more to this story. I need to fully analyze what we have."

"Yeah, okay. It'll give me time to get more answers. Just get it done, please."

Brown reviewed his computer again. "I'll do what I can as quickly as I can."

"Hang on," McCallister called out as Ellis left Brown to his work and hurried through the hall. "What are we doing?"

She reached the doors and turned around. "I'm done spinning my wheels. I'm being watched. This case is being watched. What Brown just found turns this investigation into something a hell of a lot darker than skimming money off a church. It's time we go to Concord to see your friend. We'd better start figuring out how these pieces fit together. I will tell you this, Townsend's our lynchpin. I can feel it. Allen was clean before he got tangled up with the pastor, who has a history, so we'd better turn every stone where he's concerned. That starts with Concord."

"And Allen?" he asked.

Ellis glanced back into the lab. "Brown needs time to finish the job. When he does, we arrest Allen for possessing illegal images. Maybe it'll be enough to get him to turn on Townsend, and tie him to Claire's murder. In the meantime, we look at every one of those emails they recovered from her laptop. She changed her password and kept it from her husband. You don't do that unless you know something you shouldn't."

12

Days after his wife's murder and having drained two bottles of Jack, Scott Allen mistrusted everyone. Friends, family, even his own pastor. Now, he hunched over a bar top with an empty shot glass in front of him and stared at the television screens. He hadn't wanted to be here any more than he wanted to be at home. Being surrounded by Claire's things had seemed a blessing at first. Not anymore. He'd failed to protect his wife and she cursed him for it.

"Sorry I'm late."

Allen glanced over his shoulder. "I wasn't sure you'd show."

Townsend pulled out a barstool to sit before garnering the barman's attention. "Draft Sam Adams, please."

"You betcha." The barman grabbed a pint glass.

"It's slow in here today," Townsend said.

Allen closed his eyes a moment. "I'm not interested in shooting the shit, Zeke. What did you want to talk about?"

"Not here. Let's grab a table."

Allen pushed off the stool when the bartender returned

with Townsend's beer. "I'll take that. We'll be just over there."
He joined Townsend at one of the booths and set down his
drink. "Here you go."

"Thanks. It's time we move everything out of the storage
unit. Bury all transactions. You said you wiped your
computer; that's a good start." Townsend sipped on the beer.
"Bangor PD is going out of their way to make their presence
known, especially to me. With the warrant they served on
you, it's only a matter of time before it's my turn."

"They don't know about the storage unit. They don't know
shit, but they think I killed my wife, given the way I'm being
treated. And since I know that's not true, where does that
leave you, Zeke?"

"Just calm down, Scott, all right? You know damn well I
had nothing to do with what happened to Claire. I'm sorry
she's gone, you know I am. But I didn't do it. I could never
hurt anyone. My God, what kind of person do you take me
for?"

"All I know is that Claire's dead and someone killed her."
His voice faltered. "They're coming after me, man. I'm in their
crosshairs now."

"Are they going to find anything?"

Townsend's accusatory tone was unmistakable. "What?
No, I told you that already. Why are you looking at me like
that? You calling me a liar? You think I did it?"

The pastor shrugged. "Let's just say you had other issues
going on that could lead one to believe you played a part.
You're not exactly above the fray on this."

Allen scowled at him. "What the hell is that supposed to
mean?"

"Take a hard look at your marriage. I'm sure it'll come to
you."

THIS WAS the last place Ellis expected to meet McCallister's friend from the state police up in Concord. The four-hour drive had come to an end, and she parked at the entrance. "He wanted to meet here?"

"The guy's an avid golfer. If it isn't raining, he's at a driving range somewhere." McCallister opened his door. "Let's go see what he has to say."

Ellis hurried out to join him. "How did you say you knew this guy?"

"I didn't, but since you asked, we were in the Guard together."

"What, the National Guard?" she asked.

"Does that surprise you?"

"No," she replied. "I guess I thought you were a cop from birth."

"In a manner of speaking, I guess I was." He chuckled. "I was a weekend warrior for a few years in my younger days. Mainly because I didn't know what I wanted to do with my life after high school. Anyway, it was only a few years, and then I got out. I met Riley there. We didn't keep in touch too much after that until I ended up on the force in Boston. I reached out and asked for his advice because I knew he'd joined Long Island PD before transferring to State Police in Concord. So, yeah, now you know."

Ellis regarded him a moment. "You're more interesting than I expected."

"Back at you." He opened the door at the entrance to the driving range. "I'll introduce you and give Riley a quick rundown of what's been happening. He knows some of it, but I'll need to fill him in on the rest."

"I'll follow your lead," she said.

He turned to her with a smile. "You want to say that again so I can record it for posterity?"

Sergeant Greg Riley stood at the tee box on the second

floor of the range and shifted into position. A stocky man, his full hips swayed, and his bulky arms flared out while he prepared to take the swing.

"Your grip's too high," McCallister called out as they arrived.

Riley whipped around. "McCallister, you made it. Figured you would've been here sooner. Your grandma drive you?"

"I didn't drive. She did." He thumbed to Ellis. "This is my partner, Detective Rebecca Ellis."

"Oh, man, I'm sorry, Detective. I was just busting his balls," Riley said. "Good to meet you."

"Hey, I've seen McCallister behind the wheel. We would've been another hour, easy." Ellis offered her hand. "Nice to meet you, too. Riley, is it?"

"Yes, ma'am."

"Thanks for sticking around long enough to meet us," she added. "I understand you and McCallister go back a ways."

"A long ways, yes, we do," he replied. "I was surprised when he called asking about this case you're working. Honestly, I thought I'd never hear the name Zeke Townsend again. After all that happened, the guy looked the type to keep a low profile."

"He's been successful at it so far. But when a woman gets burned alive in her car in the church parking lot where he's the head pastor, it tends to bring a few things to the surface," Ellis told him.

"So I hear." Riley glanced at the detectives. "Tell me, how can I help?"

"We've combed through the files you sent over," McCallister began. "But in all that paperwork, we couldn't find who authorized dropping the investigation. So we thought it was best to hear firsthand what went down and do a little digging while we're here. We have leads we're following, but they're taking too long. Getting something on this man now is how we move forward."

Riley removed his glove and returned his titanium driver to his bag, then leaned against the nearby column. He wore a troubled gaze.

McCallister regarded him. "That look on your face concerns me. What's going on, man?"

"Listen, that whole situation was messed up, all right? Heads rolled, but not the ones that should've, you catch my meaning?"

"I'm trying to," Ellis replied.

"The thing was, the accounting firm initially reached out to us. Whoever was working the church's accounts got suspicious. Enough that they called us before their own client. That was a big red flag for me," Riley explained. "Anyway, we got a warrant and searched the church's records, came up empty-handed. Strike one. Then we searched Townsend's computer, zilch. Strike two. Finally, we tried to garner support from the church staff, but every damn one of those folks said Pastor Zeke was an upstanding citizen and that we should've been ashamed of ourselves for raking him over the coals."

"I read the missing money was somewhere in the range of thirty K. Not an insignificant amount of cash, but nothing to retire on," Ellis said.

"No. Enough to make a dent without shining a spotlight as far as I'm concerned," Riley replied. "When we got a little deeper, started rooting around in that pigsty, my partner and I were able to trace some of the funds back to a dummy corporate account. We kept pushing and pushing. The parishioners weren't happy with us."

"I don't get it. Who would protect someone who was stealing from them?" Ellis asked.

"That's the thing. They didn't believe it. And when we

couldn't prove it, and the money seemed to magically reappear, well, that was that."

McCallister drew back in surprise. "The money was returned?"

"Not all of it, but enough that the police department's Citizen Review Committee claimed we were harassing the pastor, and that any remaining missing funds was likely an accounting error."

"And that's when it was dropped?" Ellis asked.

"That's when it was dropped. My captain didn't like it. None of us did, but we had no case anymore. Someone bailed this guy out for whatever reason. Probably someone on the committee. Hell if I know why."

"And you said the accounting firm alerted you to all this?" she continued.

Riley smiled as he returned the glove to his hand. "Yep. They were just as shocked as we were when the accounts were flush again. The guys who came forward got fired, that much I know."

"Any chance you can reach out to them?" Ellis asked.

"I'll bet I could. Not sure it'll do you much good, but since you're here," Riley said.

She turned to McCallister. "I don't know if it'll do us good either, but if we can find the system that Townsend used to move money, a system those accountants recognized, it could give us a path to take for our investigation."

Riley picked up his driver again. "Your partner's got a point."

"One other thing," McCallister cut in. "They've got Ellis in their sights. Picked up a couple tails recently. You have any reason to believe it's anything more than a scare tactic?"

Riley examined his club, smoothing some specks of dust from its grip. "I had an inkling Townsend was friends with some sketchy folks. I couldn't prove it, but I took a gander at the nonprofit that ran that particular church, where he ministered." He set his sights on Ellis. "Affiliations with a powerful family here in Concord popped up. Could've been the family that bailed him out, not wanting the spotlight to shine on them. I will say this, if you're being followed, it ain't gonna be those guys. No offense, but you're small potatoes. They wouldn't risk exposure, especially if you're talking murder."

She raised her chin. "What if we're talking a child porn ring?"

Riley jolted back. "What's that now?"

"We seized a laptop from our victim's husband," McCallister began. "We just got news that Forensics uncovered explicit images. They're still working on it, but it's forcing us to look at things differently."

"I'll bet. You got something on Townsend in that regard?" Riley asked.

Ellis shoved her hands in her coat pockets. "Not on him, but on the man we suspect is his partner."

"I don't know anything about that. Nothing we came across so much as hinted at child porn. But it's starting to make sense why someone's got you in his crosshairs." Riley returned a sideways glance at McCallister. "Unless that boy turned down a dark path, I'm not sure you ain't barking up the wrong tree on that front."

IT WAS ALMOST MIDNIGHT, and they'd returned to town. As Ellis drove along the quiet highway, she glanced at McCallister. He stared at the empty road ahead, and she seemed to notice his far-off gaze. "I can't help but think if Riley had been able to bring charges against Townsend, Claire Allen might still be alive."

"Embezzlement isn't exactly a gateway drug to murder,

especially given the dollars we're talking about. Risk versus reward. But if he's partnered with Scott Allen, and with what Brown discovered, it does cast this investigation into a different light. Hell, for all we know Townsend could be the good guy in this scenario." McCallister rubbed his smooth chin. "What concerns me more is that someone's watching you. Not me, you. If Allen was tangled up in some sort of child porn ring, Christ, this is going to get ugly real fast."

"Murder's pretty ugly as it is." Ellis turned the wheel. "You mind if we swing by the church? If we want to find the connection between Townsend and Allen, it'll start at the church. Both of them will be covering their asses and won't want people around while they're doing it. I'd like to drive by to see if any lights are on."

"It's the middle of the night. You expect one or both of them to be there?" he asked.

"We just need a reason to assume probable cause. And I'm ready to find one, so the church will be the next place we look," she replied.

"Let's tread lightly until we have some real evidence, not all this circumstantial bullshit we keep digging up. The whole congregation will want to know what's happening once we pull that trigger."

Ellis pressed lightly on the brakes as she approached. "I don't see any cars. No lights. We'll stop over here down a ways and just sit tight for a few minutes."

"If you think it's worth our time," he said.

"Maybe not." She opened her phone. "But we can go through the file Brown sent with the recovered emails. Unless you have someplace you'd rather be?"

"In my bed asleep would be nice." McCallister eyed her. "Send me a copy? We'll go through it now." He opened the file on his phone and reviewed the messages. They seemed fairly mundane, a lot of church stuff.

In the middle of the night, in front of a church, he sat in a parked car next to his partner with only their phone screens for light.

For a moment, he considered telling her. What would Ellis think of him then? If she knew the man next to her had murdered a child? The mistake had haunted him every moment of every day since it happened last year. He thought it was a gun. He could've sworn it was a gun.

"Anything catch your eye?" Her voice cut into his thoughts.

"Not yet," he replied. "You?"

"Nothing yet."

He kept his gaze on her a moment and she must've felt it.

"You okay?" she asked.

"Yeah. Yeah, I was just thinking. Sorry." He returned to his phone.

"Holy shit." Ellis shot him a look. "She knew."

"What?"

"Claire knew about the affair." A half-cocked grin spread on her lips. "Look at this." She held out her phone. "It's from Ann Kemper's husband."

McCallister read the exchange. "He told her. What's the date on this?" He spotted the header. "Last week."

"Days before she was killed," Ellis replied. "So it was Ann's husband who told her. What do you think she did? Neither Ann nor Scott sounded like they knew Claire had found out."

He peered at her. "Could be why Claire changed her passcode. Maybe she and Mr. Kemper were plotting something to catch their spouses in the act?"

"We'll have to keep looking..." She trailed off as her eyes were drawn to the light ahead. "What do you know? Someone decided to turn up after all."

McCallister peered through the windshield. "Looks like

your instincts are better than mine, but I don't know if it's Townsend."

Ellis narrowed her gaze. "Wait, what the hell?"

"You know whose car that is? Is it the one that's been following you?"

"No. It's Maxine Rehnquist's."

"Are you sure about that?" He shot her a sideways glance. "What the hell would she be doing at the church at this time of night?"

Ellis grabbed her door handle. "I don't know, but we should find out."

"Wait. She'll see the interior light. Let's sit tight a minute and see what she does."

The two watched Maxine Rehnquist park near the church entrance and walk inside.

"Okay, so now what?" Ellis asked.

"I guess we check it out." McCallister opened his door and stepped onto icy snow that crunched beneath his boots. Maxine's car was near the entrance, and Ellis joined him as they headed toward it. "Go around to the passenger side. I'll have a look in here."

The detectives shone their lights inside the electric Honda crossover. McCallister examined the interior and glanced at her. "Nothing. You?"

"Empty." Ellis continued toward the church's heavy wooden doors and tugged on the handle. "It's locked."

McCallister stood next to her and firmed his stance. "Okay, now we have a problem. What would the best friend of our victim be doing here at this time of night?"

13

The imposing wooden doors to the church refused to present Ellis with a way inside. McCallister had alluded to it—the notion Maxine Rehnquist could have had something to do with Claire's murder—and it was like a punch to her gut. Yet it was so obvious. For a moment, she saw Hank wagging a finger at her, telling her she'd gotten too close and let the young girl, Vanessa, sway her reasoning. What was worse was that the man next to her, her partner, would think the same, if he didn't already. "What the hell do we do? Pound on the door?"

"She hears someone pounding down the doors, she'll be terrified to come out," he replied. "And if she's involved, and she thinks we tracked her down because we know, there's no telling what..."

His words disappeared as Ellis and McCallister reeled back and fixed their eyes on the handle as it moved.

Maxine pushed open the door only narrowly enough to slip out. She turned and jumped back at the sight of them, gasping for breath.

"Maxine, it's okay," Ellis called out. "It's Detectives Ellis and McCallister."

The woman placed her hand over her chest to soothe her labored breathing. "Oh my God. You scared the bejesus out of me."

"Why are you here?" Ellis pressed on. "How did you get inside?"

Maxine closed the door. "How long have you been out here?"

"Long enough," McCallister cut in. "Is there a reason you're here at almost one o'clock in the morning?"

"Is there a reason *you're* here?"

"That would be a fair question were we not police officers investigating a crime," he persisted. "Maxine, if you know something pertaining to this investigation, you need to tell us. Why did you come here in the middle of the night?"

Was that guilt Ellis saw? The hard swallow, the shifty gaze. She rested her hand on the butt of her gun from force of habit. "You might want to think of an answer more quickly than that."

Maxine raised her hands. "Hang on. Look, I came across some recent pictures of Claire and me. One, in particular, from around Thanksgiving. Long story short, I'd seen Pastor Zeke in one of the pictures and something just felt wrong. I can't really explain it, but it kind of looked like he and Claire had had a falling-out or something along those lines."

Ellis flicked the snap from her holster. "So you came here to, what?"

"Look for something to back up my theory." Maxine appeared to take notice of the weapons they'd each taken hold of. "I haven't done anything wrong. I promise you. I came here looking for answers."

"And what exactly is your theory?" McCallister asked.

"That maybe Zeke had something to do with what

happened to Claire," she replied. "I have a key and the code to shut off the alarm. I went inside and had a look around Zeke's office."

Ellis wasn't prepared to let this woman off the hook yet. "Did you find anything?"

Maxine closed her eyes a moment. "No. I don't know what I was looking for, but nothing caught my eye. I just felt helpless, and I had to do something."

"I know what that feels like." Ellis couldn't let go of her suspicious nature, but her interactions with Maxine had been transparent. She'd willingly handed over her communications with Claire and had been open about their relationship. Plus, the obvious fact that Maxine had been out of town, as confirmed by her husband. She turned to McCallister and looked for consensus.

He nodded and released his gun. "You say you have a key?"

"Yes."

"Well, we're already here." He glanced at Ellis. "You said something about probable cause."

"This isn't it. Not to go inside the church." Ellis shone her light on Maxine. "Did you remove anything?"

"No, I promise you. I only looked. I'm sorry, it was a mistake to come here." The woman trembled from the cold and, perhaps, from fear.

Ellis considered their options. Maxine had no permission to be inside. It was too much of a gray area. If it had been Townsend, a person of interest already, she could've pushed the boundaries, but not this. Anything they found would be useless without a warrant. She zeroed in on Maxine again. "Is anyone else inside?"

"No, it was just me."

McCallister turned away with his hands on his hips. "It's your call, Detective."

His stony reply wasn't lost on her. "Go home, Maxine, okay? Get some sleep. Please know that we are working around the clock to find whoever's responsible."

As Maxine started away, Ellis called out, "Your daughter, has she said anything more about her drawing?"

She turned back around. "No, nothing yet."

While Maxine drove away, McCallister stared out at the fading taillights. "Our shot at getting in the church just took off."

SUNDAY BRUNCH with Hank had been a years-long tradition for Ellis. Or at least since her dad had retired and found himself with too much time on his hands. She'd arrived right on time and opened the screen door. "Dad?"

"In the kitchen," he called out.

The smell of bacon sizzling in a pan and the sweet scent of maple syrup enveloped her. After a long night with little sleep, she looked forward to this morning. McCallister had kept silent when they left the church in the middle of the night. If he had been in charge, they would've gone inside and had a look around, but he wasn't, Ellis was. And risking her career on a reckless move like that wasn't something she was willing to do. Even if it meant catching a break in the case. Hank always told her to work inside the lines because it was the only way to get a clean conviction. She heeded that advice.

"Good morning, Becca." Hank stood in front of the stove and flipped the pancakes. A moment later, he turned to her and wiped his hands on an apron that read, "World's Greatest Cook."

Ellis couldn't argue with that; then again, she rarely cooked for herself, opting instead for takeout. If anyone ever opened the side drawer in her kitchen, they'd be bombarded with menus from every restaurant within a five-mile radius.

"Hey, Dad. It smells great in here."

"Grab a drink. It's almost ready."

A tray lay on the buffet table that held orange juice and a bottle of champagne nestled in an ice bucket. "You spoil me." She poured a mimosa. "Care for one?"

"Heck yeah, I do. It's what I look forward to the most."

"You got it." She poured him a drink and set it on the kitchen island behind him. "Have you heard from Carter?"

"I'd rather not talk about him right now, if it's all the same to you." Hank grabbed the champagne glass, downing a long sip. "Perfect. Grab a plate and get it while it's hot." He pulled a warm plate of pancakes from the oven and set it on the island along with the rest of the spread.

"This looks delicious." Ellis served herself a healthy portion. "Thank you."

"So how's the investigation going?" Hank tucked into his fried egg.

"I made a decision last night, and I don't think my partner was very happy about it." Ellis took a sip from her mimosa.

"Was it the right decision?" he asked.

"As far as I'm concerned, yes. I wanted probable cause, and it just wasn't there."

"Then that's the only concern you should have. Look, I know this new guy, McCallister, is probably trying to win points with Abbott, maybe Serrano too, but don't let him bully you into doing something you don't think is right. He's a former Boston cop." Hank raised his hand. "I don't want to speak ill of any of my brothers in blue, but those guys do things that wouldn't fly in a lot of departments." He eyed her. "What did he want you to do?"

She shoved a bacon slice into her mouth before washing it down. "We had a chance to look around the church late last night, but I said no because we didn't have a warrant."

"Hang on, your partner wanted to get inside a place? How? By breaking in?"

"No, no. It was nothing like that. We got back late from a talk we had with a cop in Concord. Anyway, I wanted to drive by the church, looking for one of our persons of interest to be there, ideally, cleaning up their mess. That was where I'd hoped I could claim probable cause if we'd seen either one of them inside. Instead, we saw a car that belonged to the victim's best friend. In a nutshell, we caught her and asked her what the deal was. She was snooping. McCallister thought it would be a good idea to go back inside with her. She had a key."

"Oh." Hank pulled back and knitted his brow.

"Wait. You think he was right?" she asked.

"I'm not saying that."

"Yes, you are. I just don't get why. If we went inside and found something, we'd never be able to use it in court."

"You're right about that, but..."

Ellis folded her arms. "Oh, here we go."

"Now, hold on. Before you roll your eyes at me and tell me I'm old school and that's not how things are done these days."

"You said it, not me," she cut in.

"Listen, kid. Here's the thing. Yeah, you could've gone back inside because you had a member of the church let you in."

"Who had no permission to be inside..."

"But who did, as you say, have a key," Hank pressed on. "So, you go inside, have a look around. Maybe you see something. Maybe you don't. But if you had, you would've been able to go back to a judge and request a warrant on the basis that a church member suspected something. I don't know what that something could have been, but I'm sure you would've figured that out."

"So you think McCallister was right," she pressed him to confirm.

"You could've come up empty-handed for all we know. That's a more likely scenario than finding something someone just happened to leave out for anyone to see. What I would suggest you do now is go ahead and seek out that warrant. Don't tell the judge you were there last night. Just tell him or her that a member of the church, who is fearful to reveal her identity, has reason to suspect someone at the church might have been involved in your murder investigation. You're already looking at the pastor, aren't you?" Hank brushed off his hands. "Problem solved."

Ellis considered the plan. "Yeah, okay. Maybe we could get a judge to bite. But if I do this and I find jack squat, I lose my advantage. If the man I think could be involved decides to go ahead and start covering his tracks, assuming he hasn't already, then I've blown it."

Hank plunked a piece of bacon into his mouth. "Then you have to decide if it's worth the risk. You have a hunch, so you'd better be sure about it."

A STOICAL PASTOR Zeke stood at the Worship Hall entrance. Hands clasped at his front, a slight nod to greet his suffering parishioners as Sunday service was set to begin. As the last of the flock arrived, the pastor prepared to return inside, but noticed one more. "Good morning, Detective Ellis. I'm a little surprised to see you here."

She entered the hall and removed her coat. "Well, Pastor, this place was a big part of Claire Allen's life. She lived for this church, according to just about everyone. I thought it would be a good idea to see how they all felt about her, so may I sit in on your sermon this morning?"

"Yes, of course. All are welcome here." He motioned her inside. "You're free to take a seat anywhere you'd like. I would ask that you respect the members and not engage in questioning them at this time. I'm sure you can understand."

"No one will even know I'm here." Ellis slipped into a pew near the back. Faces of those around her wore grief. Whispers were subdued. She never attended church herself, but supposed they were usually pleasant, cordial gatherings. Members offering warm greetings to one another. Children scampering around. But looking out at these faces and hunched shoulders now, she had some sense of just what Claire Allen meant to these people.

One person, however, she had expected to see, but didn't. Maxine Rehnquist. Scott Allen and a few of the women she'd met the other day sat near the front, including Ann Kemper. Ellis couldn't help but roll her eyes at that slap in the face. And with the revelation that Claire knew about the affair, she had a new witness on her list, Kemper's husband.

But where was Maxine, Claire's closest friend, and the woman whom she'd seen inside this place in the late hours of last night? She reached for her phone and texted McCallister.

Confirm Maxine Rehnquist's alibi asap. I'm at the church for service, but she's not here. Alarm bells ringing.

"Good morning, everyone." Pastor Zeke towered over the altar as he took his place behind it. "I want to thank you all for coming today. It has been a trying week for all of us, but an especially difficult week for our friend, Scott Allen, who has lost his wife. This isn't an official memorial service for Claire. That, from what I understand, is set for Tuesday and I'm sure you will all be in attendance. This morning is about the broader picture of Claire's impact on all our lives. Her impact on our community."

WHILE THEIR PARENTS ATTENDED WORSHIP, Pastor Jeff Harwick began his lesson with the children. He faced the whiteboard and drew a picture of an anchor. "Has anyone ever seen an anchor hanging off a boat? Do you know what an anchor does when it's lowered into the water?"

A young boy's hand shot up. "It keeps the boat from moving," he replied.

"That's right, Hayden. An anchor keeps the boat secure. Safe. So, if you think of something that might make you feel scared...Does it help when someone holds you tight, or anchors you in place?" He turned to face the young students. "Jesus can be an anchor..." A small hand rose and drew his attention. "Yes, Abby, what is it?"

The five-year-old with short curly hair and wide brown eyes held her hands in her lap. "I have to pee."

Harwick glanced up at the clock on the wall. "Okay. Go on, but hurry back." When the girl departed, he continued with the lesson. "So, can you draw a picture of a time when Jesus made you feel safely anchored?" As his young students picked up their crayons, the pastor set down his own marker and meandered through the room, checking on their progress.

After several minutes, Harwick again noted the time and walked over to one of the volunteers. "While they're coloring, I'm going to go see what's taking Abby. She's been gone too long. I'll be right back."

The teenage girl returned a smile. "I'll hold down the fort."

He walked into the hall, knocked and then pushed open

the door to the women's bathroom. "Abby? Abby, are you in here?" Harwick stepped inside and peeked under the stalls. "Dang it."

Walking back into the hall, he carried on until a small voice called out.

"Pastor Jeff?"

He spun around. "Abby, there you are. I've been looking for you."

She clutched at her stomach and walked on unsteady legs toward him.

"Are you feeling all right? Where were you? I checked the bathroom. Kiddo, you can't just disappear like that." He studied her a moment. "You look like you might be sick. Did you get sick, Abby? Do you have a bad tummy?"

"I don't feel good," she replied.

He took her hand. "Okay, how about we let you rest in the nurse's office until the service ends?" Harwick led her along the hallway and rapped his knuckles on the nurse's door. "Hey, Julia, Abby's not feeling well. You mind if she rests in here until her parents come get her?"

"Oh boy, Abby." The nurse smiled kindly at the child. "Of course."

Harwick picked her up and set her on the padded table. "Here you go, kiddo. Just rest."

Abby lay down and curled up into a ball, and Julia covered her in a light blanket.

"There must be another bug going around. I've had a couple bouts of kids getting sick here over the past few weeks. Wintertime, I guess. I'm sure we'll get it soon enough." He turned to the nurse. "Thanks for looking after her."

ELLIS PAID close attention to how Townsend carried himself up there at the altar. His soothing tone could lure anyone into a false sense of security. He insisted the congregation was safe and that he had every faith the Bangor Police would find the person responsible. Ellis couldn't be sure of either right now.

He was good at his job, that much was clear. Here was a man who Ellis was certain was corrupt yet had been absolved of any charges. At best, he was a thief of a charitable organization, something she had no way to prove yet. At worst, he was a murderer. As that thought struck her once more, she noticed Scott Allen, observed how he kept his head hung low through the entire sermon.

When the service ended, Ellis joined the others who'd begun to file out of the hall. Her interest in Townsend hadn't waned; in fact, it had only intensified. He'd gained the trust of the people here now. Maybe it was time to sit with him on a more official basis. Three people in this church had a reason to kill Claire Allen. Another, who had been her best friend, was still a question mark. Two had alibis she couldn't yet poke holes through. The third? Well, his alibi had more holes in it than a pair of Crocs.

MAXINE OPENED the door to Vanessa's bedroom. The girl lay in her bed, her knees against her chest. "How are you feeling, sweetheart?"

She turned down her mouth. "Still sick."

Maxine sat down on the bed next to her. "Maybe you caught something Friday night at the church." She placed the back of her hand on Vanessa's forehead. "You're not warm. Still no temperature. Do you want to try to eat something?"

Vanessa shook her head.

"Well, I sure wish I knew what was making you feel bad.

If I did, I'd take it away. I promise." Her attention was drawn to the door, where her husband stood.

"Ginger ale's in the kitchen," Ethan said. "How's she feeling?"

"The same. I'm sure it's just a stomach bug," Maxine replied. "You could've gone to church without me, you know."

"Hey, that's your thing more than it is mine. I only go because you make me," he said.

"That's not true, is it?"

He shook away long strands of his dark blond hair and walked inside. "Not entirely, I guess. Still, after all you've been through, I thought it would be a good idea to stick close, you know?"

"Thank you." Maxine stood from the bed and looked down at Vanessa. "Try to get some sleep, sweetheart. I'm sure you'll feel better soon." She started toward the door.

"Mommy?"

Maxine turned around. "Yes, baby?"

"I want to see the osifer."

"I'm sorry, who's that?"

"The blonde lady. The powice osifer."

"Oh, Detective Ellis? That's who you want to see?"

The little girl nodded.

"How come?" Maxine returned a puzzled glance at Ethan.

"I want to talk to her."

14

It was time to correct an apparent error in judgment from last night. Ellis had garnered Townsend's attention when he'd finished making the rounds after this morning's service or, rather, tribute to Claire Allen. Now, she waited inside his office after he'd been momentarily called away. The office was decorated similarly to Harwick's. Pictures with inspirational adages and scripture. The epitome of hypocrisy, she thought, given his ties to an embezzlement investigation. The fact it had been dropped held little weight with her. Hank had warned about the dangers of prejudging a potential suspect.

"Sorry to have kept you waiting." The slim and polished Townsend, dressed in what looked to her like a bespoke navy blue suit, returned to his desk. "It's always busy around here after Sunday service and after what happened..." He trailed off. "So, how can I help, Detective Ellis?"

"I'm sorry to take you away from your work, Pastor, but I wanted to follow up with a few more questions." But before she could say any more, her attention was drawn to her phone, where the caller ID displayed Maxine's name.

"Do you need to take that?" he asked.

"No." She declined the call. "Sorry about that. I wanted to talk to you a little about what happened back in Concord." Ellis detected the flicker of recognition in his eyes and the minor tremor in his lips.

"Excuse me?"

"Concord, New Hampshire. Apparently, there was some confusion regarding missing church funds at your previous ministry. Can you tell me a little bit about that?"

He casually leaned back in his chair and tilted his head. "Sounds like you already know what happened. Frankly, I'm surprised you're bringing it up in light of the fact you're supposed to be investigating the murder of one of my parishioners."

"It turned up during the course of the investigation. I think it's a relevant question, don't you?" Ellis asked.

"Not really, given it was simply gross negligence on the part of the Concord Police Department. I was fully exonerated of all charges." He narrowed his gaze. "How did you find out about that? I was assured no record existed because no charges were filed, again, because I was innocent."

"Well, Pastor, I am a detective. It's my job to learn as much as I can about people."

"I see. Am I now a suspect?"

"In the murder of Claire Allen?" Ellis pulled up to the edge of her chair. "I suppose that depends on why you weren't completely honest with me the other day. I understand if you don't want to talk about Concord, but to mislead me as to your whereabouts at the time of the fire doesn't bode well for you, Pastor."

"How have I not been completely honest with you about everything, Detective?"

"Let me refresh your memory. You assured me you had already gone home when the fire happened that night."

"And I had," he insisted.

"You might want to rethink your answer." She clasped her hands in her lap. "There appears to be some discrepancy between your recollection of events and the recollections of others."

Townsend shifted in his chair and cleared his throat. "I'm sorry, but who have you been speaking to? What I said was the truth. I went home after the service. Pastor Jeff called to tell me what had happened, and I came back. End of story."

"The discrepancy lies in your timeline, Pastor. You said you left at around 8:30, shortly after the service, and you live about twenty minutes away. I have spoken with members who distinctly recall seeing you in these halls around 9:30 that night." Ellis would not be mentioning that it had been the young volunteer, Hailey, who had spoken with Townsend, aware that could see her suffer unnecessary consequences.

"I see that as nothing more than the poor recollection of whoever you spoke to, which I find strange you won't reveal to me. What happened that night was horrific, shocking. Who can recall exactly their whereabouts at a particular time during a traumatic event? Pastor Jeff had left around 9 pm and soon returned to see the fire. Maybe he's mistaken as well. I don't know how else to prove what I'm telling you is how I remember it."

Ellis held out her hand. "If you really want to help clear this up, you could offer me your cell phone."

"Excuse me?"

"Your phone. It would reveal your location when the fire began. That would clear things up, wouldn't it?"

"You're treating me as if I'm a suspect, Detective Ellis. If you plan to do that, I am well within my rights to contact a lawyer. And you're also well aware that you would need a warrant to make such a request to me or my cell phone provider. Of course, I suspect if you had any sort of legitimate reason to make that request, you would've done so by now and we wouldn't be having this conversation. Nevertheless, I won't allow you to intimidate me or any member of this congregation. This is a desperate act on your part when your focus should be on searching for the person who killed Claire."

Ellis pushed up from the chair. "I suppose I shouldn't be surprised by your knowledge of Fourth Amendment rights, Pastor, given you've been down this road before. I was hoping to get your cooperation, but I can see now that's not going to happen." She started away. "Oh, and I will be getting a warrant to open up the church's finances. Probable cause is fairly obvious, given your association with a prior embezzlement case. Dropped or not, the spotlight shines on you, Pastor, and it isn't flattering."

He showed her to the door. "Whatever you have to do, Detective. I can see you're attempting to draw some connection between Claire and me by dredging up an old, trumped-up charge. What happened to Claire was an awful tragedy, but it had nothing to do with me or any member of this church." He opened the door. "Enjoy the rest of your day."

As Ellis made her way out, she grabbed her phone and listened to the message that Maxine Rehnquist had left, stopping cold as the voicemail played. "Shit." She hurried to reach her car, making the call along the way. "Maxine, I just got your message. What's going on?"

"Vanessa wasn't feeling well today, so we didn't go to this morning's service. Can you please come over? She insists on talking to you and won't tell me why. I don't know what's going on, but she's sick to her stomach. Won't eat or drink. And now she wants to see you to tell you something."

Ellis stepped into her Tahoe and turned the engine over. "I'm on my way."

IT EXPLAINED why Maxine wasn't at the service. While Ellis awaited confirmation from McCallister regarding Maxine's alibi, this could be the moment the young girl finally came out with what she'd seen. Maybe this would be proof against Townsend.

Maxine stood in front of her open door, awaiting Ellis's approach. "You went to the service this morning, huh?"

Ellis walked up the steps, appearing surprised.

"I heard it from the other volunteers. Word spreads quickly."

"Well, that makes more sense. Yes, I decided to go. It was clear everyone there really loved Claire. I see now why you weren't there."

"Motherhood." Maxine stepped aside. "Thanks for coming. I don't know what Vanessa wants to say, but I'm glad you're here to listen."

Ellis followed her inside. "And she didn't say anything else to you?"

"Nope. Just said she wanted to talk to the 'osifer.' I took that to mean you."

"She's a sweet girl." Ellis smiled. "Where is she?"

"In her room. I'll take you to her." Maxine started up the stairs. "She said she wasn't feeling well this morning. I checked for a fever, but she doesn't have one. Hard to say whether she was telling the truth, although, she usually likes going to church. Well, until recently."

Ellis trailed her up the steps. "With all that's happened, that doesn't come as much of a surprise."

"No, but this behavior has been going on a while." Maxine stopped on the top landing. "I should've asked her, you know? I just thought, well, she's a kid who doesn't want to sit in church. Fair enough. We've all been there."

"But this is more than that," Ellis added.

"As much as I don't want to believe that, yeah, I think it is." Maxine opened the door to her daughter's room. "Vanessa? Detective Ellis is here. She came to see you, just like you asked."

Ellis looked at Maxine for approval before approaching the girl. "Hi, Vanessa. I hear you're not feeling well right now."

"My tummy hurts," she replied.

"I'm sorry to hear that. You know, I think ginger ale is good for that. I remember my mom giving that to me when I had a tummy ache."

"She did?" Vanessa asked.

"Yep. She was a good mom, just like yours." Ellis sat on the edge of the bed. "Your mom tells me you wanted to talk to me."

The five-year-old's blond hair clung to her cheeks as she sat up. "I didn't want to go to church today because I was scared."

"Why were you scared?"

But, at that question, the little girl's confidence seemed to drain away. She bit her bottom lip and picked at the reddened skin around her fingernails.

"There's no need to be afraid, Vanessa. I'm here to help you. Your mom is too." Ellis was aware that she was no expert at talking to kids. Not only did she have none of her own, but she hadn't wanted any either. That said, sitting in front of Vanessa right now, she was drawn back to the hours after it happened, after her stepfather's death when she was just 12. The policewoman who'd talked to her had been so kind, so caring. It was like she knew exactly what to say. Ellis hadn't thought about that officer in a long time. But here with Vanessa, it all came flooding back.

"It's okay, baby," Maxine began. "Detective Ellis is here to listen. You aren't in any trouble. None whatsoever. Just tell her what you—"

Ellis raised her hand to stop Maxine a moment. "If there's one more thing I can say, Vanessa, it's that yes, your mother's absolutely right. You have done nothing wrong, and you are not going to get into any trouble, no matter what, okay? And whatever you need to tell me doesn't have to be shared with anyone else if you don't want it to be."

Vanessa looked at Ellis again. "Some of my friends don't like going to the church either. They feel sick sometimes."

Ellis tilted her head. "Like how you don't feel good right now?"

"Kind of. Pastor Jeff tells them to go rest in the nurse's office. They're gone for a while, but then they feel better when they come back to play."

Ellis's mind reeled. "I'm not sure I understand."

"The church has a full-time parish nurse," Maxine interjected.

"And I don't want to go back 'cause I don't want to get sick," Vanessa said.

"Okay, Vanessa, I can understand that," Ellis said softly. "But did you feel sick when I saw you the other morning? Did any of your friends feel sick?"

Vanessa shook her head wildly. "No. Pastor Jeff thinks they're faking. He thinks they just want to go home and play video games instead of learning about Jesus."

Ellis's pulse quickened. She searched for an explanation as to why this child would say something like this. The one that screamed out in her head was one she was terrified to listen to. Scott Allen was often at the church with unfettered access, and what Forensics had unearthed so far on his computer jumped to the forefront of her mind.

She quickly pulled herself together and donned a smile. "Well, you know what? I'll bet your mom won't make you go somewhere you don't want to go. There is one last thing I'd like to ask, Vanessa. That picture you drew, do you remember who it was you saw having that fight?" After a too-long pause, Ellis reared back when she noticed the girl's pants turn wet while she sat cross-legged on her bed. "Oh, honey." She looked at Maxine and drew her attention to it.

"Nessa? Sweetheart." Maxine rushed to her. "Baby, you must be sick. Come on. Let's get you cleaned up."

Ellis stepped back and let Maxine care for her daughter.

"I'm so sorry. She hasn't wet herself in years."

"It's okay. Please don't apologize." Ellis was shaken. She knew what this was and had experienced it herself once upon a time. Fear. Vanessa was terrified to admit to knowing whom she'd depicted in that drawing. "I'll wait for you outside. Take as long as you need."

Ellis started back downstairs and made her way to the front porch. She gripped the railing and inhaled long, deep breaths. What the hell was happening? What was she dealing with? Were these kids being drugged? But, again, it was what they'd found on Scott Allen's computer that set the tone in her mind. Was there something here to worry about, or was she jumping to conclusions? Kids get sick. It happens. "Enough to make a girl afraid to go to church? Enough to make her wet herself?"

Maxine walked outside, and Ellis turned at her approach. "My gosh, Detective. I'm so sorry. I have no idea why Vanessa had an accident."

"Hey, it's okay. Is she all right?"

"I think so." The anxious mother peered out over her snow-covered front yard. "I still don't understand why Vanessa won't tell us who was in her drawing."

Ellis set her gaze ahead. "Can I ask, where's Mr. Rehnquist?"

"He just left to go check in on Scott. I'm usually the one who deals with a sick kid."

She grinned. "I hear that's how that whole motherhood thing works."

"Yeah, I guess it does." Maxine turned to Ellis and seemed to pick up on her concern. "What's wrong?"

Ellis didn't know how to say it, or whether she should. Objectivity was key, and right now, Ellis had lost it where this girl was concerned. "What Vanessa did back there just now? Look, I'm no psychologist. I don't have kids. But I have seen how a scared child reacts. That's what I saw in Vanessa."

"What is she so afraid of?" Maxine pleaded.

It would set off a firestorm of rumors and panic if Ellis said more. The potential damage it could do to her case was incalculable. "Maybe you should see if she might talk to a therapist. It could help."

IT WAS time to bring in Abbott and Serrano. Ellis paced inside Abbott's office, unable to sit, while McCallister and the head of the department, Lieutenant Abe Serrano, were briefed on the latest news.

"What can we do, Sarge?" Ellis asked. "Do we arrest Jeff Harwick? Scott Allen? Both?"

"Let's evaluate what we do know." From his desk, Abbott aimed his meaty index finger at her. "You and McCallister dug into the pastor's background and uncovered a previous embezzlement investigation that had been dropped. And that was after you'd been approached by an employee of the church's current accounting firm suggesting something similar had happened here."

"Right," McCallister jumped in. "We drove to Concord

yesterday to talk to the lead investigator on that case. He offered us the names of the previous accountants and a few other details. We followed up, got a clearer picture, but that's about it."

Lieutenant Abe Serrano was in his late fifties; he still had most of his hair, though it had turned completely gray. Fit for a man of his age, he rested an elbow atop Abbott's filing cabinet and eyed Ellis. "And how long has this pastor been with Grace Community?"

"About two years," she replied. "And as far as we know, no complaints have ever been filed, no concerns brought to the department. Apart from the former accountant who voiced his concerns about the church's accounting irregularities, nothing had happened at this church until one of its members burned to death in her car last week."

"Now you have this story from the girl." Abbott nodded as he appeared to wrap his head around the situation.

"That, along with what's been discovered on Scott Allen's laptop, yes," Ellis added.

Serrano shoved a hand in his pants pocket. "And you believe she's telling the truth? She's a child, who could've easily been mistaken about what she saw."

"I've tried to keep that in mind, but my gut tells me she knows more," Ellis replied. "I can't shake the idea that Scott Allen, who strolls into the church whenever he wants to help out with the books, supposedly, was found to have accessed child pornography. Now, if he's abusing these children..."

"Hold on a second." Serrano raised his palm. "That's a hell of a giant leap, Becca. A couple of sick kids resting in the church nurse's office. Scott Allen, what, comes inside, takes pictures or God knows what. You don't have nearly enough to make that jump. Not even close."

"Until we find explicit photos of *children* on Allen's computer," she jumped in. "I understand your point, sir, but these events cannot be a coincidence. I'll grant you that the money, the affair, even if we've confirmed alibis, those seem more plausible explanations as to why Claire was murdered, but you didn't see that little girl this morning. She has seen, or been part of, something bad. Why else mention her friends being sick, too? What else could make a five-year-old wet herself at a simple question, 'who was in your drawing?'"

Serrano turned away. "Hell, I don't know. When is this forensics report due out?"

"Today," McCallister replied. "We'll know exactly what's on that computer." His phone alerted him to an incoming email and he glanced at it. "Oh, hang on. This is the airline." He opened the message and read it. "Okay, yeah. Maxine Rehnquist was, in fact, on the flight she claimed to be on. She was telling the truth, Becca. It doesn't mean she can't still be a part of it, but I'm not seeing any justification given what her daughter's got going on."

Ellis nodded. "Sarge, what this girl said and what we found on Allen's computer has to be enough to warrant a search of the church grounds. And we do have cause to search their financials based on Townsend's previous problems and the witness from their current accounting firm. I'm telling you, all this ties together. We just have to find the link. Hell, Townsend even pushed back when I asked him to verify his whereabouts on the night of the fire. I asked him to show me his GPS, and he basically told me to go fuck off." She finally stopped pacing and squared up with Serrano. "Give me access to the church finances right now and we'll find discrepancies, just like Nate Caulder did. That's where we'll start until Forensics is finished. These are things we can explore, and maybe...maybe it'll lead us to the truth about these men and whether the children in that community are being harmed."

Serrano rubbed his eyes. "Becca, I see you're passionate about this and I get it. But the moment you let your emotions take over, objectivity goes out the door. We get sloppy, and we make mistakes. Your dad would tell you the same thing."

"Shit." Abbott cut in. "Give the lab the rest of the day to find out what exactly is on Scott Allen's computer." He eyed Serrano for an approval. When they appeared to be in agreement, he turned back to Ellis. "Then you'll get your warrant."

15

There were few days working for the Bangor Police Department that left Ellis feeling beaten, but today was one of those days. As early evening arrived, she and McCallister pulled into the apartment complex that Jeff Harwick called home. The Oakwood Apartments lay northwest of the I-95. Two large buildings housed the units that looked a lot like a prison compound without the barbed wire. The exterior was painted a dull gray over top of masonry block with seafoam blue on the fake shutters and trim.

"This is it." Ellis pulled to a stop.

"I know you're hesitant to do this, but this kid had access and opportunity. You know as well as I do, those are strong components to motive," McCallister replied.

"No, you're right. We have to understand his role. He just..." She trailed off. "Doesn't matter. We have to talk to him."

"We'll keep it direct and to the point, then decide if he should be brought in for questioning. Because once he's brought in, it's likely the church will fire him, or the parents will campaign to get him fired. Even if he's found innocent of whatever the hell is going on."

She cut the engine and opened her car door. "Yeah, we'll ruin this kid's life if we screw this up."

"Hey." He reached out for her arm.

"Yeah?"

"Why didn't you tell brass you're being followed?" he asked.

Ellis glanced away a moment. "Serrano would've pulled me off the case."

"Why?"

She closed her eyes and rubbed her forehead with her fingertips. "Because my father made him promise to keep me safe. If he thought I was in greater danger than what we usually face? If he thought I was a target, I'd be on desk duty until this case was over."

They started ahead to Harwick's apartment, and Ellis knocked on the door. The moment the young man opened it and he spotted them, his body tensed.

"Detective Ellis." His gaze darted between them. "What are you both doing here? Is everything okay at the church?"

"No need to be nervous," Ellis replied, taking in the baby-faced kid's outfit of a college T-shirt and sweatpants. "We just want to talk to you."

"Oh, okay, sure. Come in." He gestured into the apartment. "Please don't mind the mess. I'm not a very good housekeeper."

Ellis observed the room. Pizza boxes, a few dirty dishes in the sink, a laptop on the coffee table. Pretty much what she would expect from a twenty-something who lived alone. And as she regarded McCallister, it seemed they'd both considered the same thing. If this kid was guilty, he might not be so willing to let them waltz right in.

"Can I offer you something to drink? I have some pop."

He rubbed his hands on his sweatpants as though they'd been clammy.

Body language. Always something she kept in mind. "No, thank you."

"I'm fine, thanks," McCallister said.

"Okay, then why don't you both take a seat?" Harwick followed them to the modest living room complete with worn furnishings and a large television screen fixed to the wall.

Ellis sat down on the sofa and took note of the gaming system, his tablet, and a laptop. A few pictures of what she assumed were his family. "We'd like to talk to you about being the youth pastor at Grace Community."

"Sure. What do you want to know?" He sat down on an Ikea chair next to the couch.

"We understand you've been there since this past summer," McCallister began. "And by all accounts, the kids seem to have taken to you."

"Oh, yes. I really enjoy teaching them and talking with them. You know, the important thing that people forget sometimes is that kids don't like it when adults talk down to them. Like they're not smart people. Kids know a lot more than adults give them credit for. I especially connect with the teens." He chuckled. "Maybe because I'm not much older than they are, huh?"

"Maybe so," Ellis replied. "As you know, we're investigating Claire Allen's murder."

"Yes, ma'am." He appeared serious again.

"And during the course of the investigation, we've had some unusual situations come up."

"I'm sorry, situations?" he asked.

McCallister eyed Ellis a moment and jumped in. "Jeff, what do you do for work?"

"I'm a pharmaceutical associate with Bangor General

Hospital. That's what I went to school for. I hope to open my own pharmacy someday."

Ellis straightened her back. "You work in a pharmacy?"

"Yes, I do. At the hospital. Why?"

"Do you have access to prescription drugs?" she asked.

"Well, yes and no. I can't prescribe drugs yet. I can distribute them at the hospital under the supervision of the pharmacist only." He peered at them with an inquiring smile. "What's this about exactly? Am I in trouble for something?"

"Jeff, how well do you know Scott Allen?" Ellis asked, deflecting him.

He shrugged. "Not well. He and Claire didn't have kids, so I didn't have a reason to associate with them much."

"Are you ever left alone with the children at the church?" McCallister cut in.

There it was. The look that people got when they suddenly realized the cops thought they were the guilty ones. Ellis had seen it plenty of times. But how Harwick handled the next few moments would reveal whether he had anything to do with what she suspected. This kid's life teetered between ruin and redemption, and she wasn't sure he knew that.

Harwick swallowed hard and wiped his hands on his pants again. "Well, sure, sometimes. What's going on? Did someone say something? I haven't done anything wrong. I swear it. Go. Go have a look around here. You won't find anything. I don't know what's happening right now. I just thought you were here about Claire..."

"Calm down, Jeff," Ellis said. "No one's said anything. It's just a question."

WITH THE WARM mug in her hands, Ellis sipped on the steaming coffee. She stared out onto the quiet street from the coffee shop window as Sunday drew to a close. "Did we make the right call?"

McCallister returned his gaze to Ellis, who sat across from him. "You know we did. Harwick didn't do anything to those kids. He turned over everything to us without hesitation, without a warrant. That doesn't happen if you're guilty. I'll admit, I was sweating it a little when he said he worked at a pharmacy."

"Same here. And you know, Vanessa never flinched when she mentioned Harwick. Never shuddered or looked fearful of him. Just whoever was in her drawing," Ellis added. "Problem is, we're no closer to learning what happened to Claire or whether Vanessa's account of the situation is as bad as we think it is. But I won't pass judgment on that until we know what's on Scott Allen's computers. Harwick may not have done anything, but that doesn't mean nothing happened."

"I agree."

She ran her finger over the rim of the mug. "You ever deal with something like this?"

McCallister tilted his head into the palm of his left hand. "With the kids? No. And I don't mind telling you, I'm afraid of what we might find. Look, I'm sure this isn't the right time, but earlier, with the lieutenant, he seemed to pick up on some strong feelings you had. And this apparent pact he has with your pop..."

Ellis shrugged. "Serrano was a junior detective when he first met my dad. They worked quite a few cases together. Eventually, Serrano moved up the ranks."

"But not your dad?"

"You'd have to understand the type of man he is," Ellis added. "My dad was never one to kiss anyone's ass. That kind of cop doesn't get very far. Maybe that's why I haven't been promoted much."

"Probably." He smiled.

"No, in all seriousness, Dad felt his talents lay in investigation, and he was right. So Serrano eventually became his boss, and shortly after that, Dad retired from the force."

"And the other stuff?"

"What other stuff?" she asked.

"Serrano feeling like, you know, maybe he didn't want to push your buttons." McCallister turned away his gaze a moment. "Look, I don't mean to..."

"Yes, you do." She glanced through the window again. "Anyone ever tell you you're about as subtle as a brick?"

McCallister returned a smile. "On occasion."

"I suppose it's better you hear it from me rather than through the rumor mill, where shit never comes out the same way twice." Ellis swirled her coffee mug. "So, you probably heard that when I was a kid, I killed someone." She eyed him. "Or maybe you didn't hear that. Well, you would've soon enough. Anyway, he wasn't just any man. He was my stepfather, and I was twelve."

His eyes appeared to soften. "Did he hurt you? Is that why you feel connected to the girl?"

"Me? No, but he beat the ever-loving shit out of my mom —a lot."

"I'm sorry to hear that, Becca."

McCallister's display of compassion made her feel weak and was the main reason she rarely told people about this part of her life. But he deserved to know the baggage his partner carried, just as she would want to know the same in return. "Don't be. Happens to a lot of families. So, anyway..." She cleared her throat, determined to tell her tale now she'd begun. "John came home—that was his name—drunk like he usually did. Mom had made dinner and it had gotten cold.

She was mad at him for turning up late and drunk. He got pissed because he didn't have a hot dinner waiting for him. I was upstairs when all of it started, but the walls were thin." Ellis took another sip of her coffee. "Things got heated pretty quickly. They were both screaming at each other. I'd sort of gotten used to that part. Then the hitting started. John had put Mom in the hospital twice before. Once for a broken jaw, the second for a sprained wrist. Never pressed any charges."

"Can I ask where your dad was during all this? McCallister asked. "I get they were divorced, but did you tell him?"

"He knew. He tried to talk to Mom more than once to get her to leave John. She wouldn't. I'll never understand why. I mean, I do in theory, but..." She shook her head slightly, still puzzled. "So, going back to that night. John started smacking her around. Pushing her. Whacking her across the head." Ellis looked away a moment and scratched her palms, distracting herself from the rising emotional tide. "I guess you could say I'd finally had enough. I walked into their bedroom, walked right to the locked safe where my dad insisted Mom keep a gun. I knew the code. I took it out, loaded it with a few bullets, and walked downstairs." She turned up her gaze, drew in a deep breath and exhaled slowly. "I remember my hands shook so badly, I thought I would drop the gun, but I didn't. I was sick and tired of that asshole hurting my mom. If she wasn't going to do something to stop him, then I would." Ellis took a sip of coffee from her mug. "I warned him. I warned him to stop. And do you know what that son of a bitch did? He turned to me and laughed. I'm holding a gun, aiming it right at his head, and the fucker laughs. Then he turned back around and grabbed my mom's throat. He was choking the life from her. They fell to the ground, and he wouldn't let her go. I screamed and I screamed. I cried so hard, I couldn't hardly see. And then I fired."

McCallister closed his eyes a moment. "Jesus."

"Well, it was a good thing Hank taught me how to use a gun. Bullet went right through the back of John's head." Ellis made a finger gun and pressed it against her skull. "Except that I was too late to help her. He'd throttled her so hard that her windpipe was crushed. She'd stopped breathing by the time I got to her. I did all that, and I still couldn't save my mom." Ellis's heart beat in her throat and she finally swallowed it down. She'd told the story many times before, yet it failed to get any easier.

"Becca, I'm so sorry." McCallister's face masked in disbelief. "I can't imagine going through something like that."

She looked across the table at him. "Hank told me that if I hadn't done what I did, John would've killed her anyway. And this way, I made sure he didn't hurt anyone else ever again."

McCallister captured her watery gaze. "Thank you for sharing that with me. I appreciate your trust and I won't abuse it."

She waved him off. "I told you because, like I said, things get twisted. I wanted you to know the truth. The guys we work with, they all know. They understand. I just thought you should know who you're working with."

———

SCOTT ALLEN APPEARED in the doorway of Townsend's office. He glanced down the hall and waited for it to clear of stragglers.

Townsend looked up from his desk and took notice. "What are you doing here, Scott? Have you been here all this time?"

"No, I went home after the service, but I had to come back. I need to know the truth." He walked inside.

"About?"

"You're not stupid, Zeke, okay? Don't act like you are." He sat down. "I saw that detective at the service this morning. I saw her in here, too."

"She has a right to worship just like everyone else," Townsend replied.

Scott slammed his fist on the desk. "I'm not in the mood to play games with you today. I'm here because you need to tell me what happened that night. You know, I went home this morning, had to listen to my mother-in-law cry on the phone for an hour. Then I stared at a full bottle of whiskey and decided I needed more. You have any idea what the fuck is happening to me right now? And you sit here smug and perfect and..."

"Scott, we've been through all this..."

"Yeah, we have. And I still don't believe you. The cops don't believe you either, or I don't think they would've shown up today. So why don't you do me a goddam favor and tell me the truth about what happened to Claire."

Townsend walked to his door. "How about we keep this between ourselves?" He closed it and returned to his desk. "What more do you want me to say, Scott? Do you really think I'd jeopardize everything we've got going on by killing your wife, of all people?"

"I think she figured out what we were doing. That's what I think. She came to you and confronted you," Allen snapped.

"If she suspected us, why not ask you, her husband?"

"I don't know. But if I don't start getting some goddam answers from you, I'm going to the cops myself. I'll tell them we've been skimming from the church. I don't give a shit anymore, Zeke. My fucking wife is dead. You hear me? What the hell more do I have to lose?"

Townsend returned a fiery gaze. "I'll tell you what you have to lose—everything. Your job, your family..."

"Claire was my family."

"Your home and your freedom," Townsend added. "Should I go on?"

"Look, I only agreed to help you so I could pay off some debt. That's it. Claire wanted a good life. Nice clothes, expensive shoes. I gave her all that."

"But you couldn't afford it, so you came to me," Townsend reminded him. "And we worked out a deal. Now you want to go back on that deal?" He leaned over his desk with steely resolve. "Listen to me carefully, Scott, because this is the last time I'll say this. I didn't kill Claire."

Allen wiped the tears from his cheeks with the back of his hand. "Then who the hell did?"

"If I knew, I'd tell you," Townsend replied. "I know you're grieving. We all are, but you have to see this through. I told you to start closing the accounts. Move the money. Have you done that yet?"

"Not all of it," Allen admitted.

"Get it done." Townsend folded his arms and leaned back again. "You know, maybe you should think about where you're at in your life right now before you decide to chuck it all away. The cops will find out who killed your wife. They always do. But until then, you need to keep your shit together, you hear me? Don't screw this up now. You're in way too deep, my friend."

ELLIS UNLOCKED her driver's side door and climbed behind the wheel, waiting for McCallister to step in. "Now that we feel comfortable ruling out Harwick, we're left to uncover the correlation between Townsend and Allen. I think the only way we find it is by getting Allen to turn on his partner. We have circumstantial evidence to suggest embezzlement. Let's talk to Allen about what's been found on his laptop."

"You want to hit him up again before we have hard evidence?" McCallister asked.

"I want to scare him. Whatever Brown ends up finding on that laptop will be bad, I'm sure, but will it be enough to prove he and/or Townsend murdered Claire? Two things need to happen fast. Connect these men and stop either or both of them from hurting any children, if that's what's been happening. A warrant will give us authority to search, but unless a kid comes forward or we find clear-cut evidence..." Ellis pulled out onto the road and headed north. "Look, Allen was at the service this morning, but the temperature between him and Townsend plunged to below freezing when the two shook hands after it was over."

"If things are turning sour, that'll work in our favor," McCallister replied. "Hammering a wedge between them is our best bet for now."

Ellis turned down the road and parked at the end of the driveway near the nice new BMW. "It's up to us to get Allen to change his tune, and my guess is that mentioning his wife knew about his affair, too, will prod him along."

McCallister joined her and the two walked the long path to the front door. Ellis knocked, and a moment later, the door opened. "Mr. Allen."

"Detectives." He glanced at them. "I thought I'd seen enough of the Bangor Police. You here to take more of my possessions?"

"No, sir. We'd like to talk to you about what happened the day of Claire's death," Ellis replied.

"Christ." Allen shook his head. "Come in; like I have a choice."

"Your choice is to talk to us here or at the station." McCallister followed Ellis inside. "I'd say this is the right call."

"The pastor offered some very nice words about Claire at the service this morning." Ellis meandered toward the living room. "She was clearly a valued member of the church."

"I was there, I heard. And yes, she was." He closed the door. "I suppose I should be a gracious host and offer you two a drink."

"Thank you, no." Ellis walked to the fireplace, where photos of the couple rested on the mantel. "Claire was a beautiful woman. You were lucky to have her."

Allen sat down on the sofa. "I know that."

Ellis took a seat on a side chair while McCallister remained standing. "We've struggled to gain traction on this case, Mr. Allen."

"You're saying that you have no leads," he replied.

"A few, but we've come up against some troubling information, so that's the real reason why we're here," Ellis continued. "The lab is still analyzing your electronic devices as well as Claire's. Which, by the way, revealed emails between her and Ann Kemper's husband. Your wife knew, Mr. Allen. And so did Mr. Kemper. I imagine that was the reason she changed her passcode. We haven't uncovered any further correspondence, but we thought you'd want to know."

Allen turned away and shook his head.

"But going back to Forensics, a preliminary report suggests some disturbing findings on your laptop," Ellis continued.

Allen glowered at her. "What is that supposed to mean?"

"It means that it's in your best interest to tell us everything about your relationship with Zeke Townsend," McCallister cut in. "Because I'll tell you, Mr. Allen, what we've found so far is discouraging. And your attempt to erase the hard drive makes the findings all that much worse. If more is uncovered, life as you know it will cease to exist."

"Now, hang on. What the hell is happening here?" He stood in protest. "I've done nothing but cooperate with you."

"Selectively, I should add," Ellis replied. "Look, Mr. Allen, just tell us what your role was at the church. What did you do for Townsend? If you want to help us find your wife's killer, help us learn more about the pastor. Right now, that's your best option."

"No. You don't get to drop a bomb and say threatening shit to me only to pull back and not disclose what you think you found."

McCallister glanced at Ellis. "We're hesitant to say more because we don't have all the facts, but since you insist. Preliminary reports suggest the presence of child pornography on your personal laptop. That's a felony charge that would see you behind bars for a couple of decades, depending on how you received it or used it."

"What? No, your people are wrong. I would never. Are you screwing with me right now? Is this some sort of intimidation tactic?"

"I promise you, it's not," Ellis replied flatly. "Now, you can sit down and cooperate, or you can deny what's been found and when the final report comes out, we'll be back to put you in cuffs."

Allen paced his living room with clenched fists. He finally stopped and turned around to Ellis. "First of all, I didn't kill my wife."

"So you've said," McCallister shot back.

"Secondly, whoever put that disgusting shit on my computer is out to get me. If what you're saying is true, then it's nothing more than an attempt to frame me."

"We hear that a lot," Ellis said. "Do you have proof of anyone who would want to frame you, and why?" She noticed a shift in his demeanor. He grew hesitant. "Mr. Allen, if you know something relevant to the investigation into your wife's murder, you need to tell us now."

16

Behind Scott Allen's eyes lay a truth that Ellis plainly witnessed. He wanted to speak out, and her heart raced in anticipation. Her desire for answers regarding Claire's murder and, now, the vague notion that not all was right with the children at the church left her nearly breathless.

Allen dropped onto the sofa, where he appeared to slump in defeat. "I don't know why you found those things on my computer. I swear to you, I've never looked at that kind of vile stuff in my entire life."

Ellis unleashed a heavy sigh. Whatever he was about to admit to had vanished, and the truth in his gaze was replaced with fear. "Did you go to the church earlier that day, the day Claire was killed, to meet with Townsend for any reason?"

"I told you where I was every minute of that day. Maybe it's time you guys start doing your jobs, huh? My wife was a good woman. She cared more about the people of this community than they will ever know." He wiped away a tear. "You think I don't know that I didn't deserve her? You have to find whoever did this."

The tear was a nice touch, Ellis thought. Very convincing. "Just so you understand, Mr. Allen, there will be a continued police presence outside your home until all the evidence in our possession is fully analyzed, given the nature of the discovery. If you try to leave, they will follow."

"So I'm a prisoner in my own home?" he asked.

"Call it what you want. But as long as you're a person of interest, we will be watching you. And the moment we get what we need to bring charges..."

Allen raised his gaze to her. "Sounds to me like you've made up your mind."

"What we do have is already damning, Mr. Allen," McCallister replied.

Ellis had crossed the line, and she knew it. She jeopardized her case by lobbing unproven allegations at a man who hadn't yet been considered a suspect, and she was doing it out of anger. Heeding Lieutenant Serrano would've been wise. But it was the fear she'd seen in Vanessa that set her on this path. "We'll be reviewing the church's finances as well as continuing to analyze your personal devices. Know that your relationship with Zeke Townsend will be put under the microscope as well. You've chosen to partner with a man who has a checkered history, Mr. Allen. Or maybe you already knew that?"

"He's not my partner in anything."

McCallister cleared his throat. "We'll be in touch very soon. Thank you for your time." He led the way to the door and held it open for Ellis.

The detectives returned to her SUV, and she stepped behind the wheel.

"You all right?" McCallister asked.

Her shoulders sank low, and she closed her eyes. "I'm sorry. I shouldn't have said those things to him."

He grabbed the handle above his door and stared through

the windshield. "Yeah, well, that's a conversation that could've gone better."

Ellis turned over the engine and backed out of the driveway. "You know someone got to him, right?"

"I think that was pretty clear. Unfortunately, we still don't know if he's actually done anything wrong. We're assuming his relationship with Townsend is what implicates him. Whether he's right about someone attempting to frame him by creating a whole new set of charges, I don't know."

"It's like we're dealing with two separate investigations, but they have to be connected. I just can't figure out how." Ellis turned to him. "There's no mistaking what I saw in Vanessa Rehnquist. Something is going on at that church. Right now, Scott Allen is the only one where we have direct evidence to suggest his involvement."

"Let's be careful about that because all Brown has uncovered are websites. Nothing to say those kids at the church were harmed in any way. I understand your concern over the Rehnquist girl, but her fear could be based on something entirely different. I'm not dismissing it, but that's a serious accusation that needs to be based on solid evidence."

"Okay, but then let's do something to prevent anything further. Even the suggestion something could be happening warrants a response. I say we talk to the church and get them to shut down all youth activities," she replied.

"That won't go over well, especially without proof. But considering their other problem of a parishioner being murdered in their parking lot, they may be open to discussion."

Ellis arrived at the station, and they walked inside to the relative quiet. Patrol officers filled out paperwork as they prepared for a shift change on this Sunday evening. And as the detectives made their way upstairs to the bullpen, a few of their co-workers remained on duty.

"You're still here, Bevins?" McCallister asked.

"Filling out bullshit paperwork, as usual. What's going on with you guys? Why are you two here so late?"

"Waiting on computer forensics," Ellis replied.

"The Claire Allen case. How's that going?"

She shrugged.

"That good, huh?" Bevins clicked his tongue. "Sorry to hear that."

"Thanks." Ellis turned to McCallister. "Brown's time is up. You ready to see what he has?"

"After the day we've had, dear God, he'd better have something." He followed her back to the lab.

Brown drew his gaze from his bank of screens when the door opened. He spotted the detectives heading his way. "I'd say I'm surprised to see you, but..."

Ellis reluctantly grinned. "What do you have for us on the Scott Allen seizures?"

He spun around in his chair to face his computer. "We retrieved several files on the laptop. Whatever program the guy used to wipe his hard drive left behind remnants that made it fairly easy to recover quite a bit. If someone's going to go through the effort of scrubbing his computer, don't skimp on the software. Anywho, we recovered several images, many of which involved child exploitation. They were installed via an external storage device."

"Goddam it. Installed via USB?" Ellis asked.

"Yes, ma'am."

McCallister narrowed his gaze. "What's the significance of that?"

Brown turned to him. "Well, it means that Scott Allen didn't download the files onto his computer from a website and—"

"It would be easy to deny that he added the files at all,"

Ellis cut in. "But those files were still erased, so it's not a leap to assume he knew they were there and tried to delete them."

"The guy may not have known they were there." Brown raised his hands after Ellis shot him a look. "I'm just saying. He wiped his hard drive. That's all we know for fact."

She peered over his shoulder. "I need to see the images."

"You sure about that, Detective?"

"Yes."

"Okay." Brown typed on his keyboard and retrieved the information. "The metadata for each photo indicates the date they were taken and what device they were stored on. However, it doesn't show whether the jpegs originated from another device."

"Again, making it easy to deny he'd installed them on his computer," Ellis added.

"Uh-huh. So here's what we found. You don't mind if I step out while you view these? I have no need..."

"I understand." Ellis looked at McCallister. "You ready?"

"It's not like we have a choice."

After Brown stepped away, Ellis opened the files. She feigned detachment, calling on a part of her brain she hadn't engaged since the night her mother was murdered. Each image seemed worse than the last. Young children, not older than eight.

"Christ." McCallister turned away.

"That's all of them," Ellis said.

"Did you recognize anyone? Not that many showed the faces," he pressed on.

"No, but I don't know all the kids at that church. It didn't look like they were taken there. We'll have to ask the church elders to view these to determine whether they know who any of these children are."

"That'll be enough to convince them to shut it down,"

McCallister said. "And their first question will be who had the images."

"If we give them Allen's name, his life is effectively over. So what do we do about him? If we arrest him, will it hold up?" she asked.

"That depends on whether we can identify the victims here, which we'll jump on ASAP. On charges of having these on his computer, yes, but if you want to tie him to murder or even partnering with Townsend, this won't do it," McCallister began. "And if we bring him in, we might lose Townsend. Look, for all we know, whatever the hell this is could be a joint effort. We're keeping eyes on Allen. Now's the time to make the connection to Townsend and the embezzlement, something we're close to getting. Then we bring both these sons of bitches in, and we'll find a way to get them for murder too."

ELLIS'S straight-and-narrow approach had cost her an opportunity to gain access to the church while only bending the rules. Of course, she thought it had been the right decision. Clean case, clean conviction. But given what she knew now, the time lost and the potential evidence that the kids of Grace Community Church were at risk, the mistake haunted her. Now, rather than bend the rules, she was about to break them. And whatever the end result, it was unlikely Hank would forgive her.

Getting inside would be the easy part. Ellis stepped out of her SUV and canvassed the area around the church. The late hour and darkened grounds eclipsed her progression as she reached the youth building, where large windows faced the road. She had arranged ingress this morning while awaiting Townsend; a single window left unlocked. The last-minute notion derived from a prickly feeling at the back of her neck that struck as she watched Townsend and Allen speaking after the service. A quick rundown of the security system proved it to be as half-assed as the absence of cameras on the exterior. An alarm tied to the doors only. No window sensors. No interior sensors.

Nevertheless, the strength to follow through on her hunch arrived only after she forced herself to set eyes on photos of children grotesquely displayed for the vile pleasure of degenerates. The hunch wasn't enough for a judge to issue a warrant on the church, but it was enough for her to take action.

With gloved hands, Ellis pushed open the window and climbed inside. The building was bathed in darkness except for the hall. Red exit lights glowed above her. Townsend's office was where she would start. The small flashlight she carried inside shone on the neatly stacked papers and the computer on his desk. She turned to the filing cabinet and pulled the top drawer. It wouldn't budge. "Shit." After tugging on each one beneath with the same results, Ellis moved on into the hall again until she spotted a door marked "closet." Inside, black filing cabinets lined the walls and again she tried the drawers. Expecting all to be locked, she yanked the handle on one, and it opened. Ellis nearly stumbled back from the force. "All right. Let's see what we have." She held the small flashlight between her teeth, aiming it inside the drawer while her fingers flipped through the files.

A door creaked on its hinges. Ellis dropped the light into her hands, switched it off and jumped back from the cabinet. She stood fixed in place. Her heartbeat echoed in her ears and her eyes widened to pull in every ounce of light they could. It wasn't enough.

Ellis pulled her weapon from her chest strap and took measured steps into the hall. The noise had traveled from farther down, she believed. Townsend's office? Her throat dried as she advanced along the dark corridor with a faint red glow from above. No one knew she was here, not even her partner.

A classroom lay on the right, its door open. She stopped just outside it and listened, but there was nothing. Ellis continued with a steady hand on her revolver. It had been a long time since she drew on anyone and even longer since she'd fired. But here in the dark, in a place she shouldn't have been, killing someone had just become a distinct possibility.

A percussive echo rang out from behind the nearby bathroom door, as if something had been dropped. Ellis spun around and pressed her back against the wall, crawling along it until she reached the bathroom door. With her right hand, she pushed it open, keeping her body clear of the entrance. Her gun trained ahead, Ellis stepped inside. "Bangor PD. Identify yourself." Sweat poured from her neck and her heart raced like she'd run a marathon, but her finger was steady. Her trigger finger was always steady.

The stall doors were closed and she glimpsed down, but didn't see any feet. "Step out of the stall and show me your hands." The light switch was behind her. If she turned it on, the split-second distraction could cost Ellis her life, but it was too dark to see. She firmed her stance and peered down along each stall, looking for signs of life and then she saw it. On the floor was the cover of a smoke detector. Her eyes were drawn up to wires that dangled from high on the wall. "What the hell?"

A metal stall door flew open and knocked Ellis to the ground. As she struck the tile floor, her gun slipped from her hand and slid toward the sinks. A shadow sprinted around her and into the hall.

Ellis pushed off the ground, wincing from the pain on the

side of her head. She snatched her gun before darting after the moving figure. "Stop! Bangor PD!"

Indistinct under the red glow, the burly figure swathed in dark heavy clothing ran toward the exit at the end of the hall.

Ellis pumped her legs. Her head throbbed and stars swirled before her eyes as she blinked to clear her vision. "Police! Stop!"

The door flew open and he bolted.

"Goddam it!" The door had slammed shut by the time Ellis reached it and she thrust it open again. The snow-covered ground revealed his tracks and she followed them around the building toward the nearby basketball courts until a car's engine roared in the distance. White smoke billowed into the night sky as the tires squealed. He was gone.

Ellis returned inside and stopped cold as she entered the hall. With her fist clenched, she screamed. "Fuck!" And in that moment, she spun around and gazed at the door. "Sensors. Then why the hell isn't the alarm going off?" The doors were tied to the alarm, she'd confirmed as much. Whoever he was had the code. "Jesus."

Her flashlight had dropped inside the bathroom and she returned to find it. On retrieving it, she spotted the broken smoke detector cover on the floor and picked it up. Flipping it over, she looked at it closely, but it looked like every other alarm. "What the hell were you doing in here?"

Ellis pushed open the door to one of the stalls and walked inside. She removed the lid to the toilet tank and shone her light in. Nothing. Squatting low, she trained the light around the bottom of the toilet. Nothing. She returned to her feet. "Why the smoke detector?" It was the cover that had fallen to the floor that caught her attention and set off this chain of events. "Were you already here?" Her hands at her hips, Ellis considered the idea.

Either way, she couldn't stay for much longer. The risk

was already too great because whoever it had been knew she was here and could make an anonymous call to the cops. Her car was right out front. Getting caught would mean the end of her career, so she'd better find something or get the hell out.

Ellis dropped to her knees at the front of the toilet and with a blind reach, she felt along the back of the tank until her hand touched something. Her lips curled into a smile as she wrapped her fingers around it and yanked it out. She pulled upright again and examined it. "Oh my God."

McCALLISTER KEYED the lock and opened the door to his one-bedroom apartment near the Waterfront. He'd gone for a late-night walk along the river to clear his head in hopes of piecing together a case that had more moving parts than a clock. Instead, all he succeeded in doing was freezing his balls off.

He dropped his keys on the kitchen counter and tossed his coat over the barstool. This was the first significant case he'd been assigned since joining Bangor PD. The sergeant had put him on a couple of other cases when he'd arrived a month ago and that had given him a chance to learn how things were done around here. The other guys seemed great. He'd worked with Bevins and Lewis and now Ellis. Bevins was his least favorite among them, but he knew he wasn't alone in that assessment.

He liked Ellis, though. Okay, so she wasn't bad to look at, if he was being honest, but it was more than that. The fact that she'd opened up to him meant a lot. It was crazy to think a 12-year-old could've gone through something like that, but he knew that worse things happened to kids. Being raised by Hank must've helped Ellis keep her head on straight.

The fridge light kicked on when he opened the door and

grabbed a bottle of beer. The weekend had been long, and the clock hadn't stopped, though it was nothing he wasn't used to. He sat on the sofa and slipped off his shoes before raising his feet to the table.

The idea occurred to him whether Ellis, or any of the other detectives, would be accepting of his own past. McCallister was a good cop. He followed the rules, except for the one time. He'd been called out, and things were different after that. His coworkers lost respect for him. Hell, he'd lost respect for himself.

Unlike Ellis's, his tale wasn't a heroic one, so telling her wouldn't be so easy. Bad things went down in Boston all the time. Things that would make most people's heads spin. McCallister believed he had done the right thing. It hadn't cost him his job, but it had cost him the respect he had built at that department. After a while, he saw the writing on the wall. Nothing was going to change, and he realized it was time to leave. His lieutenant offered to write him a recommendation letter, insisting his career shouldn't be defined by that one moment. So he left. And now he was here in Bangor.

Ellis had a lot to lose by revealing her past to him. He acknowledged that. But would she feel the same if he told her that he'd shot a kid no matter the circumstance? McCallister drew the beer bottle to his lips and pondered the idea. "I'm not sure I want to find out."

He was still lost in thought when his phone lit up with an incoming call, which he answered immediately. "Becca, what's going on?"

"I need to meet you somewhere. Now."

"Now? Are you all right?" He swung his feet to the floor and perched on the edge of the sofa. "Did you pick up another tail?"

"No."

The hesitation in her voice concerned him. "What did you find, Becca?"

"Cameras. Miniature video cameras."

"I'm sorry, cameras? Where? Where the hell are you right now?" He got to his feet and walked to the sliding glass door. Moonlight reflected off the river and he saw his own troubled reflection in the glass.

"About a half mile away from the church. Listen, I'll explain in person. Can we meet?"

"Yeah, sure. Text me a location. I'll leave now."

———————

Sometimes Ellis went against her better judgment. Who was she kidding? She often went against her better judgment. That was what made her a good detective, or so she told herself. Now, she waited for McCallister to arrive after texting him her address. Where else could she go but home?

The one thing Hank had drilled into her head was to color inside the damn lines. And what had she done? She colored so far out of the lines, she couldn't see them anymore. But the results were there. This was going to change the trajectory of the entire investigation, if she didn't get arrested first.

The knock on her door came and she opened it. "Thanks for coming. Sorry it's late."

"Don't be. I wasn't busy." McCallister stepped inside. "You ready to tell me what the hell you found?"

"Have a seat." She walked to the kitchen. "You want a beer? Because I sure as hell do."

"Yeah, why not?" He sat down on the sofa and let his eyes wander. "Nice place."

"Thanks. Bought it with my ex-husband." She handed him a bottle and sat down on the side chair.

"You were married?" He twisted off the cap.

"I was. Not for long. But we're not here to unpack more of my bullshit." Ellis reached for the plastic bag on the coffee table. "We're here for this."

McCallister examined the contents. "That's the camera you were talking about."

"Yep. I went back to the church and got inside…"

"How did you manage that?" he asked.

"You really don't want to know. Point is, I wanted to find something. Something that would get us Townsend. And maybe I regretted not getting inside the church when we had a legit shot at it."

"So you broke the law?" He raised his hands and pressed together his lips. "Continue."

"I put the plan in motion when I attended the service. Didn't think I would go through with it until after what we saw on Allen's computer."

"You really want Townsend, don't you?"

"No way he's innocent, so I went to prove it. I got inside the place, rooted around in couple filing cabinets…then I heard something. Went and checked it out. Couldn't see anything, so I started opening doors and then I heard a noise from the women's bathroom." As she recalled the events, her pulse quickened again and she rubbed her hands together.

McCallister appeared to notice the nervous movement. "It's all right. Take a breath."

She raised her eyes to him. "Yeah. So, anyway, I got knocked to the ground by the door of a stall." Ellis pushed away her hair from her right temple.

He pulled close. "That's one hell of a lump. Do we need to get that looked at?"

"No, I'm fine. Long story short, I saw a big guy in a big hoodie; then I lost him. I couldn't tell if the car he took off in was the same one I'd seen following me. Could've been. But here's the thing, whoever it was must've been there before me. I expected him to set off the alarm, but it wasn't on. I don't think he knew I was there." She picked up the evidence bag again. "I think he was removing the cameras. There was probably one inside the smoke detector, too; it was the sound of the cover dropping that drew my attention."

McCallister pulled back and knitted his brow. "And this happened after we told Allen about the prelim findings on his laptop."

"The porn, yeah," she replied. "But it wasn't Allen in the church tonight. We have a unit watching him, and the guy I saw was big."

"He looked big," McCallister added. "You said he wore a large hoodie."

"I did. And it wasn't Townsend either. Not tall enough. Well, let me rephrase that. It's possible it was Townsend given how dark it was and the clothing, but I don't think the guy I saw was that tall."

"No one else knows what we found on Allen's computer, though," he added.

"Nope." Ellis sat back on the chair and laid her arms in her lap. "I found cameras behind all of the toilets. I grabbed all of them. They're in that box over there on my table."

"Are you serious?" He glanced over his shoulder. "What the hell's on these? Who put them there? How long have..."

"I've already asked myself these questions and I don't have answers." Ellis tapped gently on the lump at her temple. "I don't know who was there, but the extent of this goes beyond Townsend. It goes beyond Allen."

McCallister set his elbows on his thighs and leaned toward her. "What are you saying?"

"I'm saying I want to know where Townsend is. Right now. I want to know if he's home because if he isn't, then he's in CYA mode, and so is the guy he's working with."

"I'm game." McCallister told her as he pulled upright again. "Let's go find him."

———

THE MOMENT they arrived at Townsend's home and Ellis spotted the pickup truck in his driveway, she knew she'd been wrong. "Looks like we can rule out Townsend as my tail. No large sedan here. And if he's looking to cover his tracks, he sure as hell doesn't seem to be in a hurry to do it." She turned off her headlights and rolled to a stop several yards from the pastor's home. "Not to mention, for a man who stole money from his last church, he doesn't live like he's wealthy."

McCallister looked through the passenger window at the modest brick home. Screened by a tall hedgerow, only the steps to the porch were visible in the clear night sky. "They never do. That's how they get away with it."

"Maybe we should be working on how the hell those cameras fit into this case." She shifted into gear again. "I didn't think he'd be here. Now that he is, maybe this is just a waste of time."

"Hang on. We're not leaving yet. If he's connected to the man you saw tonight, we need to let this play out. It's only been an hour or so since this happened. He could be getting ready to make a move."

Ellis noticed an air about her partner. The way he clutched the handle above the door. His firm jaw and pursed lips. "You're pissed, aren't you?"

McCallister drew his gaze to her. "I suppose I don't get why you went into the church when you wouldn't before. At least with Maxine Rehnquist there, we weren't breaking in."

"I didn't break in. A window was left unlocked."

"Nice try." He scoffed. "Doesn't count when you're the one

who left it unlocked. I'm just saying you took a big risk, not only with your life but with the case."

Ellis set her sights on the house again. "I know I did. I was trying to make up for the mistake. Even Hank thought I made the wrong decision."

"Does he know about tonight?"

"Absolutely not, and I don't plan on telling him. Somehow, whoever that guy was...I don't think he plans on speaking out either." She caught a glimpse of light flickering behind a closed curtain inside Townsend's home. "Hold up. We have movement." Her eyes remained fixed on the front of the home when the door opened and Townsend stepped out, walking to his truck.

McCallister noted the time on his phone. "Where the hell is he going at 12:30 in the morning?"

Townsend backed his truck out of the driveway. Ellis waited for him to drive ahead. "Like you said, he's making his move."

17

T ownsend's Ford turned into a storage facility only a few miles from his home. Ellis slowed down to keep her distance while he pulled up to the gate. "What is he doing here?"

McCallister fixed his gaze on the truck as Townsend's arm thrust from the rolled-down window to key in a code. The gate rolled back, and he drove inside. "You think he could be meeting someone here?"

Ellis smacked her palm against the steering wheel. "I don't know, but we're not getting in there." She reached for her phone and took pictures of the sign on the building. "We'll hang back and wait it out. Maybe someone else will turn up."

"We need to think about what those cameras mean to the investigation," McCallister began, reiterating his point. "Given what's been found on Scott Allen's computer, I don't see how this doesn't end with him in handcuffs for recording without permission and likely exploitation. And we're not just talking about minors anymore."

"Anyone who used that restroom." Ellis kept her focus on

the gates of the storage unit. "The thing is, we know the man inside was someone connected to Allen because of the timing. We'd just confronted Allen about what we saw. And the security alarm. He had the code."

"And you got the connection between Allen and Townsend."

"Which we haven't firmed up yet, so who does that leave us with?" She caught sight of Townsend's truck once again. The gate rolled back, and he drove through, stopping at the end of the driveway. "That didn't take long. Where are we off to now?"

The truck exited the facility and headed south along the barren roadway bordered by mounds of snow and a white haze of salt atop the asphalt.

"Don't get too close." McCallister squinted through the windshield. "There aren't enough cars on the road to keep us camouflaged. He sees us, we're done."

"Yeah, I got it." Ellis pulled out behind him and maintained her distance. "He's heading back in the same direction. Could be going back home."

"Keep on him for a little longer till we know for sure."

She canvassed the street and the upcoming intersection. "No, I gotta pull back. He's going to see me." Ellis turned down the first street on her right while Townsend continued ahead. "Shit."

"No choice this time. Roads are empty," McCallister said. "Townsend's got something to hide because who drives to a storage unit in the middle of the night?"

"If I had a reason to pull over his truck, I bet we'd find out real quick. No doubt he went there to remove something." She regarded him. "Might be a good idea to find out what he might have left behind inside that unit."

DETECTIVE BRYCE PELLETIER had transferred from the Portland Police Department, where he'd worked in Robbery/Homicide, almost two years ago now. He preferred Bangor to Portland and when a position opened in the Criminal Investigation Division, he'd requested the move, which was a decision questioned by his family and friends. Portland was twice the size and had a larger police department with more opportunities for advancement. And Portland was located on the coast. But Pelletier wasn't interested in the larger city, and he'd wanted a fresh start. He'd lost his mother to cancer about a year before the move. He had brothers and sisters to care for their father, and while they accused him of being selfish, it was really the only way he felt he could move on from his mother's death.

So now he was here, in Bangor, where he'd wanted to be. He loved the department and his colleagues. They were a family here. And he'd grown close to Ellis, partly owing to their shared experience of loss, but partly because they just clicked.

They were about the same age. Pelletier was only a year younger. Both were single, although he'd never been married, unlike Ellis. Neither had children, and both made work their lives.

Pelletier was early to arrive at the station this morning. A call had come in during the early hours, and Sergeant Abbott requested he and Detective Gabby Lewis be assigned the case. They were set for a briefing within the hour. He returned to his desk with a coffee in hand and a day-old bagel wrapped in a paper towel. As he sat down, he spotted Ellis arrive. "Good morning."

She took notice of him. "Hey, good morning. You're here early."

"Abbott's got a case for Gabby and me. We'll be briefed in

about an hour. There was a carjacking at around 3 am that looks to be connected to a series of recent carjackings."

"Let me know if I can help," Ellis replied.

"Yeah, of course. How's the Allen investigation coming?" he asked.

"We got a break. I'm not sure what to make of it yet."

"That's great. Isn't it? Somehow, you don't look like it's a good thing." He noted her hesitation. "Becca?"

She cocked her head and shrugged. "I can't figure out how it fits together. It's like I'm dealing with two different investigations and neither one is helping me find out who killed Claire Allen."

Detective Gabby Lewis headed toward them. "Morning, Becca." She turned to Pelletier. "Bryce, you ready for the briefing?"

"I'll let you guys get back to work." Ellis continued to her desk.

He waited for her to step out of earshot. "I just need to gather up everything, but, um, can I ask you something?"

"Shoot," Lewis replied.

"What do you think of McCallister?"

"He's all right. Seems to know his job. Decent sense of humor," she replied.

"But what about what happened in Boston?"

Lewis regarded him. "What happened in Boston?"

"I don't know. I thought you did."

"Not a clue. Does it matter? Becca seems to get along with him well enough." She returned a sideways gaze. "That's the problem, isn't it?"

"What? No." He pushed back his shoulders.

"You sure about that? Come on, Bryce. We all know how you feel about her," Lewis said.

"What do you mean, 'we all know'?"

She placed her hands on her hips and returned a stern

look. "It's not like you're good at hiding your feelings, okay? Look, Becca's got some crazy big baggage she's carrying around. Her divorce. What happened when she was a kid. Her brother. Now her dad's not doing all that great, I hear. As much as I love her, and you know I do, you're better off setting your sights elsewhere. Particularly, outside of this department. Never a good combination, Bryce."

IN AN INVESTIGATION that had splintered into various theories and numerous suspects, Ellis had done little to narrow their field of vision. Last night's tail on Townsend only added to the scope with a mysterious storage unit now having come into play. However, the cameras were a more pressing concern, and it was time to make a move.

McCallister arrived at his desk with a coffee in hand. "Did you manage to get any sleep after last night?"

"Nope. You?"

"Nope. You ready to talk to Abbott and shut down the church?"

She stood from her desk and grabbed her coffee. "Hell yes."

They arrived at the sergeant's office and Ellis knocked on the open door. "Hey, Sarge, you have a minute?"

Abbott wiped his reading glasses with a cloth. "Come on in. You two were here late last night, and neither one of you look like you got any sleep. I'd say something opened up. What is it?"

McCallister sat down while Ellis opened the file and placed it on Abbott's desk.

She took a seat and gave him a moment to examine it. "First off, we have the results from Scott Allen's laptop that was seized from his home. Nothing more was found on the victim's laptop other than emails from Kemper's husband to Claire. I'd hoped to find more, but that was it. And without her phone, we have no way of knowing whether she was in communication with anyone through a secure messaging app. So that didn't end up helping us as much as we'd hoped. What was recovered on her husband's computer, however, is disturbing. You know we mentioned the initial report indicating he'd accessed illicit websites."

"Yeah." Abbott continued to study the file.

"On top of that, the hard drive was wiped, but more importantly, Brown recovered several files. Sarge, they were explicit images of children," McCallister added.

"Goddam it." Abbott turned away a moment.

"We can't prove he was the one who put those images on his computer," Ellis cut in. "But he can't disprove it. We talked about what happened with Claire Allen's friend. Her five-year-old daughter, and what she may or may not have seen concerning her friends. Now, with this information, I'm starting to think the little girl was right."

He set down the file and directed his sights on Ellis. "You got something else to back that up?"

She eyed McCallister, who returned a nod. "Sarge, I found miniature web cameras installed behind every toilet in the women's restroom at the church."

Abbott yanked off his glasses and zeroed in on her with a hard stare.

Before he had a chance to ask what she knew he would ask, Ellis continued, "Someone was at the church late last night. I interrupted whatever it was they were doing, although I suspect they were trying to remove those cameras. I gave chase. He got away."

The sarge sucked on his teeth and looked away. His chest heaved and his face turned red. He finally turned his eyes back to her. "Are you hurt?"

"No, sir. Just a little bump on the head."

"Good. Then tell me how you two plan to move forward with this new information."

McCallister cleared his throat. "First of all, Sarge, I think what Becca and I considered was to have the church board members identify the children in these images."

"You want me to ask them to peruse those pictures on Allen's computer?" Abbott asked. "For what purpose?"

"In the event any of them can be identified as members of families belonging to the church," Ellis interrupted. "If they are, then we arrest Mr. Allen."

Abbott raised his chin. "Did he kill his wife?"

Ellis and McCallister traded glances before she continued, "We don't have proof of that."

"What about these cameras, then? Can we find out what's on them?"

"It's not a case of what's on them, Sarge," McCallister added. "It's a case that they recorded whoever used the bathroom. The data is likely stored on a computer or cloud drive. For what purpose, we don't know yet."

Ellis shifted in her chair, anticipating Abbott's wrath for her decision to enter the church without a warrant. "Our number one suspect was the pastor, Ezekiel Townsend. And that's based on his shady history with skimming money from his previous church, which, unfortunately, was not proven. We do have a witness from the church's current accounting firm who suspected he was doing the same thing here. Our second thought was, had Claire discovered what her husband had done with regard to the child exploitation? We don't know. Had she learned that the pastor was stealing money from the church? We don't know that either."

"Well, Jesus H. Christ, Becca, what the hell do you two know?" Abbott shot back.

If she hadn't known any better, Ellis could swear that

Abbott was channeling her father right now. His reaction would've been the same. "That either or both men had something to do with Claire Allen's murder. And that we're certain they're working in concert, but unclear as to what extent. There could be another person in this scenario. Whoever I chased last night...we have to find out who he is."

"The concern right now, Sarge, is the children, the cameras," McCallister said. "While we untangle this web, they have to be at the forefront."

"So these board members must already be aware of what's happening in the investigation?" Abbott continued.

"They know we've homed in on their pastor," Ellis replied. "Without alarming the entire community, this has to be kept in a small circle until we can be sure. An arrest warrant against Allen is imminent. One more thing, Sarge. Regardless of whether these particular kids belong to the church, the church likely has in its midst a child pornographer. Given that, for the safety of the community, and until we can discover the origins of the cameras, it's best to insist the church halt any and all activities until this case is over."

Abbott eyed his detectives. "All right. Then that's what'll happen."

A UNIFORMED OFFICER from the first floor led the two gentlemen to Abbott's office. Owen Gibbons trailed his legal counsel. The older Mr. Gibbons was in his sixties and wore a dark suit with a single button that stretched over his full waist. Sweat was visible on the sides of his face, and he kept his hands clasped behind his back while he walked. As the church elder, it was his duty to answer for the disturbing investigation into not only his head pastor, but also a member of the church who had been murdered. He appeared as though a dark cloud hung over him.

Lieutenant Serrano waited inside Abbott's office along with Ellis and McCallister.

As they entered, Abbott approached with an outstretched hand. "Thank you for coming down, Mr. Gibbons. I'm Sergeant James Abbott. This is my boss, and the man who runs the Criminal Investigation Division, Lieutenant Abe Serrano."

The reticent man returned a faint nod. "Sergeant, I'm sure you know that these past few days have been extremely difficult for our community and our congregation."

"I have no doubt. Please, sit down, Mr. Gibbons." Abbott gestured to a chair at the nearby table. "You might already know Detectives Ellis and McCallister."

"We have not directly met, but I'm aware, yes." The man turned to his lawyer. "This is George Norris; he serves as the church's legal counsel. I've asked him to accompany me here today."

Abbott tendered a greeting. "Mr. Norris, I won't pretend I'm surprised you've been asked here, given the circumstances. Please take a seat."

A middle-aged man, smaller in stature than his client, Norris unbuttoned his suit jacket and pulled out a chair. "I would like to make a note for the record that Owen Gibbons of Grace Community Church has willingly offered to assist the police with this investigation."

Serrano made his way to the table to sit down. "Your cooperation is noted. As you both are aware, our investigators have recovered some disturbing findings on the personal computer of one of your members, who, incidentally, has provided services relating to the church finances."

"Claire Allen's husband, Scott," Gibbons confirmed.

"Yes, sir." Abbott opened the files on the table. "More

recent findings, which Detective Ellis discovered, were miniature cameras installed in the ladies' bathroom at the church."

"I'm sorry?" Norris aimed his sights at Ellis. "This is new information."

She stepped forward. "Yes, sir, it is. We've recovered five in total, but we aren't ruling out that more could be elsewhere inside the church."

His lips parted and his brow knitted. "Why on God's earth would there be cameras in the women's restroom?"

"We don't know yet, Mr. Gibbons," Ellis replied.

Abbott returned his attention to Gibbons. "Our goal today is not to send shock waves through your congregation, but to decipher whether there exists an immediate threat to some of your members, particularly children. Gentlemen, setting aside the discovery of the cameras, you're here today to help us identify the children in these pictures. Before I continue, please know that I have attempted to conceal the worst of the images I'm about to show you. They are not meant for shock value or to distress you. If you are able to identify the children we see here, we will move to immediately arrest the man responsible. But be assured, he will be arrested for the crime of possessing these images, regardless. However, if these victims are members of your church, then this man will face additional, harsher charges in accordance with the law."

"And if we are unable to identify them?" Gibbons asked.

"Then they will remain among the many children who are victims of exploitation, and the case will be turned over to the appropriate federal agency to include in their database for subsequent investigations." Abbott placed the photos in front of the men. "If you recognize any of these children..."

Gibbons and Norris peered hesitantly at the disguised photos, and it was Gibbons who continued after a few moments of uncomfortable silence. "I don't believe any of those children belong to members of our church. I know everyone there. I'm at every Sunday service and participate in youth Bible study on occasion. I can assure you that these poor souls are not familiar to me."

"Thank you, Mr. Gibbons," Serrano replied. "Under these circumstances, and given the uncertainty of how the new evidence fits into our investigation, we would prefer for the church to halt all services and youth activities until this investigation can come to its conclusion. Of course, you have the right to refuse, but there is still the matter of Scott Allen's culpability in possessing these images, and given that his wife was murdered, it makes it difficult to separate the two circumstances at the moment."

"You'll get no argument from me," Gibbons confirmed. "And you'll have the full support of the other elders. That said, we are scheduled to conduct the funeral services for Claire Allen in a few days' time. With your approval, we would like to continue that as scheduled."

Serrano glanced back at the detectives.

"We can post uniforms around the grounds to ensure everyone's safety," McCallister offered.

Serrano turned back. "Then I don't see that as a problem. Thank you, gentlemen, for your cooperation."

Gibbons made his way to the door, then stopped to look again at the police officers at their seats. "I feel quite ill knowing all this has happened at my church. Never in my worst nightmares could I imagine one of our members hurting children or..." He exhaled through his nose. "Recording them when they are most vulnerable. Please know that you have the church's full cooperation."

As Serrano led them out, Ellis turned to her partner. "Why do I feel like I need to take a shower?"

"Yeah, that wasn't pleasant," McCallister agreed. "But we got what we wanted. We have the authority to get inside the church."

"That means we'll have access to their files," she added. "Including whatever the hell Townsend keeps locked away in his office."

"You're still convinced the pastor had something to do with the murder? Or is your focus now on the man you saw?" he asked.

Abbott gathered the photos and quickly homed in on Ellis. "What man? Becca, is this where you tell me how the hell you found those cameras? You're goddam lucky those men didn't ask the same question."

Ellis's phone buzzed in her pocket and she glanced at the message. "It's from Caulder."

McCallister shot her a look. "What's he say?"

Abbott planted his hands on his hips. "Am I the last person to be informed about what's going on with this investigation? Who the hell's Caulder?"

"The guy who tipped us off about Townsend's previous embezzlement case. He says we should pull the church's bank statement from July of this year. Apparently, that's the month he noted the cash deposit drop significantly from the previous month."

"Is this something we need to be putting our focus on right now?" Abbott continued. "Seems to me like we got a more serious situation on our hands."

"Yes, sir." Ellis slipped her phone back into her pocket. "A link exists between Townsend, Allen, and whoever is responsible for those cameras. We already know Allen was found with explicit images on his laptop. That thread leads to the man I saw trying to yank the cameras before we found them. The timing of his attempt to remove them isn't coincidental. We went to Allen; Allen made the call to pull the plug."

"And the pastor?" Abbott cut in. "Where's he fit?"

"He's the money. He's funding whatever operation Allen's

running. A child porn ring. I don't know, but he's part of this. We're still putting it together," Ellis replied.

"Sounds to me like you got nothing on the pastor except skimming money. You're grasping at straws, Becca, if you think you can tie him to Allen," Abbott replied.

"You're right, sir. It is circumstantial. We need time. I'm not wrong. I just can't prove I'm right."

Serrano stepped in. "So let's get Allen off the goddam streets, yeah? We got him on possession of explicit images. That's enough to haul his ass in."

"We have eyes on him, sir," Ellis replied. "But before we pull that trigger, we have to tie him to Townsend, which we're close to doing, and when that happens, the other player will be exposed. We hit Allen too soon, Townsend and our mystery man won't stick around after that."

"Townsend will be the first to be notified of the church's cooperation and that we've insisted on shutting it down. You might lose him anyway after that." Abbott regarded his detectives. "We have permission to search the grounds. Get out there and do it. Make the goddam connection so we can arrest these assholes before this entire thing falls apart."

Ellis nodded. "Yes, sir."

THE DETECTIVES RETURNED to the bullpen, and as Ellis sat at her desk, she grabbed her phone. "If Caulder's telling us to look at certain statements, we can request those from the accounting firm now that Gibbons authorized access. I'll ask him where else we need to look." She glanced at McCallister. "The church's cash receipts would be useful too. There has to be a system where they would log in amounts collected before making the bank deposits. Problem is, the only person who would have those receipts is Townsend."

He appeared to consider the idea. "Without them, all of this is just circumstantial, but I think it would be enough to warrant a deep dive into Townsend's personal accounts."

"Let's consider that for a second because depositing that kind of cash consistently into a personal account would raise all kinds of flags from the bank. Currency transaction reports would have been filed. Which makes me think the money's not in a bank," she concluded.

"In that case..." McCallister raised a single brow. "What about a storage facility?"

18

Ann Kemper never believed she had a jealous streak. A devoted member of the church, the notion of such an emotion being part of her personality was an anathema to her. Nevertheless, when Claire Allen appeared, her feet clad in Jimmy Choos and a Louis Vuitton casually slung over her shoulder, envy sparked in her. She tried to remember that the Allens had no children and that Scott Allen's job afforded them certain luxuries. And then something changed.

Some months ago, Scott had come to spend more time at the church, usually to meet with Pastor Zeke. They would cross paths on occasion. His warm smile felt inviting and reminded Ann that she was still a woman, not just a mother and wife. Polite conversation soon turned intimate. Calls and texts grew more frequent. And then, that once-nagging envy she'd felt toward Claire changed because she had taken what was Claire's. She had Scott.

Ann arrived at the Allen home and did a double take when she spotted a patrol car parked out front. She stepped out of her SUV and buttoned her pea coat. The cops fixed their eyes on her, and their scrutiny raised the hairs on her nape. For a moment, she considered whether she should speak to them, but what would she say? She was the other woman. They all knew it now. Ann's name was in Claire Allen's file and so was her witness statement. And so now was the time to show her support for Scott. She loved him and he loved her. They would get through this together.

Her head held high, Ann carried on to the front door and knocked. "Scott, it's me. Can I come in?"

He opened the door and stood behind the screen. "What are you doing here, Ann?"

"I needed to see you. We need to talk, Scott—about a lot of things. I know how hard this has been for you and I understand why you haven't answered my calls and texts. I know you must be upset about what I told the police..."

"Jesus, Ann, it was just a fling, okay? Get over it. My wife is dead. You think I don't feel shitty enough for what I've done? I don't need to see my mistake standing right in front of me. I haven't called you back because I don't want to see you. Don't you get that?"

She felt her heart shatter into pieces. "What? How can you say that? I was the one who told them we were together that night. I helped prove your innocence, Scott. I thought, now that we can be open about our relationship, I could be here for support. I want a future with you. We're free to move on together."

"Stop, okay? Just stop." He pushed open the screen door and stepped out. "A future for us? That was *never* going to happen. My God, my wife was murdered and you're asking me about a future. I thought you'd figure it out when I didn't call you back." He stepped back inside, his face stony. "Go home to your husband, Ann. I don't want you here. I don't want you at all."

He let the screen door slam shut and then the entry door.

The blunt reality struck her squarely in the face. Anger heated her chest and she clenched her fists. "Fuck you, Scott!" That word hadn't been part of Ann's vocabulary in years, but he'd just ripped her heart from her chest. She thumped on the door once in fury, then marched back to her car, nearly slipping on the icy driveway.

One of the officers stepped out and leaned against his patrol car. As Ann neared, he folded his arms and tilted his head. "Everything okay, ma'am?"

"No, everything is not okay," she shot back. "I'd keep an eye on that man in there if I were you."

He pushed off the car and started toward her. "Do you need to tell me something right now?"

Ann swallowed hard and stopped cold in front of him. "No, Officer. No, I don't have anything to say." She stepped back behind the wheel of her SUV and steadied herself while tears streamed down her cheeks.

The officer kept his eye on her a moment longer before returning to his car, where he conversed with his partner.

Ann reached into her handbag for the detective's business card. "You think you can treat people this way, Scott? Don't count on it."

THE AUTHORIZATIONS HAD BEEN SIGNED and the time had come to shut down the church and find out exactly what the hell had been going on inside. Disciplinary action awaited Ellis for what she'd done and it was anyone's guess how Abbott planned to handle it, but that had to be set aside for now.

McCallister insisted on driving this afternoon out of concern for Ellis's safety. And the nasty bruise on her head still ached, so she didn't push back. Much. She wasn't the type to take a back seat, or passenger seat, to anyone. But in this instance, an exception could be made.

She stared out at the road ahead. "Not only does this open us up to whoever else is working with Townsend and Allen, but if we find more today, no doubt it'll give us cause to open up Townsend's life like a book."

"Which means we'll get into that storage unit and find out what he's hiding, assuming it's still there," he replied.

"That's the goal." Ellis's phone rang with an incoming call. She looked at the number and drew in her brow before answering. "Detective Ellis."

"Yes, hi, this is Ann Kemper."

"Hello, Ann." She returned a curious gaze to McCallister. "What can I do for you?"

"I'd like to talk with you now if you have the time," she replied.

"Uh, yeah, of course. Where are you? We can meet you anywhere."

"My house. I'll be there in ten minutes. I'll text you the address. Thank you, Detective."

"We'll see you soon, Ann. Goodbye." Ellis ended the call and slowly turned to McCallister.

He mirrored her surprise. "What the hell was that all about?"

"I have no idea, but she wants to meet. She's got something to tell us, and I know we need to get to the church, but we'd better let her talk before she changes her mind."

"She already told us about the affair. Confirmed both of their whereabouts, which essentially cleared them of murder. What could she possibly have left to say?" he said.

"I don't know. She sounded different. Kind of pissed off, actually. Something or someone set her off."

"Give me the address."

"It's not far. Take a right on the next street. It's toward the

Preserve just north of the highway. About a mile from the church." Ellis chewed on her lip, desperate to know what it was Ann Kemper had to say. Her statement was in the books. Changing it would be a big deal. "So what happened?" she whispered.

"What's that?" McCallister asked.

"Nothing. I'm talking to myself." She pointed ahead. "Here. Turn left down this street. She's the third house on the right."

"Got it." McCallister rolled to a stop in the black Ford Police Interceptor. He joined Ellis as they stepped out.

But just as Ellis was about to knock, the front door opened. "Ann, hello."

"Detective Ellis, Detective McCallister, come in." She stepped aside. "Thank you for arriving so quickly."

"You made it sound pretty urgent," Ellis replied. "What's on your mind?"

"Don't you want to sit down or something?" Ann said. "I can make you a coffee."

"It's a kind offer, and I don't mean to be rude, Ann, but for the sake of time, we'd like to get down to business," Ellis replied.

"I understand." She clasped her hands. "In that case, I guess I'll just come out with it. I lied to you when I said Scott and I met at his house the night Claire died. I was trying to protect him."

Ellis noted the look in Ann's eyes. She'd clearly been crying, and emptiness seemed to linger behind them. Distance, too. Maybe anger. "Protecting him from who?"

"From you," Ann said. "We did meet after last Tuesday's service, but not at his house. We stopped by a hotel."

McCallister looked at her. "Can you prove that? Forgive me, but this is quite a change from your previous statement."

"I used a credit card my husband doesn't know about,"

Ann replied. "We weren't there for long. We both had to hurry back home. The thing is, I left the hotel around 9:45. I was home by ten, which can be backed up by my mother, who'd dropped off my kids at that time. I don't know when Scott left."

Ellis folded her arms across her chest, her posture unforgiving. "Are you saying no one was in fact with Scott Allen between 9:30 and 10 pm when we suspect the fire happened?"

"That's what I'm saying," Ann confirmed. "I know I should've told you before…"

"Yes, you should." Ellis looked Ann in the eye. "So why are you telling us this now?"

"I swear to you, I had nothing to do with Claire's murder. I would never…could never do something like that." Her eyes stayed locked onto Ellis's. "But I'm not sure I can say the same about Scott."

Ellis turned to McCallister. "Allen insisted he'd been at home working. We confirmed it through his employer."

"We checked his IP address, and yes, he'd been logged into his company's server. Doesn't guarantee that he was at home," McCallister replied. "But he went out of his way to make it look like he was."

And here Ellis thought the rest of these pieces would just fall right into place. They had the images on Allen's laptop. The cameras inside the church. And they were about to have Townsend on a silver platter too. Now, the most logical suspect, who had motive and who she thought had an alibi, no longer had the latter. "We'll be in touch if we have any other questions," she told Ann.

Ann opened the door. "Thank you for coming over, Detectives. I really hope you find whoever killed Claire. She didn't deserve to die. No matter what, she didn't deserve it."

"We agree on that." Ellis stepped out into the cold afternoon air. The detectives walked back to the Ford when she stopped and turned to McCallister. "This changes things."

He nodded. "Is it possible Allen was the one who came after you? The hooded man inside the church?"

"How would that have been possible? We've got a unit at his place," she said.

"I don't know, but from what you told me, Scott Allen matches your description."

"What little description I had." Ellis considered the idea. "Let's make sure our guys keep a closer eye on Allen at his house for the time being. We need to get to the church. Now."

McCallister stepped out from behind the wheel as they arrived. "Townsend's here. I wasn't sure he would be after Caulder pointed us to the questionable bank statements. He must know we're coming after him and for more than reaching his hand into the donation basket."

"We're about to find out how cooperative he's prepared to be now that we have the full weight of the church behind us." Ellis led the way into the administration building to the left of the main sanctuary. Inside, she spotted an elderly woman. "Good afternoon."

"Detective Ellis, hello." The white-haired woman returned a guarded smile upon noting the detective's expression. "What can I do for you today?"

"We're here at the request of Owen Gibbons and the rest of the church elders. They've authorized us to search these grounds. I'm happy to wait if you'd like to make a call to confirm."

"Oh, my goodness. Please do what you must," she replied.

"Yes, ma'am. Thank you," Ellis said.

The two started down the corridor toward the offices. A

few of the volunteers noted the detectives and quickly stepped aside to allow them through.

"Feels like a parting of the seas," McCallister quipped.

"Word's already gotten around, by the look of it." Ellis knocked on Townsend's office door and opened it. "Excuse the interruption, Pastor."

Townsend glanced up from his desk and returned a knowing gaze. "I'd say I'm surprised to see you, but I'm not really. Come back to harass me some more, Detectives?"

"We're here at the request of Owen Gibbons and the church elders. We've been authorized to search the premises and seize the church's files and equipment, including anything in this office."

"Are we going to have any problems, Pastor?" McCallister asked.

"No, sir." He pushed back from his desk. "I won't stop you from doing your jobs. I have no doubt the board has felt the pressure from your department."

She examined his posture, his body language, wondering if it had been him she'd chased after. But to look at his face, he was either one hell of a good poker player, or he wasn't the one. Still, she noticed something in his eyes, like maybe he knew this was the end. "Then if you wouldn't mind waiting in the cafeteria?"

He gave her a sideways glance. "Whatever you say, Detective."

When he disappeared into the hall, Ellis surveyed the office. "We should send everyone else home; then we lock the doors. I think we could use some help. Let's call in Bevins and Fletch. We'll go through Townsend's files, search for more cameras. Search the youth building. Whatever it takes to find something on that asshole and Allen too. The sooner we get through this, the better for everyone."

19

S cott Allen pulled back the curtain on his living room window just enough to see that the patrol car was still outside. "What the hell is going on? First those other cops and now these guys." He picked up his phone and tried to call Townsend again. "Come on, answer." The call rang through to voicemail. "Damn it."

They'd found everything. That's why they were waiting outside. Townsend had promised him he'd handle it, but now the cops looked like they weren't planning on leaving at all. His in-laws were due to arrive in a matter of hours. "The hell, Zeke?" He threw down his phone on the sofa and paced.

The detectives already had his laptop. Claimed they found some bullshit porn he knew he never downloaded, but that hadn't seemed to matter to them. He had no idea what was happening. He was a prisoner in his home, and all because Zeke convinced him it would be easy to take the money. They'd never figure it out because the church collected so much of it in cash; it was like a goddam ATM ready for him to pluck out a few bucks every now and again.

Scott dropped to the sofa and lowered his face into his hands. "I'm going to prison. I am going to prison." The worst part of all of this was that his wife was dead, and he had no idea why or who did it. "It had to be you, you son of a bitch. Why'd you kill her?" Scott screamed into his hands to muffle the sound of his rising anger.

"I have to do something." He bounced his knee to dispel his nerves; then he looked at his phone on the sofa and grabbed it again to make the call. "Yeah, it's me. Listen, I'm sorry about before. You gotta come get me. Cops are sitting in front of my house right now. I'll go out through the back and head down the alley and meet you there." He sighed. "I don't know yet. I'll figure it out afterward."

***

WITH THE EXCEPTION of Zeke Townsend, the entire church staff had been sent home. And now that backup had arrived, the detectives prepared to search the grounds.

"Fletch, will you search the other bathrooms for more recording devices? Smoke detectors, sinks, toilets. The whole thing," Ellis began.

"You got it."

"Bevins, you and McCallister can start in the youth building. Check out the nurse's office. All of it."

"Yep." Bevins slapped McCallister on the back. "Let's go, buddy."

McCallister eyed Ellis a moment. "Don't do anything I wouldn't do."

That stung, but he was right. She couldn't jeopardize this investigation more than she already had. The time had come to figure out how Townsend fit into this picture. No more excuses.

With a key in her hand, Ellis opened the file cabinets and pulled out everything, placing the files into banker's boxes. She cleared out his entire office and would recruit the team to scour all of it. She walked to the filing room and retrieved everything that was relevant to Townsend, tossing all of it into the boxes.

Her thoughts went back to the man in the hoodie. She'd been in this very room when she heard him. The bump on her head throbbed as though the memory brought the pain to the surface again.

Ellis stepped out of the room and into the hall, where she peered at several boxes that lined it. She faced the exit that was down about 50 feet or more. The bathroom was just ahead on her right.

"Hey, Becca?"

She turned around to see Fletch. "Yeah? You find something?"

"No. I wanted to tell you I cleared the other bathrooms. Nothing there. Nurse's office was a bust too. So I thought I'd see if you need a hand while the guys search the rest of the place."

"Yeah, thanks. I was about to check out these classrooms down here, and there's a room at the end of the hall. I don't know what it is, so we'll want to scope that out too."

"Cool. Let's do it." Fletch started ahead. "I'll take this room."

Ellis entered the room, where she'd met with Claire's friends, including Ann Kemper. Now the woman who had been having an affair with Claire's husband had just stripped Allen of a legitimate alibi when she'd confessed only an hour ago to meeting with Scott Allen at a hotel that night. Ellis set her hands on her hips. "It's enough." With the new lead Caulder offered on the bank deposits, and their search here, it was time to bring them both in. If they didn't do it now, Townsend was free to leave. And Hank had assured her he would without hesitation. This had to happen now.

Ellis headed toward the youth building and tracked down McCallister. "I'm going to bring him in."

"Who?"

"Scott Allen. With what Ann Kemper told us, and the images, Euan, we have enough to bring him in. Townsend, too, thanks to Caulder. We're almost finished here. I thought you three could wrap it up and then you can haul in Townsend for questioning. The time's right, and it needs to happen now."

"I agree, but you're not going in alone." He glanced back at Bevins. "Let's wrap this up. You and Fletch can bring in the pastor. Put him on ice. He'll want his lawyer. In the meantime, I'm going with Ellis." He turned back to her. "We bring him in together."

―――――――

A PATROL UNIT had maintained a presence in front of the house for the past two days in the event Scott Allen decided to take flight.

Ellis rolled to a stop just inside the driveway. "His car is still here. That's a good sign."

McCallister opened his passenger door. "I'll go have a word with the uniforms." He made his way to the patrol car as the officer behind the wheel lowered his window. "Afternoon. How's it been out here?"

"A woman came by and had words with Allen by the sound of it. I asked if she needed to talk, but she said no and left. That was a few hours ago. Man hasn't stepped foot outside since."

McCallister squinted toward the home. "I have a feeling I know who that was."

"We saw him peek through the curtains maybe an hour ago, but that's about it," the officer added. "What's going on? We ready to take him in or what?"

"Oh, yeah. It's time to bring him in. It'd be a good idea to have you both lend a hand."

"You got it, Detective." The officer stepped outside, and his partner joined him.

McCallister waved over Ellis, and when she arrived, he continued, "Sounds like Ann dropped by for a word. Apparently, it didn't go well according to those guys."

"That must've been when she called us," she replied. "I'll bet he turned on her."

"And she stabbed him in the back for it." He walked to the front door and knocked. "Mr. Allen, Bangor PD. Open up." After no reply, he eyed Ellis. "If just one thing can go smoothly today." He knocked again. "Scott, open the door. This doesn't have to get complicated."

Ellis assessed the house. "Curtains are closed. I don't hear any footsteps coming."

"Damn it. Now I'm going to have to break something." He walked around the porch.

"Hey, hang on." Ellis stepped toward the kitchen window. "What the hell is that?"

McCallister joined her. "Is that blood on the curtain?"

"Son of a bitch." Her jaw clenched. "We need to get inside. Now."

McCallister opened the screen door and tried the handle. "It's unlocked." He walked inside. "Scott?"

Ellis trailed him. "Head straight for the kitchen."

The two officers, along with Ellis and McCallister, came upon the gruesome scene.

"Oh, God." Ellis hurried to press her hand on Allen's carotid artery. "No pulse."

McCallister shot around to the officers. "How the hell does this happen when a unit's been parked outside his house for two days?"

Blood pooled on the table and floor around Allen. Ellis scanned the kitchen when her eyes landed on the back door. "There's blood on the door handle."

"His wrists are cut." McCallister turned stone-faced. "He committed suicide?"

Ellis had already opened the back door and stepped outside.

McCallister trailed her onto the salt-covered stepping stones that led to a back gate.

She opened it and peered into the alleyway. A small pool of blood lay just outside the gate. "He didn't commit suicide. Someone tried hard to make it look that way. Must've cleaned up the blood from the back door to the table too. And I'll bet it's the same son of a bitch who came after me."

One of the officers ran out to catch up to them. "Detectives?"

They walked inside the gate when Ellis glanced at him. "Do me a favor and photograph the tire tracks out there while we look—"

"Detective, I don't mean to interrupt, but there's something else you two need to see."

They returned inside. The other officer stood near Allen's dead body, which lay slumped over the kitchen table.

"A cell phone," the officer said.

Ellis approached him. "Locked?"

"Yeah."

She grabbed latex gloves from her pocket and slipped them on. Ellis picked up the phone and pressed the button to turn it on.

"It'll be password protected," McCallister said.

"I know. Give me a second." She waited for the phone to load and pressed the home screen. "It's hers."

"Claire's missing phone?" McCallister stepped toward her. "How do you know?"

She held it up. "The picture. It's Claire and Scott and she's holding the camera. It's Claire's phone and the knife is right there too. The only person who would've had that phone is the person who killed her. And it has to be the same person whose prints will be on that knife."

"What are the odds we'll find prints on it?" he asked.

She looked at McCallister. "If we do, they won't be Scott Allen's."

ELLIS WANTED a reason to bring in Townsend. Now she had one. His partner was dead. She headed to the interview room and opened the door. "Sorry to have kept you waiting, Pastor."

"I'm sure you are," he replied. "I have a right to a lawyer."

"Yes, you do." She set down her cell phone in front of him. "Go right ahead and make the call. I'll wait." When he didn't pick up the phone, Ellis continued, "Something wrong?"

"I don't have a lawyer."

"Well, I suppose the one you had back in Concord wouldn't do you much good here."

"Those charges were dropped, Detective. You know that. I've done nothing wrong," Townsend insisted.

"Then why the hell did we find cameras in the bathroom at the church?" she pressed on.

"You can think what you want, but I had no idea those were there. Just as I told your people at the church. Some sick, depraved person put them there and is trying to frame me for it."

Ellis paced between the table and the wall. "Scott Allen was murdered today, Zeke. He had child pornography on his laptop. We're left to assume the cameras were part of something you two had going because I know he wasn't acting alone." Ellis sat down in the chair across from him. "Your church has been shut down. Children are at risk, so if you want to prove you had nothing to do with that, then you'll need to offer us something."

For the first time since she'd met this man, he looked terrified. It was clear he didn't know about Scott Allen.

"I don't know why anyone would've killed Claire or Scott. I don't know who put cameras inside the church bathroom, I promise you. But I can see that's not what you want to hear," he added. "Get me a lawyer. I'm not saying anything else until you do."

"Then we'll talk again soon, Pastor." She stepped out into the hall, where she spotted McCallister. "He won't talk without a..."

"I have something," he cut in. "Scott Allen's bank records just came through. Payment to a certain storage facility shows up on a recurring basis."

She turned stone-faced. "The same place Townsend went?"

He gave a grim smile. "The same place. Could be the same damn one."

Ellis glanced back at the interview room. "I think while we're waiting for the pastor's lawyer, we should take a look inside."

THIS WAS THE PLACE. McCallister set his hands on his hips. "Open it up."

The manager of the facility cut off the padlock and raised the metal rolling door. "Have at it, Detectives."

McCallister stood at attention and glanced at Ellis. "Okay, let's see what we can find, yeah?" They walked inside the ten-by-twenty unit, where several pieces of computer equipment and cardboard boxes lay against the walls. Along one wall, he pulled out a pocketknife and sliced open the seal on one of the boxes. "Don't suppose you're a computer expert, huh, Becca?"

"Gabby is our resident hacker." She approached him. "What'd you find?"

"Hell if I know. Looks like CPUs maybe. I don't know if these are for resale or what."

Ellis picked up her phone and snapped a picture. "Looks exactly like what I saw in Allen's office that day before we served the warrant. I'll send this to Gabby and get her take." She only waited a moment and a response arrived. "Here we go. She says it looks like a processor. It's like a CPU, but it processes data quickly, more like a server."

"What would it be used for?" McCallister asked.

She typed the question. "Gabby says these could be used for a website operator to store and transmit data." Ellis peered at her phone again when another message arrived. "Says something like what a company like Amazon would use, but obviously theirs would be much larger."

"So a website operator," McCallister replied.

"I guess so, but all we can do is haul all this in and have the lab take a look," Ellis said. "But you might want to come over here and take a look at this."

He approached her as Ellis opened the box and laid down the flaps. "Found this tucked near the far back wall inside a safe."

"A safe?" McCallister asked.

"I know, right? It wasn't locked. Just a keypad code that hadn't been activated, like someone was in a hurry or something." She peered inside. "So, how much you think is in here?"

McCallister eyed the contents. "Thirty, forty grand, maybe. I wonder how a banker gets hold of this kind of cash?"

20

Townsend had been in the hot seat for almost three hours, awaiting his court-appointed lawyer. Ellis let him stew, knowing he wasn't going to talk. Now, however, with the knowledge that Scott Allen had been murdered, and they'd found money and computer hardware in the storage unit she'd tracked him down to, she might have an opening.

Word reached her that the attorney had arrived and was given an opportunity to discuss the pending charges with his client. The time to strike was now. She returned to the interview room. "Mr. Nichols, it's been a while. Nice to see you again."

"The junior Detective Ellis." Nichols presented a smoker's smile replete with yellow-tinged teeth and deeply lined lips that stretched wide. "How's your father doing? Managing retirement all right?" His cheeks puffed as he spoke while the overhead fluorescent light bounced off his smooth head.

"He seems to be enjoying it. I'll be sure and let him know you asked about him." Ellis tucked a swath of blond hair behind her ear before sitting down at the table. "Now that your lawyer is here, Pastor, are we going to have a conversation?"

Nichols raised his index finger. "My client maintains his innocence on the allegations of illegal recordings on the property of the Grace Community Church, embezzlement of church donations, and child exploitation."

"Uh-huh," she replied. "Then let's talk about what was found in Scott Allen's storage unit. Mr. Allen, of course, being a close acquaintance of Mr. Townsend. Tens of thousands of dollars, various pieces of valuable computer equipment. And, on our attempt to arrest Mr. Allen on charges of possessing child pornography, he turned up dead. Does your client wish to comment on any of that?" Ellis captured Townsend's gaze.

Nichols eyed his client, who remained stone-faced. "Not at this time."

Ellis raised her eyes to meet Townsend's. "You have no one left to bail you out, Pastor. Scott Allen is dead. If you know who killed him, you should really consider your options carefully."

MAXINE HOVERED over her kitchen stove, preparing dinner. Vanessa played in her room. Tomorrow was Claire's funeral, and she'd gone out to buy dresses for herself and Vanessa, along with a new jacket for Ethan. Scott refused help making the arrangements, so Maxine hadn't known anything except to arrive at the appropriate time. Claire had been her best friend and she'd been shut out of everything.

Her phone rang on the kitchen counter, and she wiped her hands on a dishtowel before answering it. She recognized the number. "Mrs. DuPont, hello. It's so good to hear from you."

"Maxine, hello."

Her eyes imbued with tears at the sound of Claire's mother's voice. With her emotions so near the surface, the Band-Aid had been ripped off again. "I'm so sorry about Claire. I miss her so much. I just can't imagine losing a daughter..."

"I know, honey, thank you. But before we get into that, I need to tell you that we're in town. Claire's father and I just arrived."

Maxine cleared her throat and wiped her eyes. "Oh, I see. Are you with Scott now?"

"I'm afraid we're at the police station." Mrs. DuPont's voice faltered. "I-I don't quite know how to say this, but Scott's dead."

Maxine reeled in confusion. "I'm sorry, you're at the station now? I don't understand." Ethan walked through the front door and drew her attention to the foyer. "What do you mean Scott's dead?"

"When we arrived at the house. The police...they were everywhere. Sweetheart, I can't talk right now. Please, just call the detective. You have her number?"

"Yes, yes, I have it. I'll call her. We'll speak soon. Goodbye." She set down her phone and stared off in the distance.

Ethan hung his coat and made his way into the kitchen. "I'm sorry I was at the office for so long. Boss called an impromptu meeting I couldn't get out of." He stopped cold just steps from her. "Max, you're white as a sheet. What happened? Are you okay? Did they find out who killed Claire?"

She slowly raised her eyes to him. "That was Claire's mom. They got into town a little while ago and went to Scott and Claire's house. Apparently, cops were everywhere."

"Oh, my God. Why?" he asked.

"Scott's dead. I don't know the whole story. I have to call Detective Ellis. I have to know what's going on."

He pulled out a kitchen chair and slowly dropped onto it. "Dead? How? Are they sure?"

"That's what Claire's mom said. My God, Ethan. What is happening? First Claire and now Scott?" Maxine grabbed her phone and walked into the living room to make the call. "Hello, Detective Ellis? It's Maxine Rehnquist. I just got a call from Mrs. DuPont. She told me Scott was dead."

Ellis remained silent for a moment. "He-uh, he was murdered, Maxine."

She braced herself against the wall as her knees buckled. "Murdered? What are you talking about? Did you find out that he killed Claire? Did someone else find out and kill him for it?"

"I wish I could say more, but I can't. Maxine, other things are happening at the church. I can't get into it right now, mainly because I don't have all the information yet, but I'm working on it."

"But Claire's funeral is tomorrow. What's going to happen now?" Maxine pressed on.

"I don't know. I honestly don't know right now. I would recommend that you stay put for a while, and when I have more information, I'll contact you, okay? I promise," Ellis assured her.

She regained her footing. "What about Claire's parents?"

"They're being taken care of. Like I said, a lot's happening right now that I can't get into yet. I'm so sorry you had to find out about Mr. Allen this way and maybe even sorrier that Claire's parents learned of it like that too. Please sit tight. I will call you when I know more."

"Yes, of course. Thank you, Detective." Maxine ended the call and walked back to the kitchen. Ethan remained at the table. He appeared to swallow down his emotions when she captured his gaze.

"What did she say?" he asked.

"Not much." Her voice was barely above a whisper and as she sat next to him at the table, her chin quivered. It was time Ethan knew what she and the detective suspected. Their two best friends were dead, murdered; this was no coincidence. "Look, I have to tell you something."

He eyed her with apparent hesitation. "Okay."

"Things have been going on at the church outside of what happened to Claire and now Scott," Maxine began. "But I can't ignore the possibility it's all connected in some way. It must be. I haven't said anything because, well, I'd left it up to the detective to figure out if it's something or not. I was afraid to believe it could be real."

He turned up his palms and furrowed his brow. "What are you saying, Max?"

"I'm saying Vanessa thought she saw things happening with the other kids at the church. She doesn't want to go back, and we shouldn't take her. In fact, I heard they're shutting it all down for the time being."

His jaw clenched, and with a hardened gaze, he peered at Maxine. "Why? Has someone hurt our daughter?"

Her entire body trembled as she fought to voice the unthinkable. "Someone, maybe Pastor Zeke, might have been exploiting the kids. But as far as I can tell, Vanessa hasn't been harmed. And now Scott's dead." Tears spilled again from her eyes. "Could it have been Zeke? Could he have killed Claire because she knew the truth? Maybe Scott did too?"

"He would've said something. I know he would've." Ethan gazed through the breakfast window and drew back his shoulders, appearing stoic. "I don't know what's happening, but I do know my best friend is gone."

Maxine reached for his hand to offer comfort. "I'm so sorry. I should've said something sooner. I didn't want to believe it. I didn't want to think our friends were dead because of it. But, my God…" She shook her head in disbelief. "And this is still all speculation. Regardless, I don't believe for one minute our daughter would fabricate a story like that. It was enough for the detective to insist the church shut down everything until the police can get to the bottom of it. She asked me to stay put and wait for her to figure this out, but I don't think I can do that."

"What can you do, Max? Don't even think about going anywhere. Are you kidding me? No way am I letting you leave this house."

"Detective Ellis says Pastor Zeke may be tied to what happened to Claire and I'm starting to think maybe Scott was too. Pastor Jeff has to know something, right, or at least suspect something? Especially if it involves the kids too. I mean, how could he not?"

"What if he is part of it? You can't go near him. If he's involved, you could be putting yourself in danger. This isn't a joke, you understand? People are dead."

She stood from the table. "Maybe he's just afraid to speak out. He's a kid. I don't believe he's part of it, but he might have some idea, a sense that something's been wrong. He'll tell me the truth. Look, dinner's finished. Can you fix a plate for Vanessa? I can't sit here and do nothing. My best friend was murdered and now her husband has been too. I feel like the world is crashing down around my shoulders and I'm just letting it happen."

"That's all the more reason to do what the detective asked," Ethan insisted.

"Please, I have to do this and I have to look into his eyes to know for sure if he's being honest. I won't let you stop me. Not when this involves the children in our church and, God forbid, our daughter. Can you take care of her while I talk to him?"

He jumped from the chair. "Then let me go with you."

"No. You need to stay with Vanessa. Besides, I can't let Pastor Jeff think he's under attack. He won't say a word then. I have a good relationship with him. I can do this." She grabbed her keys and headed out into the dusky evening.

The church was only minutes from the Rehnquist home, and she had no idea whether Pastor Jeff would be there, but she had to start somewhere. On her arrival, the doors were locked, and she used her key to enter. To her knowledge, no events had been planned for that evening while they prepared for Claire's funeral service scheduled for midday tomorrow, assuming that was still happening. Something Detective Ellis seemed uncertain of at the moment.

She noticed a few cars in the parking lot, but not whether Jeff's was there. Instead, she bolted inside and searched for anyone who could talk to her. But the first thing she spotted was the bathroom. It had been taped off. And as she continued down the hall, Pastor Zeke's office was also taped off and locked. "What is happening?"

It wasn't until she reached the sanctuary that she spotted one of the church elders arranging the stage with flowers and candles. He appeared to notice her and stopped what he was doing.

"Maxine, what are you doing here? We aren't operating at the moment."

"Hello, Owen. I'm looking for Pastor Jeff. Is he here?"

"I don't believe so." He stepped down and made his way toward her. "Maxine, I'm so sorry about Claire. And I've just been informed about Scott as well. I don't think any of this has really sunk in yet, and here I am preparing for Claire's service tomorrow."

"So there is still going to be one?" she asked.

"Yes. I was asked to reach out to Claire's parents, since they're the only people who can now make decisions on behalf of the family. They want this to be over. Pastor Zeke won't be delivering the service. I'll be stepping in. Are you aware of all that's been happening?"

"Some of it. I've been in contact with the detective, but she says she can't tell me everything yet. Where is Pastor Zeke?"

"He's being held at the police station. From what I gather, he'll be charged with..." Gibbons averted his gaze. "I'm sorry, it's so difficult for me to say." He pulled in a breath. "Suspected embezzlement from our church as well as charges related to the cameras they found in the bathrooms."

"I'm sorry, what?"

"Oh, Maxine, I just can't understand any of this. The police were here to search Zeke's office..." Owen's eyes watered.

"Oh no. That was what Detective Ellis couldn't tell me."

He placed his hand on her shoulder. "After tomorrow's service, the church will be closing down for a while until all of this is resolved. I'm not sure we'll recover from this, but if we come together as a community, maybe hope remains."

"Were our children hurt in any of this, Owen?" she pressed on.

He swallowed down the lump in his throat. "Dear Lord, I pray not."

21

E than Rehnquist studied his daughter while she picked at her food. The girl appeared sullen and kept her eyes fixed on the plate in front of her. He sipped on his glass of water and tried to capture her attention. "Hey, Nessa, you love mac and cheese. How come you're not eating it?"

She shrugged and pushed the food around her plate. "When's Mommy coming back?"

"Soon. She just had to run some errands. I'm sure she'll be home to tuck you into bed." He took a mouthful of his own food. "Mommy told me you don't like going to the church to play with the other kids anymore. How come?"

"It's not fun. Mommy said I don't have to go." She turned up her gaze. "Are you going to make me?"

"No, honey. No, of course not. I was just wondering if something happened to make you feel that way. Do you want to tell Daddy?"

She pushed away her plate. "Can I go to my room now? I'm not hungry."

"Nessa, please tell me what's making you unhappy. Daddy

is here for you, honey. And if something happened at church, it's important I know about it," he continued.

Vanessa refused to make eye contact. "I don't want to talk. I don't want to eat. My tummy hurts."

He raised his palms. "Okay. You go lie down for a little while. I'm sure you'll feel better soon."

She pushed off her chair and padded away.

———

WITH SCOTT ALLEN DEAD, Ellis needed to come hard at Townsend. Direct evidence existed that he and Scott Allen worked together to skim money from the church. Townsend was seen at the storage unit, where they kept computer equipment along with a tidy stash of cash, likely belonging to the church. But what she really needed was a direct connection to the cameras. And there remained no conclusion as to what the computer equipment had been used for. Forensics was still working on it. There was someone, however, with the skills to swiftly uncover a link Ellis was sure was there, and that person sat at her desk right now. "Gabby, hey, what are you working on?"

"Sarge put Bryce and me on a string of carjackings. Why, what do you need?" she replied.

Before she answered, from the corner of her eye, Ellis caught sight of McCallister in the corridor and waved him over.

He thrust his hands in his pockets and raised his chin. "What's up?"

"If there's one person with knowledge on how to access apps and websites, it's Gabby." Ellis held up the evidence bag that contained one of the cameras. "So, Gabby, what are the odds you can research the app that operates these cameras, and if so, can you trace them to an account and an IP address?"

Lewis examined them. "You're looking for who's running these things?"

"It's tied to our murder case somehow; we just haven't put together the pieces yet. So, yeah, we need to know who was operating them. Forensics came up empty for prints except for mine."

Lewis held up the bag and eyed the device. "Do you have the manufacturer?"

Ellis pointed to the camera. "This might be the manufacturer here if you can read the lettering."

"It's a start. Let me find this company. That should lead me to their website and app. No doubt the footage is stored in the cloud," Lewis replied.

"We definitely want the footage," McCallister added. "But our goal is to find out who bought these or the account of who ran them."

"Okay. Let me see what I can do, but you might want to give the sarge a heads-up. This will take some time," Lewis told them.

"Yeah, definitely. We owe you, Gabby. Thanks." Ellis headed toward her desk with McCallister beside her.

"There is something we haven't considered," McCallister began.

"What's that?"

"We found cash inside the unit. Most of it probably came from the church. But let's assume Townsend's as smart as he thinks he is. He's not going to keep everything in cash, and some of it could've been used to buy that hardware we found. It would've taken thousands to buy all that equipment. Allen didn't have that kind of money in his personal bank account, nor did we unearth any purchases like that."

"What are you getting at?" Ellis asked.

"Crypto. It's the easiest way to move money without eyes. It's getting harder, but people can still game the system."

"I understand what you're getting at, but I don't want to take our focus off our final target. Another man is out there still. If Gabby can trace those cameras to an account holder, he could be our guy."

"We need Townsend to name him." McCallister stopped at his desk and squared up with her. "Townsend knows we don't have shit on him for murder. But if we can bring other charges, he might be more willing to cooperate."

Ellis checked the time. "Listen, I need to drop in on my dad's place and take him some dinner. You want to tag along? I wouldn't mind some food. We're only going to sit on our thumbs while we wait for Brown to cross-reference the tire tracks found in the alley. And now that we have Gabby working on the cameras, there's not much for us to do for the moment. Just a few minutes, and then we'll head back here. You up for that?"

McCallister smiled. "Sure. I'd love to meet the legend I've heard so much about."

ELLIS OPENED Hank's front door and called out, "Dad? I brought a guest for dinner."

"He doesn't lock his door?" McCallister asked.

"Don't even get me started on that. Come on." She carried bags of fast food toward the living room. The TV was ten notches too loud, and Hank had dozed off in his recliner. "Dad? Hey, Dad? Can you turn that down? I want to introduce you to someone."

Hank roused from his snooze and sat up. "Oh, Becca. You're here." He grabbed the remote and turned down the volume. "Who's your friend?"

"Dad, this is Euan McCallister. We've been working together on the Claire Allen investigation. Euan, this is my dad, Hank."

He extended a hand. "Mr. Ellis, pleasure to meet you."

"Please call me Hank." He returned a firm handshake and turned off the television. "So Becca tells me you hail from Boston."

"Yes, sir. I was a detective there for several years."

"Is that so?" Hank appeared impressed. "Not an easy gig. And if you don't mind my saying, Bangor's a little bit of a step down, don't you think?"

Ellis returned from the kitchen with plates and shot him a glance. "Nice, Dad. I hope you're in the mood for burgers and fries." She set down his plate on the side table next to him.

"Thanks, kiddo."

"Well, sir—Hank, Boston has its own challenges for law enforcement. I guess I got tired of trying to work with one hand tied behind my back. Makes it hard to get things done."

"I'm sure it does." Hank took a bite of his burger.

Ellis sat down next to McCallister. "Grab your plate. So how you feeling, Dad?"

"Fine. Same as always," he replied. "More to the point, how's your investigation going?"

"Well, we've gone from investigating one murder to investigating two. We have the pastor in custody; now we're just piecing it together. I'm hoping we can do that before we're forced to cut him loose."

"So you still don't know who killed that woman?" Hank asked.

"No, not yet. And now we're dealing with a whole other very troubling concern," she replied.

"What's that?"

Ellis reached for her pop and took a drink. "It's a long

story, but I happened across mini cameras installed in the church bathroom."

"What's that now?" he asked.

"We think this could be a child exploitation situation, but we don't have enough yet. We're too busy trying to track down whoever murdered a husband and wife," McCallister answered.

"Good God," Hank said. "Not that I should be surprised. I saw plenty in my day."

"We're leaning on Gabby to look into who was operating the cameras, and any possible websites where the material might've been uploaded," Ellis added.

Hank grunted as he swallowed a handful of fries. "If anyone can figure out that, she can."

After inhaling the rest of her food, Ellis wiped her mouth and wadded the paper wrapper. "I hate to eat and run, Dad, but we should probably get back to the station. I just wanted to bring some dinner and check in on you."

"I am an adult, Becca. You don't have to check in on me," Hank replied.

"Maybe I like to. Did you ever think of that?" She stood from the sofa and reached for Hank's plate before walking with it to the kitchen. On her return, she leaned over the recliner and kissed the top of his head. "I'll let you get back to your TV."

McCallister got to his feet. "It was a pleasure meeting you, Hank. I hope we can do it again soon when we're not in so much of a rush."

"I wouldn't hold my breath for that day. Not when you're partnered up with this one." He thumbed back at Ellis. "Don't let her bulldoze you now, all right? 'Cause she will. She's pigheaded like that."

"You mean like you?" Ellis cut in with a grin.

Hank waited for McCallister to make his way to the door

before he pulled Ellis aside. "I know you're waiting for evidence to break your way, Becca, but what I see you got on your plate right now is much more than what it appears on the surface."

"What do you mean?" she asked.

"I mean, you'd better get to talking to the families at that church. You know, about what you found...Becca, I think it could be the tip of the iceberg. My two cents is one of them kids, if they were hurt, one of them is bound to say something. That may be your best chance at identifying whoever operated those things, and maybe faster than Gabby can work. How do you think those parents are going to feel knowing what you know right now, and Bangor PD didn't come to them first?"

"Dad, I don't know exactly what I'm dealing with. Don't you think the parents, if something happened, would've come forward already? At least to their pastor?"

"Who's currently being held under suspicion of how many different charges?" Hank challenged her. "Go with your gut, Becca. You know what it's telling you."

"Yeah, okay, Dad." She kissed his cheek and hurried outside to catch up with McCallister. "You up for a beer?"

"Always." He stepped into the SUV, and after Ellis climbed behind the wheel, he continued, "That bad, huh?"

"What do you mean?" She pulled out onto the road ahead.

"Your dad must've said something that struck a nerve," he said.

She regarded him a moment. "Maybe. I'd just like to talk through a few things before we head back to the station. Hank thinks we could be focusing our efforts on the wrong problem."

"How so?"

Ellis pulled into a nearby strip mall in front of a dive bar called the Dirty Buffalo. A good a place as any for cheap beer and conversation surrounded by people who didn't give a shit what they talked about. "Let's go inside."

A handful of patrons dotted the place. Two older men played pool on the quarter tables. Ellis eyed a spot near the back. "How about there?"

They slipped into the booth, and a cocktail server approached. "What can I get for you two tonight?"

"Draft IPA, thanks," Ellis replied.

"I'll have a Stella," McCallister added.

"Coming up."

After the server walked away, Ellis continued, "We've been laser-focused on Zeke Townsend and Scott Allen."

"Sure. They stood to lose the most if Claire had learned what they were up to," McCallister said. "We put our eggs in those baskets because of Townsend's history and Allen's access; then the evidence discovered on his laptop sent us in a new direction. Unfortunately, that direction has splintered into other facets. But with Allen dead and a man still out there who's already come after you, we are dealing with something bigger, yeah? The computer equipment we found in storage, Gabby suggested it was something that would be used to handle website traffic, right?"

"Right," she agreed. "And so this money being skimmed off the church could've been used to buy this stuff and run the cameras and probably a website too."

"None of this is a coincidence," he continued. "You don't work on a murder case, uncover an embezzlement scheme, and tie it to the sexual exploitation of minors unless that's exactly what's happening."

The server returned with their drinks. "Can I get you two anything else?"

Ellis regarded the young woman who gave the impression

that she regretted some of her life's choices. "I think we're good. Thanks." She sipped on her beer, then licked the foam from her lips. "So Claire uncovered this scheme and was killed for it. Makes sense, right? But my gut tells me that what Townsend and Allen were up to was about the money. Townsend seemed genuinely shocked when I told him about the cameras."

"And Allen's reaction when we told him what we found on his laptop," McCallister added. "Your dad said it wasn't about the money, but about..."

"The kids." She looked away a moment. "What if we've been hitting at this from the wrong angle? What if they aren't connected?"

ELLIS SLIPPED OFF her shoes and padded in socked feet to her bedroom. This investigation was unlike anything she'd ever worked before, and the dread of the unknown was what haunted her.

She changed into a sweatshirt and plaid pajama bottoms before returning to the kitchen to grab a bottle of beer, her preferred choice of drink. Growing up with a cop for a father, she was certain he'd influenced her in that regard. Although Piper would always bring over a bottle of wine to share when they had their movie nights, which seemed to become less frequent as time went on.

After returning to the sofa, her attention was drawn to her phone as it rang out from the coffee table. She noticed the caller ID. "Hey, Bryce, what's going on?"

"Becca, I didn't wake you, did I?" he asked.

"It's 10:30, so, no, you didn't wake me. Are you at the station?"

"No, I'm outside your house."

"What?" She reared back and ended the call as she stood from the sofa to open the front door.

Pelletier stood on the other side, cloaked in winter gear. "Hi."

Ellis tilted her head. "What are you doing here? Is everything okay? Come in. It's freezing outside."

"You're in your PJs," he said. "I'm sorry."

"Don't be." She closed the door. "Can I get you a beer or something?"

"Yeah, thanks. A beer sounds good." He followed her to the kitchen.

"So what brings you by?" She pulled out a bottle from the fridge and twisted off the top. "Here you go."

"Thanks. I, um, I just wanted to catch up. See how your case was going. Gabby told me you asked her to run on something for you."

"Yeah, I did." Ellis returned to the couch and waited for Pelletier to join her. "This case is turning into something I can't really get my head around."

"Well, if anyone can help, it's Gabby."

She regarded him a moment. "What's going on, Bryce? Are you okay?"

He peered down at his bottle. "I got a call about half an hour ago from a friend of mine. "I-uh, I thought it was best to come see you about it."

Ellis held his gaze. "Okay. Now you're starting to scare me. What is it?"

"Becca." He picked at the beer bottle label. "Your brother was attacked tonight."

She jumped to her feet. "What?"

"He was on the street in the center of town. Got into some kind of skirmish, I don't know exactly, but the cops were called. You know Graham Yearwood?"

"Sure. He's a good cop. Works in the Downtown area. He was the responding officer?"

"He was. Look, Carter's okay. You should know that first. I would've called if he wasn't. The thing is, Becca, he was caught with an eight ball on him."

She closed her eyes. "Oh, God. Coke or meth?"

"Meth."

Ellis paced the room. "A class C felony. Jesus, Bryce, that's five years."

"I know. He's still at the hospital. They're keeping him overnight. Yearwood wanted to call you, but he figured it was best if it came from a friend."

"Does Hank know?" she asked.

Pelletier shook his head. "I thought you'd want to be the one to tell him. They'll probably release Carter from the hospital tomorrow, where he'll go into holding and await arraignment. Becca, I don't think Hank can get him out of this one."

"No, I don't think so, either, and it's going to break his heart."

Her friend set down his half-empty beer bottle and stood up again. "I should go. I'm sorry I had to be the one to tell you this."

"Don't be. I know who my brother is." She stepped toward him. "Thank you. I'm lucky to have you in my life, Bryce. You know that, right?" Ellis wrapped her arms around his neck and pulled in close.

"I'm the lucky one, Becca."

22

Visiting her junky brother in the hospital during one of the most important cases she'd ever worked wasn't how Ellis wanted to start this morning. And to top it off, she was set to attend the funeral of the victim who still awaited justice. But, once again, Carter demanded her attention.

She approached the hospital's administration desk. "Good morning. Can you tell me which room Carter Ellis is in?"

"Are you family?" the nurse asked.

"Yes, he's my brother." She held up her badge. "Rebecca Ellis, Bangor PD."

"Of course. He's in room 208, down the hall and to your left."

"Thank you." She made her way to Carter's room and opened the door. "Carter, it's me. Can I come in?" When no reply came, she walked in anyway. And there he was. Two black eyes, swollen lips, scratches on his neck. "Jesus, Carter, what the hell happened?"

He slowly turned to her with eyes that swollen tissue rendered mere slits, offering no retort.

"That's it? You've got nothing to say? Do you understand what's going to happen to you when they let you out of here?" she asked.

"I don't care," he replied with a gravelly voice. "If you would've let me stay at Dad's and quit giving him a hard time about me, I never would've been out there in the first place."

Her face heated with anger. "This is my fault? You never change, you know that? No matter how hard Dad and I try to help you, you don't change."

"What are you doing here, Becca?" he asked. "I don't need this shit right now."

She examined his scrawny frame outlined beneath the bedcovers. "When the hospital discharges you today, you'll be taken into custody, where you'll spend the next few nights in a cell until you can get in front of a judge. And do you know what will happen after that?"

He returned a sideways glance at her.

"You'll be sent to prison for up to five years. Five years, Carter. Can you even comprehend that?" She moved in. "Do you hear what I'm telling you? You're about to go to prison for a very long time."

"Dad knows people. He won't let that happen."

She heard the catch in his voice. "He can't help you this time. Not with this. Yeah, Dad knows people in this town, he knows judges, but no one will overlook what you've done. Do you understand?"

"Just go away, Becca, okay? I don't need you here and I don't want you here." His tone strengthened even while his body appeared weak. "Everything was always about you when we were growing up. Even when my mom died, somehow it became about you. Poor Becca. She watched her mother die." He shot her a look through wounded eyes.

"Well, boo fucking hoo. I watched my mom die too, all right?"

Ellis regarded him. "No offense, but it's a little different to witness your mother's murder. I loved June, you know that. She treated me like I was her daughter."

"That's right, she did. You were the special one. The one everyone had to protect because of what you did to John. You have any idea what impact that had on me? Then Dad put all his energy into turning you into some miniature version of himself. Where did that leave me, Becca? I was the loser half-brother who turned to drugs. You think I did that because I was happy?" He scoffed. "I doubt you cared."

She stood there a moment longer. "Maybe someday you'll realize not everything is about you."

"Spare me the sanctimony and just get the hell out of here." He recoiled with pain before shouting, "Now!"

"Don't worry I'm outta here. Rot in prison for all I care." Ellis took one last look at her brother before she marched out to her car. It was all she could do to suppress her emotions but the tears came anyway. She slammed the driver's side door as she sank down behind the wheel, hitting her fist against it. "Goddam it!"

Carter had been a thorn in her side for years, but she hadn't wanted this for him. After all was said and done, he was still her brother. It hadn't mattered what she did or what Hank did, Carter went his own way, and it was the wrong way. Now she was going to have to tell Hank that his son was going to prison, and there was nothing he could do about it.

Ellis turned the engine and pulled out of the parking lot. This distraction was the last thing she needed. Townsend remained in holding, but no doubt, his lawyer was working hard to free him on bail. And Claire Allen's funeral was set for a few hours from now. A killer remained on the streets and that killer knew exactly who Ellis was.

She had reached her limit and whether she could break through hinged on results from other people. Control of this investigation was lost. In fact, she'd lost it the moment she broke into the church, and a price was yet to be paid for her transgression. If there was ever a moment she needed her father, it was now. "Guess I'm more like my brother than I thought."

She returned to the station and removed her coat. Dressed in a dark suit and white silk blouse, she looked like a woman in mourning, suitable attire for a funeral.

Officer Angie Morgan sat behind the desk. "Morning, Becca."

"Morning." The look on the officer's face was unmistakable. "Does everyone already know?"

The officer held sympathy in her gaze. "Sorry."

"Don't be." Ellis continued upstairs to the CID and stopped at Lewis's desk. "Good morning. You have any news for me?"

Lewis peered up at her. "Yes and no. I tracked down the company's website based on the manufacturer's name, but I don't have any account details yet on these particular cameras. I'm looking for some kind of identifier that will tie them to an account. These guys sell cameras with wireless connections and they have an app that controls them. I haven't given up, though. It's just going to take some time."

"Thanks, Gabby. Hey, you want me to grab you a coffee or something? I feel like I owe you more than that, but..."

"No, I'm good. You know I got your back." Lewis smiled.

"I know." Ellis continued to her desk, where McCallister had already arrived. "Morning."

"Back at you." He regarded her with concern. "What happened?"

"You haven't heard?" She raised her hands. "Long story,

not worth repeating. It has nothing to do with the case anyway."

"Fair enough. We should head down to Forensics and talk with Brown. See if he's found anything on those servers or, better yet, the tire tracks."

"Yeah, let's go." She started ahead without him.

He jogged to catch up. "I can see you've already had a rough morning, but we'll get through this."

She slowed her steps. "You're right. I'm in a bad headspace. Sorry. I'll explain after we get through this funeral. People at the service are going to ask us questions. They're going to want to know about Claire and now Scott too. They're going to want to know where their pastor is, and we can't tell them anything."

"They'll be on edge for sure," McCallister agreed. "Once word gets out about the cameras..."

"If it hasn't already." Ellis pushed through the glass door into the lab and headed back to Brown's office. As they walked in, she wasn't given the chance to speak; instead, Brown jumped in.

"I think I may have been on the wrong track before," he began.

"How so?" Ellis asked.

"Okay, so you know we found some shady stuff on Scott Allen's computer, right?"

"The uploaded images, yeah," Ellis replied. "That was a wrong track?"

"No, not exactly."

"So the child porn, was it on his computer or not?" McCallister pressed on.

"Yes, like I said, it had been uploaded via a USB drive. But I found nothing indicating anything like that on these servers here. These were not used to run any website, let alone child porn."

Ellis folded her arms. "Okay, let's set that aside for a minute. What *have* you found, then?"

"Transactions," he replied. "Cryptocurrency transactions, to be more precise. And a lot of them."

"Can you elaborate?" McCallister asked. "Was that how they converted whatever cash they stole from the church? Definitely much harder to trace, but that doesn't explain all that equipment in the storage unit."

"No, on its surface, you're right. It doesn't. Moving cash to crypto is the best solution for laundering; however, this equipment is designed for and was used to mine crypto."

"I'm sorry, to mine it?" Ellis asked.

"Yeah, it's a whole thing," Brown replied. "Kind of complicated to explain, but the gist of it is, these heavy-duty computers, or rigs, run programs, if you will. And to jump to the simplest explanation I can offer, the result of the mining programs is that they generate income." Brown looked at them. "Have I lost you already?"

"No, go on," McCallister replied.

"But this equipment is expensive. Very expensive. It takes a ton of power to run each one of these rigs, and they have to be kept cool, like most servers. But they run twenty-four seven and generate a lot of income in the form of cryptocurrency."

"Okay, let me see if I understand this," Ellis began. "Scott Allen and Zeke Townsend were stealing from the church and, what, buying this equipment as a side gig? Why would anyone risk doing that?"

"Because it is very lucrative—and often difficult to trace. The money is earned in crypto coins, and as we all know, that's still a little bit of a wild frontier," Brown replied. "Dodging taxes, skimming cash, well, this makes that a lot easier."

"So that's it?" Ellis asked. "These guys were stealing

money to buy equipment to make more money. That part I understand. What about the USB-uploaded images? Someone put them there. Someone obtained them. You said yourself that you'd found illicit websites that Allen had tried to wipe from his hard drive."

"I did, and there were some. But here's the thing I haven't worked out yet," Brown added. "It's possible someone got hold of his computer and uploaded the images without his knowledge."

"Probably the same guy who killed him," Ellis scoffed. "He knew we were about to find out what he was doing with those cameras. What about the tire tracks?"

"That particular brand and size of tire is stock on about a dozen different vehicles. We're still running them through the database for a match."

"Look for a sedan. Don't bother with anything else, just home in on a full-size sedan," Ellis replied.

"Will do."

McCallister checked the time. "We'd better head over to the church. There's nothing more we can do until Brown puts all this together."

Ellis returned a closed-lip smile. "I know you're only doing what you can do. It's appreciated."

"Hey, we're getting close," Brown assured her.

"I know, thanks." Ellis returned to the corridor while her partner followed. "So who accessed Scott Allen's computer? Why would someone upload those images if Allen was already going to get busted for embezzlement with Townsend?"

"In case we uncovered the cameras would be my guess. It would put our focus on Allen, which it did. And the only reason we know there's another involved is that he came after you."

She stopped on a dime. "Is Hank right? Do we reach out

to all the parents and tell them what we know? Maybe it is the shortest way to get from point A to point B."

McCallister scratched his head. "Talk about Pandora's box. But everyone who attends that church has a right to know we found cameras, regardless of the fact we don't know who operated them or for what purpose. Some of those people were violated, women and children. Maxine's daughter knows something but won't say. Shit, I don't know. Let's go to the funeral and we'll figure out what direction to take."

THE LOCAL NEWS had aired Claire Allen's story and word had spread through the neighboring communities, so it was no surprise to Ellis and McCallister that when they arrived at the church, it spilled over with those who wished to pay their respects.

As the detectives entered, Ellis focused on the rear pews. "Let's hang back here. I don't want to draw attention."

McCallister followed her to the bench and took a seat. "I see Claire's parents up front."

Ellis peered beyond the backs of heads to see. "I can't imagine what they must be going through right now. First Claire and now their son-in-law. Looks like Maxine and her husband are up there too. Doesn't look like Vanessa's with them. They're talking to the DuPonts."

Owen Gibbons approached the altar. "Good afternoon." The church went quiet, and the parishioners listened. A few children muttered, but otherwise, all eyes and ears were on the man at the podium. "I know I have never experienced a more difficult week in my lifetime than I have this week. We have lost two beloved members of our church and it is incomprehensible how our lives will not forever be changed by these horrific events."

Ellis noted that he failed to mention their pastor, who remained in holding. Still, she let her gaze roam, capturing the mood of those in attendance. But it was the children she watched most carefully. Little legs that couldn't touch the ground kicked back and forth. They squirmed in their seats as children did. Her eyes soon landed on Pastor Jeff, who sat near the front in a folding chair. She nudged McCallister and leaned in to whisper, "What kind of drug would make a child feel sick, and if something happened to them, would it also cause a lapse in memory, or are we dealing with a fear issue?"

He regarded her and seemed to notice her eyes fixed on the youth pastor. "We ruled him out already, but he's the only one we know with access to drugs. My sense is that GHB might do it."

"The date-rape drug." Ellis nodded. "Possibly."

"Was it Harwick you saw?"

"The more I look at him." She exhaled through her nose. "Maybe. But he drives a compact car."

"Cars can be borrowed." McCallister glanced around and lowered his tone further. "If we need to take another pass at him, then we will."

The service continued, and Owen Gibbons handed it over to a few people who stepped up to speak of Claire.

Finally, Maxine took her turn. "My best friend is gone." She raised her eyes to look out among the congregation. "Someone took her not only from me, but from this community and her family. I loved Claire. She never failed to help when called upon, sometimes even when she wasn't. Her thoughtful gestures, the giving of her time, these were gestures that touched every one of us in this church right now."

Ellis captured Maxine's gaze a moment, and then she went on.

"I know the police are doing everything in their power to seek out the truth. Our church has been shattered into a million pieces." Her eyes welled. "Mr. and Mrs. DuPont, please know that your daughter was dearly loved, admired, and respected in this community. You only need to look out into this church to see that. And now, she and her beloved husband are together. May that bring you some peace." Maxine stepped off the raised platform and returned to her seat.

Ellis tuned out the remainder of the service. Instead, she considered whether they had dismissed Harwick too soon. He was the first one to return to the scene. He was close to Townsend, making it likely he could've been part of the embezzlement plan. But he'd claimed to not know the Allens well because they had no children. Still, if she looked at him long enough, she would start to see what she wanted to see.

"Becca?" McCallister tapped on her shoulder. "Hey, you with me? It's over."

"Huh? Oh, okay." She reached for her bag and stood up.

It took several minutes for the pews to clear. The mourners wandered the Worship Center lobby like sheep without a shepherd. Ellis and McCallister navigated through the flock and reached the entrance.

Maxine drew near and called out, "Detective Ellis?"

She captured her gaze. "Maxine, Ethan, nice to see you. Your tribute was very moving."

"Thank you. And thank you both for coming," she said.

Ethan offered his hand to Ellis. "The Allens were our best friends, Detective. I hope you find whoever murdered them." He turned to his wife. "I'll be back in a minute, Max. I want to talk to a few of the guys."

"Sure, hon."

Ellis looked beyond Maxine for a moment. "Where's your daughter?"

"She's with her grandmother."

"Of course." Ellis noticed Claire's parents approaching. "Mr. and Mrs. DuPont, it was a lovely service in honor of your daughter."

Mrs. DuPont, an elegant woman in her early sixties, wore a Chanel dress. She reached into her handbag for a tissue and dabbed at her eyes. "Scott arranged the whole thing on his own and now he's dead too. It doesn't feel real. None of this feels real to me."

Her husband wrapped his arm around her and pulled her close, exuding strength while offering comfort to his grieving wife. "Claire's at peace now. That's all we have to cling to." He set a firm gaze on Ellis. "Please, Detective, please tell us you're closer to finding whoever murdered our daughter."

She glanced at McCallister, who shoved his hands in his pockets. "We are continuing to follow leads, Mr. DuPont. It's difficult to say much more than that, though you deserve more."

"I understand. I'm sure you're doing the best you can. We'll be staying in town a while. It's up to us to clear out Claire and Scott's home. There's no one left now but us."

"I'm here to help," Maxine added. "Please know that."

Mrs. DuPont turned to her. "Thank you, honey. You're a true friend. She just adored you."

Maxine smiled, her eyes filling once more with tears. "You know, I think I'll track down Ethan so we can get going. You'll keep us posted?"

"Of course. Please do the same. I know Vanessa is having a hard time, so if she needs to talk to me, I'm here." Ellis returned her gaze to Claire's parents. "I am so sorry for your loss, Mr. and Mrs. DuPont. Rest assured, we are working hard to find the person responsible." She offered a polite nod and followed McCallister toward the exit. "God, I hate this stuff."

MAXINE RETURNED to the Worship Hall, where a few people remained and she approached Owen. "Thank you so much for what you did today. Claire's voice came through you."

"It was the Lord who guided me, Maxine," he replied.

She canvassed the hall. "I don't suppose you've seen my husband? He came back through here and was going to talk with a few of our friends."

Gibbons turned down his mouth. "No, I'm afraid I haven't. He must be outside. The police put up tape around the entrances to the other buildings."

"Of course. I must've just missed him. I'll keep looking." She kissed his cheek. "Thank you again, Owen." Maxine returned to the lobby, where she spotted the double doors that led to the church offices. They were locked with a chain. She made her way outside and zipped up her coat, meandering through the grounds. Cars exited the lot and only a few people were left, though she spotted the detectives at their car. Still no sign of Ethan. "Come on, hon. Where are you? It's freezing out here."

She surveyed the area one more time and finally picked up her phone. "Guess I'll have to call you." With her phone at her ear, the line rang through. Maxine shuffled in place to keep warm and the call went to voicemail. "Seriously?" She keyed a quick message to ask that he meet her in the parking lot.

Maxine rubbed her arms and continued to canvass the grounds when her eyes landed near the basketball courts. A figure appeared. "What in the world?" She started that way and quickly recognized her husband. "Ethan? What are you doing over here? I've been trying to reach you."

"Sorry. I went for a walk."

"Why didn't you answer my call?"

As he neared, he retrieved his phone. "Oh, my ringer must be off. I see your text, though. I'm sorry, babe. Let's get out of here. It's freezing."

AFTER THE PARKING lot had virtually cleared out, Ellis pressed the remote to unlock her SUV and soon spotted an older gentleman approaching.

"Excuse me, you the detectives in charge of Mrs. Allen's investigation?" he asked.

Ellis turned to him. "Yes, we are. Have we met before?"

"No, ma'am. I figured you two were cops by the way you look. No offense. Name's Bill Neelan. I live just over there." He pointed across the street. "I heard all the commotion that night last week and came to see what was what."

"You saw the fire?" Ellis asked.

"Yes, I did. It was a beautiful thing had it not been so awful and terrifying. Course, at the time, none of us knew someone was inside the car. Not that we could've done nothing about it, mind you."

"No, sir," Ellis replied. "What can we do for you, Mr. Neelan?"

"Well, I saw all the cars and figured it was the young woman's service and all, and I got to thinking I should probably come tell you folks about something I saw that night."

Anticipation arose in her chest. "What'd you see, Mr. Neelan?"

"Well, I hadn't figured it was important at the time. Came out... hell, all of us on this street came out after the explosion.

And as I came out, well, there was this car speeding on down the road. Fast, you know? Much too fast for this street. And, like I said, didn't think much of it at the time. In fact, it wasn't until yesterday I was talking to my neighbor, she lives right there." He turned and pointed back again. "Well, she said I ought to say something 'cause it might be important to your investigation. I shooed her away and told her it wouldn't matter to you folks, but, you know, I had second thoughts."

Ellis glanced at McCallister. "Mr. Neelan, what did you see?"

"This car, like I said was speeding like crazy. Looked to come out from the parking lot over there, near the church's basketball courts. It was too dark to see the plates or anything, but I do remember the kind of car it was."

"We're listening," McCallister replied. "Go on."

"It was a Chrysler 300, black or dark in color. Newer-looking model, of course. Fast as can be. Yep. I saw him come out right from over there. Damn near run me over." He pointed toward the back lot of the church. "Spun out his tires a little on the ice, I figured. Then just zoomed on by as I was walking into the street." He tugged on his wool hat. "Don't know if it'll help you folks, but figured it can't hurt, right?"

Ellis returned a closed-lip smile. "No, sir, Mr. Neelan. Can't hurt at all."

23

THE NIGHT OF

Claire waited until the Tuesday evening service was finished before she arrived at the church. She sat inside her Lexus SUV, playing out every possible scenario as to how she would handle this. Her chest heaved and her lips quivered with the unimaginable comprehension of what had occurred inside those walls. But she couldn't jump to conclusions. It was time to see for herself if what she suspected was, in fact, true.

Her gaze turned toward the youth building, where lights still burned through the windows, but she couldn't see who was left inside. The doors at the main entrance were solid wood and any hint of movement in the sanctuary could only be seen through the narrow stained-glass sidelights. A glow emanated. Someone was still there.

Claire had to be ready for whatever she might find. Go straight to the police. Don't talk to anyone because the extent of the crime was unknown, and putting her trust in anyone was a risk she was unwilling to take.

The doors to the youth building opened and Claire hunched down in her seat. Pastor Jeff walked out with a few of the teens who helped run the programs. The three of them waved goodbye and headed toward their cars. Claire had parked away from the streetlamps and in the dark, blustery skies, her black Lexus was virtually invisible. They pulled away, oblivious to her presence.

The time had come to go inside and see for herself. To make sense of his unusual behavior for what seemed like the past several weeks. But...had she been crazy all this time? No, something was off. And after glancing at his phone, unintentionally seeing what she'd seen, Claire had better be damn sure she was right about this. This would change everything for the entire community.

She stepped out of her car and hurried to the main entrance. Claire had keys to the building, but the doors were still unlocked, so she walked inside. The idea was to avoid being seen and while it would've been better to arrive later, that would mean she would have to make up something to tell Scott, and she never could lie to him.

Claire slipped into the corridor and made her way to the back of the building. At the far end, near the exit to the outside courts, lay a room that had once housed students. Years ago, the church had been used as a school. That part of the building needed repairs but the church hadn't enough money, so it remained closed off. Claire had been in that room before. Two years ago, the church elders planned to renovate, but the plans fell through thanks to city ordinances and bringing the building up to code. So it sat decaying with each passing day.

She arrived, unseen, and stood in front of the door. The lock no longer worked. Claire wrapped her hand around the handle, trembling with fear of what lay inside, though she already knew.

Pastor Zeke noticed the time. He should've left 30 minutes ago after the service but had been mired in requests from the church's accounting firm regarding discrepancies. He couldn't risk forging signatures and erasing written receipts from the collection box during the day. Too many people demanded his attention. His partner, Scott Allen, needed the next day to process the cash and create new paper trails.

Now, however, he'd finished the task and prepared to leave. He slung his carrier bag over his shoulder and walked into the hall toward the front exit. It appeared that no one else had been inside, except that he was sure he saw some movement in the hall that led to the youth building. Never mind. It was best to slip out unnoticed, but it was too late for that now.

"Pastor Zeke, what are you still doing here?" The wide-eyed young woman dressed in black skinny jeans and a long sweater approached him.

"Hailey? What are *you* still doing here?"

"Just finishing up in the youth center. I came over to see if I needed to do anything else before I left."

"I can't think of anything," he replied.

"Okay. I'll see you on Sunday, Pastor." She turned and walked away.

Townsend's expression hardened as he continued toward the exit and pushed outside to a blast of arctic air that took away his breath. He hurried to his car parked near the front when a glint of light captured his attention. He gazed out into the parking lot and noticed an SUV. "Claire?" What was she doing here? She hadn't been at the service. In fact, if he recalled, she'd been distant lately. If he hadn't known any better, he would've suspected she knew of his partnership with her husband. A potential problem to be quickly nipped in the bud.

Townsend unlocked his car and slipped behind the wheel. He turned the engine and drove away.

———

THE MUSTY ODOR, the thick dust, old desks piled against the wall. It all looked like Claire remembered, until she made her way to the back corner, where a door led to a storage room. Her knees weakened and her throat dried as she turned the handle. No one ever came in here anymore and certainly not back here into a room that was practically obscured by old furnishings.

As Claire stood here in this room now, this was what she'd seen on that phone. A mattress on the floor and a drop cloth that hung behind it. "What in God's name?" She recognized the poster on the wall, too. It was of the Tree of Life. This was it. This was the place. It was time to tell the cops.

Claire darted out of the room and hurried into the hall. The lights were off now except for the emergency signs above. She glanced over her shoulder, feeling like the devil chased her.

———

TODAY

THE SUN WARMED the surface of the roads and turned the top layer of snow to slush. Salt kicked up under Ellis's Tahoe as she drove back to the stationhouse. Late afternoon arrived and so had a viable lead that could quickly bring this case to a head. She approached Lewis's desk. "Tell me you have something good for us, Gabby."

"That depends on your definition of 'good,' but I think I have something you can use." Lewis typed on her keyboard. "The church is assigned an IP address, which would reveal the location of anything connected to it. I searched the logs of that address and ruled out any connections that would be considered normal usage by the church and its network. What I found, eventually, was software connected to the church's network, but it used a hidden identifier. In other words, I couldn't determine its origin."

"But you found something?" McCallister asked.

"Yes. A VPN that was utilized by this software."

"That's a virtual private network, right? It hides your location," Ellis said.

"Exactly. It makes it difficult, or impossible, as some would say, to obtain the user's IP address, so they wouldn't know who you were or what you were doing online. Whoever connected to the church's network used a VPN for that very reason."

"And you don't know who that VPN belonged to," McCallister added.

"Not yet. But now that I know it's outside the network, I have something to work with. I can now go to the ISP, the church's internet service provider, and ask them to view the actual IP address of the VPN. It sounds a little complicated, but it's really not. People who use VPNs think they're free to roam the internet for whatever nefarious reasons they want, but that's not the case. And especially if someone is using a free VPN service. Those services generally sell your information to marketing companies, much like all the Big Tech guys do. So that's my next step," Lewis continued. "I'll contact the church's service provider and work with them to uncover the real IP address of this VPN. It'll give us the location of whoever is operating the account for those cameras."

"Who and where. This is exactly what we needed," Ellis replied. "How long do you think this will take?"

"I can urge the ISP to put a rush on it. Doesn't mean they will, but it's all I can do. I'd like to say a day or two, maybe less if we're lucky."

"We do have a run on something else," Ellis began. "A witness has just told us they saw a car leaving the church after the explosion. Gave us a make and model, so we're going to look into that. Should help us narrow down the database search for the tire tracks." She turned to McCallister. "Let's jump on that while Gabby works her magic. I have a contact at BMV who can help us out with anyone who has a registered Chrysler 300 in Bangor."

Maxine unlocked her front door as the afternoon sun dipped below the tree line. She walked inside to find Vanessa in the living room, watching television. "Hi, sweetheart, where's Daddy?"

"In his office," she replied without a look back.

"Are you okay? Did you have a good day with Grandma?" Maxine squatted beside her.

"Yeah. And when we got home, Daddy said I could watch cartoons."

Maxine stood again. "So that's what you've been doing since you got home? Great. I'll go say 'hi' to Daddy, then." She started into the hall and made her way to Ethan's office, which was just a den with a small desk inside. "Hi, I'm back."

He glanced up at her from his desk and closed the lid of his laptop. "Hey. How did it go at the house?"

"Strange. It was weird being in there again, especially knowing both of them are gone. But Claire's parents took a few boxes with them. They're hiring a moving truck next week to clear out the rest."

"That must've been so hard for them." Ethan stood from the desk and walked toward her. "Hard for you too, huh?"

"It was." She walked into his open arms and, with her head against his chest, gently sobbed. "I miss her so much. I can't believe all of this has happened. In our community? It doesn't make any sense."

He wrapped his arms around her. "I know it doesn't. It's hard to know what goes on in people's lives. I mean, yes, she was your best friend, but you never really know what's happening with them."

She pulled back and held his gaze. "I thought I did. I thought we told each other everything. But she became more and more distant and I still don't know why."

"I'm sorry, honey. Maybe you should try to take a nap. It's been a long and stressful day for you," Ethan said. "I can look after Vanessa and make sure she gets her bath."

Maxine set her hands on her hips. "She says she's been watching TV since you brought her back from Mom's house. You can't just leave her be. She's only withdrawing into herself. What have you been doing? I didn't think you had any work today."

"Just a few things to take care of. I guess I lost track of time," he replied. "Vanessa's fine, anyway."

"I don't think she is, Ethan. Don't you see the change in her? And with what Owen said...those cameras they found."

He turned straight-faced. "What?"

"I didn't want to freak you out because last night Owen said the police don't know anything yet. I asked the detective about it after the service, after you left to get Vanessa. Apparently, they were found in the bathroom stalls. I mean, my God. What kind of sick person...and then, the kids..." She wiped away a tear. "That's why the police made the church shut down everything. That was what Detective Ellis couldn't tell me. Ethan, what we talked about...what Vanessa said about her friends..."

"You said you'd talked to Pastor Jeff. Did he tell you this?"

"No, he wasn't at the church. I talked to Owen, and I saw the police tape everywhere," Maxine replied.

"Have the police talked to the parents about any of this?" Ethan appeared incensed and thrust his hands into his pockets. "You'd think this was something the parents should be made aware of...Jesus!"

She pressed her hand against his chest to calm him. "I don't know the whole story. The detective asked me to give her time, said that she was close to figuring it all out. I said I would. I still don't think Vanessa was hurt, but the time's come to ask her, point blank. Our friends at the church don't know about any of this, and many of them have kids...but we know. We can get to the truth, if Vanessa knows anything more and isn't terrified to speak. Give me a little time to figure that out. I'll take a bath, clear my head, and try to figure out how to talk to our daughter. You'll be okay on your own for a while longer?"

"I'll manage." Ethan kissed her lips. "Go. Take care of yourself for once. We'll sit down with Nessa and figure this out as a family."

Maxine wore a reluctant smile as she walked out of his office. She returned upstairs to her bedroom and dropped onto her bed. The world spun out of control around her. She should've been there for Claire. Rumors had swirled at church about Ann and Scott. She had wanted to talk to Claire about it, but the delicate subject seemed taboo. Turned out, Maxine hadn't been a very good friend to Claire, and she would have to live with that. The rest of it? Whatever was going on with her daughter, the kids, all of that. Well, it seemed like just the beginning of that nightmare.

Maxine pushed off the bed and walked into the bathroom. Their large soaking tub lay beneath a window that revealed the harsh reality of winter. Cold and bleak. It seemed to surround her every move, encompass every aspect of her life.

The story of Claire remained so muddled, it was hard to wrap her head around it. What was happening in her community? Trust was gone. Love was gone. Only death and pain remained in an unforgiving season.

Maxine turned on the water and filled the tub. She perched on its edge and scrolled through her phone, going back to the messages and voicemails Claire had left in the days leading up to her murder. She'd handed over all of this to the police, and it hadn't helped. Much of it made little sense to her. Claire had been concerned, no doubt, but hadn't so much as hinted at the source of her anxiety.

Maxine dipped her hand into the water and adjusted the temperature. She placed her phone to her ear and listened to Claire's final voicemail.

"God, how I wish I would've answered." But she hadn't. The call had come late. Late for Maxine, who'd just put down Vanessa and then packed a bag in preparation for the work trip. That was the night before Claire was murdered, and those were the last words she'd heard Claire say.

24

Sergeant Abbott arrived in the bullpen and Ellis grew concerned. It was late in the day, past time to clock out. And the man never came out of his office unless it was to call on someone directly. That happened, and whoever it was prepared for an ass-chewing.

Abbott set his hands on his rounded hips. "Doesn't anyone in here have a life?"

"No, sir." Bevins displayed his bright-white smile. "Bangor PD is our lives."

"Feel free to pull your head out of my ass any time, son." Abbott slapped him on the shoulder. "I'm giving you shit. I appreciate what all of you do, which is why I need to have a chat with those two over there." He pointed to Ellis and McCallister. "Feel like coming to my office for a quick word?"

"Sure thing." Ellis pushed up from her desk.

McCallister joined her, and as they walked through the bullpen, scattered whispers sounded about who was going to be on the receiving end this time. Mostly it was in jest, but then again...

Ellis stepped into Abbott's office, where Lieutenant Serrano waited. "Lieutenant."

"Becca, Euan, come in and close the door."

The detectives took a seat across from Abbott's desk while he returned to his chair.

"Everything okay, Sarge?" she asked.

Abbott and Serrano eyed one another before Serrano began. "Calls have been coming into the station about the Grace Community Church and their pastor, who we all know is sitting in our jail cell right now."

"He's about to be charged with embezzlement, sir," McCallister replied. "And we're working on more charges."

"They aren't just concerned about him. This case was about Claire Allen's murder," Abbott cut in. "Where are you with that? Last I checked, you're no closer to finding her killer than you are to figuring out who murdered her husband."

"We got a new lead from a witness who says he saw a vehicle tear out of the parking lot on the night of the fire," Ellis stated. "We're working with a contact at BMV to pull the registration of that make and model for Bangor and the rest of the state. And we've given the details to Brown's team to cross-reference against the tire tracks we picked up in the alley at the back of the Allen home."

"And when do you expect to have that?" Serrano asked.

"Soon. By tomorrow morning, I'd say," she added. "Gabby's working on uncovering whoever was operating the cameras we found in the church. As you know, the entire facility has been shut down until we learn more about that. The funeral service was the only thing on their schedule."

Serrano pushed off the corner of Abbott's desk. "I'm just having a real hard time figuring out how a murder investigation has turned into embezzlement, child exploitation. Look, I'm getting calls from everyone on this. Leaders in the community. The other church elders. The media. I have to give these people something, Becca. Come on. If your dad had been on this case, it'd be solved by now."

McCallister shot her a look while she remained stone-faced.

"Damn it, Becca, I didn't mean that," Serrano said. "I'm sorry. First of all, that's not true, and those words never should've left my goddam mouth. I'm just saying, this thing has blown up in our faces and we need answers."

"I know we do, sir," Ellis replied. "And this has been a challenging case from the beginning, but we're close. I promise you. I won't lie and say there aren't a lot of moving parts here." She glanced at McCallister. "We need another day, maybe two. Lieutenant, there is a chance we're dealing with unrelated crimes."

"How do you mean?" he asked.

"We're certain that Scott Allen and Zeke Townsend were working together to steal money from the church. We have strong evidence in the church's records. The lab was able to figure out what that computer equipment was being used for in Allen's storage unit. Point being, that part of it seems resolved."

"What remains," McCallister cut in, "is how these cameras fit into this situation, or if they fit into it, and more importantly, who murdered the Allens. We know there's a third party in this deal. He's the lynchpin, and when we get the details on the car, it'll lead us right to him."

Abbott sighed. "Listen here, bring me something by tomorrow. You say you got BMV helping. Gabby helping. Someone's gotta come through, all right? I have to feed something to the vultures. There's no two ways about it, you got that?"

"Yes, sir," Ellis said.

"Then go. Both of you get home and get some sleep. Things aren't going to happen tonight anyway. Might as well sleep on this, and who knows, maybe you'll have some sort of epiphany," Abbott continued.

Ellis stood. "Yes, sir."

"Becca, hold back a minute, would you," Serrano called out.

She looked at McCallister and nodded for him to leave before turning back. "Yes, sir?"

He approached her. "You know if Hank ever heard me say something like that to him, he would've socked me in the jaw."

Ellis grinned. "I doubt that, sir."

"I don't. Look, despite my sharp tongue, you know you're one of the best detectives I've had the pleasure to have under my charge. You do rival your dad's skills; there's no doubt about that. So I am very sorry for what I said." He paused a moment. "But I also wanted to mention about Carter. I know he's going to be spending some time here until his arraignment and then get transferred to County. You talk to Hank about this yet?"

"No, sir. It's not a conversation I'm looking forward to having," she replied.

"I bet not. Let me do it. Let me talk to Hank and we'll figure out something to try to fix this."

"I appreciate that, Lieutenant, but nobody can fix this. Carter's going to have to suffer the consequences and I know that sounds terrible coming from his own sister, but Hank and you and everyone else at this station, you can't keep bailing him out of trouble. If it keeps happening, he'll wind up dead."

Serrano lowered his gaze a moment. "I'm not sure I can sit back while Hank suffers through that much pain, Becca. I've known your dad a long time. I've seen him in too much pain as it is. Do me this favor, let me tell him at least."

Ellis shrugged. "Okay, if that's what you want. I'd better

get going." She returned to her desk and noticed McCallister's eyes following her.

"You okay?" he asked.

"Fine. I don't think I'm ready to call it a day yet. And after the lieutenant talks to Hank, I don't think I want to be around after that." She glanced out at the team. "Who's up for a beer?"

ELLIS PULLED off her heavy coat as they walked inside their usual bar on the Waterfront. "Hey, Austin, how's it going?"

"Becca, good to see you." He eyed her partner a moment. "McCallister, right?"

"That's me. Nice to see you, Austin. I wouldn't mind a Blue Moon when you get a chance, and whatever she wants."

"I'll take a Sam Adams, thanks." She walked inside and found a high-top table. A moment later, she spotted Pelletier walking in. "Hey, you made it."

"Figured I could use a beer." He thumbed back. "Brought some friends with me."

Bevins, Fletcher, and Lewis trailed him.

"The gang's all here. Thanks for coming down, guys." Ellis patted the seat beside her. "Come join us."

McCallister sat next to her while the others made their way to the table. "Gabby, I can't thank you enough for the work you're doing on this case for us. It's a huge help."

"Anytime. That's the thing about our department. We all work together and pitch in when we're needed. It'll come back around, trust me on that," she replied.

"How are your boys? Still growing like weeds?" Ellis asked.

"Of course. Eli's over six feet now, if you can believe that. Kid's only fifteen. Martin isn't far behind either."

"I have no doubt he'll catch up to his older brother soon," Ellis joked. "Hey, so I heard someone tried to take Duck the other day. Any of you guys around when that happened?"

"I was," Pelletier said. "Some high school kid came in and tried to snag him, but he didn't get very far. One of the guys downstairs said they put the fear of God into him and he promised he'd never do it again."

McCallister creased his brow. "I'm sorry, did you say Duck?"

"Yeah, the Duck of Justice." Ellis eyed him. "You know, the stuffed duck in the station museum. Come on, you've seen it. You can't miss it."

"Oh, right. Yeah, I guess I have seen it. I just didn't think much of it. What the hell is the Duck of Justice anyway?"

"Oh, now, hang on," Fletch cut in. "You've been here, what, a month, and no one's told you about Duck?"

"Sounds like I'm missing out." McCallister grinned.

"So a while back, hell, I don't even remember when it was," Pelletier began. "But a stuffed duck, like you know, a taxidermy thing, well, it was found in the dumpster near the station. Someone fished it out, cleaned it up, rescued the damn thing, and now it sits on display in the station's museum. It's our official mascot, the Duck of Justice."

McCallister chuckled and took a drink. "I knew I'd like working here."

"I see you both still have your asses attached," Bevins observed. "I figured Serrano would've chewed 'em up and spit 'em out."

"He's getting pressure from above," Ellis replied. "That church had a good-sized congregation. They're losing money every day it's shut down. They don't like it, even if it means we're cleaning up their mess. Their pastor is sitting in one of our cells. That's not going over well. So, yeah, Abbott and

Serrano are taking heat for this. I don't blame them for wanting answers."

McCallister glanced at her a moment as if prepared to say something, but he turned away.

Pelletier appeared to pick up on the exchange and eyed Ellis. "You're doing your job. That's all you can do. That's why top brass gets paid the big bucks. They keep everyone off our backs so we can do what needs to be done."

"That's how it's supposed to work," Fletch replied. "Doesn't always. I'm not saying Serrano isn't a great boss, but when he feels the pressure, he makes sure we know it."

"Someday, that'll be your job, Fletch," Bevins added. "And we all know it."

"That day won't come for a long time. Serrano isn't going anywhere, which means neither is Abbott. But that's fine. I'll bide my time." She laughed. "Besides, I can't leave you guys. You need me too much."

"Uh-huh, so says the girl with the tape measure ready to order drapes for the lieutenant's office." Lewis patted her on the back. "We love you, Fletch."

"Sure. Yeah."

Ellis hadn't realized how much she needed to get outside her head for a little while. And these guys were just about the only ones who could help her do that. Piper, too, but in a very different way. "So, listen, I know we're all swamped right now, but I thought we should do something for Abbott next week."

"Why?" Bevins asked.

"Because it's his twentieth anniversary with the department." Fletch peered at him with a furrowed brow. "The man deserves at least a damn cake for being here that long. I have a friend who's a baker. I'll ask her to whip up something nice for him. Maybe by that time, things will be a little less 'hair on fire.'"

"I doubt it, but we'll make it work." Lewis checked the

time. "Listen, I should bounce. Can't leave my teenage sons alone for long. They'll stay on their video games and homework will go right out the window." She retrieved her wallet.

"No, I got this, Gabby," Ellis said. "You're saving our asses right now. It's the least I can do."

"Well, thank you. And I'll know more tomorrow. This will start to come together, Becca. It will." She stepped away. "Night, everyone."

Ellis tipped back her bottle and finished off the last of the beer. "I should probably get going too."

"Already?" Pelletier asked. "Come on, stay for one more."

"I wish I could, but I'm exhausted. I need to clear my head and get ready for whatever tomorrow brings. And I'm sure I'll hear from Hank tonight and that'll take up a fair amount of energy."

He looked away. "Right. I forgot about that."

"Forgot about what?" Bevins asked.

"Nothing. Just family stuff," Ellis replied. "Hey, thanks, everyone, for joining me for a drink. It's nice to know I can lean on you guys."

McCallister pulled on his coat. "I'll walk you to your car. I should check out too."

"Sure, if you're ready. You realize that I carry a gun, right? Don't feel like you have to walk me out."

"I didn't say you needed protection. I'm saying I'm a puss and I should get some rest too. So you want to walk out together, or should I wait for you to leave?"

"In that case, we can walk out together." She turned back to the others. "Thanks, guys. See you tomorrow."

Pelletier swirled his beer and kept his gaze trained ahead. "Night."

She walked outside and turned to McCallister. "Thanks for joining us tonight. It's good for you to get to know the guys better. Aside from some quirks, they're all good people. And I'm probably the quirkiest among them."

McCallister pulled on his hat. "Somehow, I doubt that's true. I got my eye on Bevins. I have no doubt that kid has a few kinks to work out."

"You might be right, but he's a good guy overall. He'll have your back." She reached her car. "So I guess we should have some answers tomorrow, huh?"

"God, I hope so. And hey, about what Serrano said..."

She raised her hands. "He didn't mean it and he apologized. Trust me when I say he's not that kind of boss. He's been a friend of Hank's for years and sometimes I think he sees me as Hank, you know? But don't worry about it. I'm fine. I can handle criticism."

"Okay, fair enough."

Ellis unlocked her door. "Don't see any tracks around the car. That's a good sign. Hey, see you tomorrow?"

"See you tomorrow."

She felt his gaze linger in a way she recognized. Ellis was no stranger to that look from men. But the last thing on her mind was Euan McCallister and whatever complication that would bring. She had fought hard to come out of Hank's shadow, and her fight still wasn't complete, as evidenced by Serrano's outburst. So for her to tangle with a colleague wasn't an option that was on the table. Not to mention, it was never a good idea to cross that line.

IT WAS ONLY a matter of time before Hank called. Ellis walked inside her house and dropped her keys in the bowl on the entry table. The brief outing with her coworkers had helped to clear her head. But what lay before her was a tidal wave of uncertainty, pain, and confusion for her family. Carter had never been to prison. He'd always gotten off with a rehab sentence or been placed under Hank's care, but this time was going to be different, and it weighed on her.

She looked at the time and rolled her eyes. "It's only nine o'clock?" It felt like midnight. She retreated to her bedroom to change clothes and secure her service weapon. She tried not to let Serrano's words get to her, but it was hard not to. He was a good boss and rarely said such rash things to her, so it had come as a surprise. Nevertheless, she would have to put on her big-girl pants and deal with it. Being Hank Ellis's daughter was a double-edged sword. His stellar reputation left others expecting the same from her. And while she did her damnedest to live up to that expectation, she wasn't Hank.

Ellis curled up on the sofa and switched on the TV. Her thoughts turned to Claire Allen and the events revolving around the case. She still couldn't see how all of it tied together. Brass was right to question their progress. Still, she held out hope the owner of the car would be ID'd and Gabby would track down the cameras' account holder by tomorrow. They were close, and she needed to remember that.

As the TV broadcast another mind-numbing reality show, Ellis slowly pulled up to the edge of the couch. Her brow knitted and her mind spun as she glanced up. "Holy shit." She grabbed her phone and pressed her partner's number. "Hey, it's Becca."

"Yeah, what's up? Everything all right? Did you make it home?"

"Yeah, I'm here now. I was just thinking." She paused a moment to be certain this wasn't a mistake. "The car that sped out of the church parking lot that night. I think I've seen it."

McCallister remained silent for a moment. "Okay, but I

wouldn't call that particularly unusual. It's a common car, isn't it? Do you remember where and when?"

"Hell yes, I remember. After drinks at the bar and at my house. It's the same car I saw drive away from the church with our hooded man inside. As I sat here thinking about that goddam car, I remembered the taillights. My God, it was there at the Allen house the morning we drove him back from the ME's office." Ellis waited a moment. "Euan, are you still there?"

"Jesus, you're right."

She got to her feet. "He's our man. The hooded man. It's Ethan Rehnquist."

25

While Maxine and Vanessa slept upstairs, Ethan stared at his laptop screen. He'd convinced his wife to hold off speaking to their daughter until the cops knew more. It was his only play until he figured out his next move. One that would have to come sooner rather than later now that the detectives had found the cameras. He should've taken care of Detective Ellis that night in the church. But she'd had the gun and her unexpected arrival had forced him to retreat before finishing the job of removing the evidence. Still, he'd covered his online tracks well and to pin the cameras on him would prove difficult, at best.

Now, as he hunched over on the sofa in the dimly lit living room, he viewed the images. They carried him to a dark place, where a history he'd kept buried climbed to the surface.

"Come here, boy."

Ethan's old man leaned back in his recliner and reached out for him. He still stank from his job at the fish cannery.

"I said come here."

Inside the living room of their shitty two-bedroom house,

Ethan stood still on the dingy gray carpet stained with food and booze and God knew what else. Ethan was almost ten and he hated it when his pop called him "boy."

"I have homework." He turned his back.

"Don't you dare walk out of this room, boy. Now, you better do as I say." He pointed a finger at the fishing rod that lay in the corner. It was the thin part of the rod, no reel. "You know what'll happen if you leave, right?"

"Yes, sir." Ethan shook away the tangled mop of curly blond hair from his eyes as they welled.

"Don't you cry either, you fucking pussy. Now get your ass over here. Don't make me get up."

Ethan swallowed down the lump in his throat and wiped his eyes with the back of his hand. Just get it over with. He'll get drunk and leave you alone, *he thought. He stepped closer.*

"Take off your shirt now, boy. And your pants too. Come on now, you know the deal."

A MILD THUD reverberated in Maxine's ears and awakened her. She'd been a light sleeper since Vanessa was born, an inherent trait among many mothers. The scant moonlight shone around her drawn bedroom shades, leaving the room cast in a somber hue. She pressed the screen on her phone to check the time. It showed 1:15 am.

Her gaze shifted to where Ethan slept, but he wasn't there. Maxine assumed the noise came from him. He must've gone downstairs for a drink of water. But as she turned to her bedroom door, light seeped in from below. She grew more alert and sat up in bed.

A robe hung on the back of her bedroom door, and she slipped it on before stepping into the hall. The light came from downstairs. Maxine padded toward Vanessa's room, where the door was cracked open. The slight hum of a sleeping child sounded, and Maxine carried on to the stairs.

WHEN ETHAN PULLED his thoughts back to the present, his right hand stung where a scratch had opened. "Damn it," he whispered. He recalled the moment it happened. Scott had fought back, but not hard enough. Ethan walked into the kitchen to wipe the fresh blood from the wound.

As he pressed a paper towel against his skin, Scott's face flashed before him, as though he stood right there in his kitchen. He hadn't wanted to kill his best friend, but planting the evidence hadn't worked and the cops wouldn't stop looking. He had no choice.

Scott opened the back gate as he stood on the other side.

"Holy shit, man. You came. I wasn't sure you would after I got pissed at Maxine and thought she knew something about Claire. Look, we don't have much time. We have to go now."

Ethan reached into his coat pocket. "Is there anything left inside for them to find?"

"Like what? They took my computer. That's how I ended up in this fucking mess. They think I killed Claire and was downloading kiddie porn or some shit. I don't know, but it's bad, Ethan."

"I know, brother." Ethan pulled out a pocketknife and flicked it open. "I know you didn't kill your wife...because I did."

Scott eyed the knife and stumbled back. "What the hell? What are you doing, man?"

Ethan had about 20 pounds and a couple inches on his friend. He grabbed Scott and spun him around, shoving him to the ground. He kneed him in the back and yanked on his arm, slicing open his wrist. With his free hand, he slammed it over Scott's mouth before he could scream. "Just relax, man. Fucking relax." He struggled to keep Scott down but managed to grab his other wrist.

"It's gotta be this way, all right?" He sliced it open and, with his knees, straddled Scott to control his arms. "I'm so sorry, man. I'm sorry. We just gotta stay here a minute, yeah? Just till you calm the fuck down and I can get you back inside."

The alley was empty, but his car would stand out like a sore thumb. He didn't have much time. "I gotta let you bleed out for a minute. It's the only way I'll be able to take you inside without a fight."

The fight was already leaving Scott as he wept. Under Ethan's hand, his voice was muffled. "Why?"

"I'm sorry, brother. She found out." Ethan got to his feet and pulled back on Scott's arms to get him to stand. "All right. Let's get you inside." He turned Scott around and pulled him close. Blood already covered his jeans. With one hand wrapped around Scott's mouth, the other held back his arms. "Just stay quiet, okay? I don't want to have to stab you in the chest and let you bleed out right here in your backyard."

He led Scott inside through the kitchen door. "I always liked Claire. I didn't want things to go down this way. I'll admit I was careless, but she saw shit that was none of her business and we both knew it."

Scott's face turned pale.

"I'm gonna put you down over here." He set him down on a kitchen chair. "This is getting messy. Goddam, I wish there was another way."

"What did you do?" Scott's voice was barely above a whisper now. "The porn?"

"I had to let the cops find it on your computer. It was the only way to keep them off me and I knew they would start looking at you and Zeke. You shouldn't have told me what you two were doing with the church's money. And when you called to tell me they found the porn, I knew it was time to clear out. Problem was, I didn't expect that cop to be there. I've been freaking out looking for a way through this, then you called and I guess I knew what I had to do."

He sat down on the chair next to Scott. "You gonna keep quiet, or do I have to finish the job?"

Scott lowered his gaze while his breath grew labored.

"I tried to prepare for the worst, but I didn't want to hurt you. Just like I didn't want to hurt Claire."

"Vanessa?"

He looked away. "It had nothing to do with her. Easy money, man. That's it. You wouldn't believe what people pay for a few pictures of kids. I was going to stop. I was. But you know, I saw you with all that money. Stealing from our own, and I thought, what the fuck, right? You got away with it, why can't I?"

Scott closed his eyes. "They'll find you."

"I don't think so, man, not with all the shit they got on you. You and Zeke. They'll think you did this out of guilt." He reached into his coat pocket and retrieved a cell phone. "Cops have been looking for it. It's Claire's." He wiped off his prints with his shirt and set it down. "When they find it here, they'll be convinced it was you who killed her." He stood again. "I'm out of time." Ethan wiped his prints from the knife and laid it on the table. "I am sorry, Scott. Shit got out of control too fast. I will tell you this, don't scream for those cops out there. I know Claire's parents are coming for the funeral. You do anything to draw those cops' attention and I swear to God, I'll kill them, too."

IN A HOME that had been built more than 30 years ago, Maxine had wanted to replace the carpet on the stairs with solid wood treads. Ethan hadn't wanted to spend the money. Now, those ugly carpeted stairs were whisper-quiet as she descended. The dim gray light seemed to emanate from the living room. Still no sign of Ethan as she reached the bottom step and turned right.

He wasn't in the living room, but the TV was on with no sound, and his laptop lay open on the coffee table. Maxine glanced to her left, toward the kitchen. She saw a light that appeared to come from the refrigerator; he must be there. She walked to his laptop and looked at the screen.

As she cleared her sleepy eyes, it took her a moment to understand what she was seeing. But when the recognition hit, she clutched at her stomach as it turned sour. Her hand clamped down over her mouth. It was the storage room inside the old church classroom. She recognized the carpet, the poster. And the child. Oh, God, it was Abby and she was...

"What are you doing?"

Maxine whipped around to see Ethan standing between the kitchen and living room, holding a bottle of water. "What the hell is this?" She pointed to the screen. The look on his face was like nothing she'd ever seen before. It was robotic with underlying anger deep in his gaze. "My God, Ethan. You're the one. The cameras in the church bathrooms, was that you, too? Why? How could you do this? We have a child."

"What the hell are you talking about? Come on, Max. It's me."

A chill crawled up her spine. She swallowed hard and wrapped her arms around herself. "Don't lie to me, Ethan. That's Abby. I'm looking at Maggie and Blake's daughter." Her voice faltered and tears welled. "What did you do to her?"

"I've never harmed Vanessa. This isn't what you think it is."

Unexpected nervous laughter erupted from her as tears spilled down her cheeks. Her mind spun with horrific thoughts about the children at the church. About Claire and Scott Allen. "I don't understand how you could do this. Did you kill our best friends?"

He stepped toward her.

"Don't." She pushed down her fear and thrust out her hand. "Don't come near me. You're a monster." Movement on the stairs captured her gaze as Vanessa appeared on the landing.

Ethan glanced at his daughter. "Calm down, Max, and nothing will happen to Vanessa. I promise you."

"Mommy?" the girl called out.

"Go back to your room, baby." Maxine wiped away her tears and waited until she heard the click of her child's door. "Claire found out, didn't she? That's what she wanted to tell me, but she was afraid. She wanted to tell me she knew what you were doing at the church."

Ethan moved in again. "I'm not going to hurt you, Max. I just want you to let me explain, okay?"

"She was going to go to the police, wasn't she?" Maxine pressed on. "You couldn't let her do that, so you killed her."

Vanessa started down the steps again. "Mommy? Isn't everyone supposed to be asleep?"

"Go to bed now, Vanessa," Maxine pleaded. "Go on, honey. Go back to sleep."

"It's okay, baby; come on downstairs," Ethan cut in. "Come see Daddy."

"No," Maxine shouted.

"Mommy?" Vanessa looked at her with narrowed, sleepy eyes. "What's wrong?"

REINFORCEMENTS HAD BEEN CALLED in and Ellis checked her weapon. Inside the Special Ops room, the team awaited instructions. Sergeant Abbott stood at the head of the conference table. "Detective Ellis, this is your op, you want to tell these guys your plan?"

She moved to the front wall, where a screen broadcast a map with the Rehnquist home at its center. "McCallister and I have confirmed that the vehicle seen leaving the church moments before the car fire belongs to Ethan and Maxine Rehnquist. And Forensics just confirmed the tires that are stock on that model match the tracks found in the alley of our victims' home." She pointed to the map. "This is their house here, and I expect them to be there now, along with their five-year-old daughter, Vanessa. I don't know what Maxine is aware of at this point, maybe nothing, so this is going to send her into a panic. We need to take caution to protect both the child and mother because once Ethan realizes what's happening, there's no way to know how he'll react. We're awaiting confirmation that the cameras belonged to him. But because of this man's connection to the victims, and thanks to a witness, we're moving to arrest him now." She eyed McCallister, who stood at attention near the back wall. "Detective McCallister and I will take point, going in at the front. Teams of two will flank us and we'll have another team covering the back exit of the house. It's the middle of the night and neighbors will be curious if they hear, so be prepared for bystanders. My hope is that Ethan Rehnquist will go quietly, but he might not see a way out except to take down himself, along with anyone else in his sights."

"Okay, you all have your orders," Abbott began. "You leave in five."

Ellis headed toward McCallister. "I wish there was a way to warn Maxine, but if I call her and Ethan gets wind of it, that could set him off, and I just don't know what he'll do. I don't know if she knows. There's too much uncertainty and it scares the shit out of me." She eyed the map again. "He's the only one who was close enough to Scott Allen to access his computer and load the images. Why? I don't know."

"Claire must have grown suspicious," McCallister offered. "He might've picked up on that and created an exit strategy."

"No doubt. We saw that son of a bitch at Scott Allen's house the morning we brought him back from the ME's office. As a close friend, he probably had a key. Probably went inside and did what he needed to do before Allen returned. He killed his best friend's wife because of what she either knew or suspected, then laid the groundwork to frame his friend for it."

"But why kill him, then?" he asked.

Ellis glanced away a moment. "Because I found the cameras. That had to have been the catalyst. I saw him and he knew that it would only be a matter of time before we had the evidence to prove the cameras belonged to him. I don't know why he would've bothered with those drive-bys. It wasn't like they were going to scare me off. Thing is, he tried to make Scott Allen's death look like a suicide. The husband kills himself, fraught with guilt over murdering his wife, case closed. Guess he didn't think we'd follow the trail he left behind. What I want to know is what he was doing with the camera footage."

"Uploading it for sale would be my first pick," McCallister replied.

"We're about to find out. You ready?" she asked.

"As I'll ever be."

Ellis turned back to the team. "Let's move." She started toward the bullpen and eyed her phone one more time.

"You expecting something?" McCallister checked his weapon as he followed.

"I was hoping Maxine would call saying she knew what her husband had done and that she and Vanessa had left. But I don't think we're going to get that ending."

"I don't think so either." He placed his hand on her shoulder. "We'll keep them safe."

She made her way outside with McCallister beside her. Three teams of officers stepped into their patrol cars and prepared to head out. "We get our share of crime here. I've busted down doors and arrested people before. But this? I've never done anything like this."

"It's okay to be nervous," he began. "I've seen a lot in Boston. Too much. I guess I thought coming here would be different."

Ellis climbed into her Tahoe and once McCallister got in, she turned the engine. "I guess you can't escape the true nature of humanity no matter where you go."

She peered into her rearview mirror and spotted the backup units rolling along behind her as she reached the neighborhood. It was almost two o'clock in the morning. The sergeant alerted the rest of the detectives, so on their return, Ellis expected they would be there for support. But the officers behind them were trained specialists. The last time they'd been commissioned was during a bank robbery where the perpetrators had taken hostages. That had been Cavanaugh's case. He was the guy before McCallister. And he had been a damn good cop.

Ellis turned onto the quiet street. "This is it." She flipped off the headlights and rolled to a stop at the bottom of the Rehnquist driveway.

The plan was for the other teams to hang back and take the final approach to the home on foot. The last thing Ellis wanted was for Ethan Rehnquist to see a bunch of cop cars out his front window. Being outmanned and outgunned put people in a state of mind that could see them act impulsively. She couldn't risk that with a child in the home.

Ellis unbuckled her seatbelt and opened her door to step out. She pulled on her Kevlar vest and secured her holster. It must've been ten below as the cold seeped through to her skin. She nodded to McCallister, who had also stepped out, and started ahead toward the front door. Light came from the front window. Ellis turned to him. "Someone's awake." She looked back to see the teams approaching. With hand signals, Ellis directed them into position. If Ethan Rehnquist was awake, chances were good he would hear their approach. This would change their tactic and required quick thinking.

McCallister moved in next to her and pulled out his gun. "We need to be ready."

Ellis readied her weapon as they reached the front door. The assumption had to be made that more than one person was awake inside. She knocked and called out, "Ethan Rehnquist, Bangor PD. Open the door." She confirmed with a glance that the other officers were in place and knocked again. "Bangor PD. Open up. Now!"

26

E than lingered between the foyer and the living room. Vanessa was on the steps and Maxine stood near the coffee table where the laptop still lay open. He fixed his gaze on his wife. "Did you call the cops, Max?"

"No, I swear I didn't." She turned to Vanessa again. "Baby, please go upstairs to your room right now."

"No, don't, honey. Come see Daddy."

Confused, the half-asleep girl heard the knock on the door again. "Who's outside?"

"It's just the police checking in on us. There's nothing to be scared of, sweetheart. Now, come see Daddy, okay?"

Vanessa took a step down, and as she did so, Maxine shouted, "No! Vanessa, run upstairs, now!"

ELLIS WHIPPED AROUND TO MCCALLISTER. "Did you hear that?"

"Let's go in." He kicked the front door. "Police, open up. Open the door now!" He kicked it again. When it refused to budge, he shoved his shoulder hard against it and winced in pain. The handle split the frame and the door finally swung open.

Ellis turned to the teams and waved them on. They had to go in with all the firepower they had because after hearing Maxine call out, she didn't know what she'd find inside.

McCallister pushed in and Ellis was right behind him. In the living room, they found Ethan clutching onto Vanessa while Maxine stood several feet away near the sofa. "Ethan Rehnquist, you're under arrest for the murders of Claire and Scott Allen."

Ellis eyed Maxine, whose face wore fear. She turned to Ethan. "Let her go. You don't want to make this worse for yourself. Let your family go."

"I don't know what you're talking about," Ethan replied. "I didn't kill Claire Allen. I didn't kill Scott Allen. They were our friends."

"Step away from the child," McCallister commanded.

Four officers walked in behind them, guns at the ready.

"Whatever you think you can do about this, Ethan, think again," Ellis cut in. "We know about the cameras. We know it was your car that fled the church moments before Claire Allen's car caught fire. Don't make us do this in front of your daughter." Her mind's eye flashed memories of that night when she was 12. John's hands clutching her mother's neck. His knees holding down her mother's arms. Ellis standing behind him, screaming for him to stop. Her hands trembling as she held onto the gun.

Ethan exposed the knife from behind his back and pulled Vanessa closer.

"Oh my God!" Maxine thrust her hand over her mouth. "Ethan, for the love of God, what are you doing?"

Ellis tightened her grip on the weapon. "Put down the knife!"

Ethan's eyes reddened and his chin quivered. He pressed the knife against his daughter's cheek. "You won't do anything. Not as long as I have her."

"Daddy?" the girl cried out. "Daddy, why did you take my friend? Daddy, please don't hurt me too."

Ellis shot a look at Maxine. They both immediately understood.

"Baby, was it Daddy you put in your drawing?" Maxine asked, but her daughter was crying too hard to speak.

"Shut up, Max. I didn't hurt our daughter. Just shut up!" Ethan demanded.

"What do you think you're doing now?" Maxine appeared to struggle for breath as she turned her sights to Ethan. "How could you? How could you hurt children like that?"

"She's wrong." Ethan pulled Vanessa even closer. "Stop crying now, Nessa. I mean it. Stop."

Ellis flipped off her gun's safety. "I'll put you down before you can harm one hair on your daughter's head. Now let her go. Don't make me shoot you in front of her. You've destroyed your life. Don't destroy hers too."

"For God's sake," Maxine pleaded. "Ethan, do what she says."

Ellis picked up on the shift in Ethan's gaze. He was looking for a way out. She glanced at Vanessa as tears poured down the girl's cheek, the knife still pressed against it. The idea that she would see her father gunned down stirred a sickening feeling in Ellis's gut. But she had faced men like this before. Desperate men. He wasn't going to back down. Ethan was a man who knew he lost.

His eyes shifted to the foyer and that was when Ellis knew what to do. She pulled the trigger. The bullet sliced through the air and struck Ethan in the chest. It was the kill shot.

He turned his eyes to her while his lips parted slowly at

the realization of what she'd done. He crumpled to the ground, pulling Vanessa down with him.

The girl screamed and Maxine ran to free her.

"Jesus." Ellis propelled herself toward them. "Are you okay? Vanessa, are you okay?"

The little girl slowly pulled herself up. "Yeah."

McCallister kept his eye on Ethan as he approached Ellis. "Get them out of here."

Ethan barely clung to life as his chest hemorrhaged blood. Ellis walked toward him and eyed the other officers, who remained in the foyer. "Call an ambulance."

One of the officers pressed the button on his radio. "We need an ambulance at 1465 Cherry Tree Lane. Suspect down. I repeat, suspect down."

The officers moved to secure the scene while Ellis and McCallister gently escorted Maxine and her daughter outside.

"I don't understand how...why? We were their friends." She set her gaze on Ellis. "His laptop. I saw a picture. I know who it was, and I know where he took them. It's a room inside the church."

Ellis shot a look at McCallister. "Show us where."

———

OWEN GIBBONS MET the detectives and Maxine Rehnquist at the church entrance. It was three in the morning, and the time had come to learn what Ethan had inflicted on the children of the community.

Ellis placed her hand on Maxine's shoulder. "Thank you for agreeing to do this now, given everything you and your daughter have been through tonight. I know it's not easy."

"There was really no choice, was there? Vanessa will be

okay with my mother for a while. She's always been close to her. The rest, well, I'll figure it out as it comes."

Gibbons unlocked the door. "I just don't understand any of this."

"We need to get inside, sir," Ellis said. "Please."

He opened the door. "Go on in."

She walked in with McCallister trailing, then turned to Maxine. "Please show us the room."

Maxine headed into the hall and started back. "There's an old storage room no one uses anymore. It used to be part of the school the church ran. In the corner of that room is a smaller storage room." She reached the door and turned back with tears in her eyes. "I can't look."

"That's okay, you don't have to. Stay out here. We'll go inside." Ellis nodded to McCallister, and he followed her.

The musty room was dark, and Ellis felt along the wall for a light switch. When she flipped it on, it illuminated a room filled with old desks, furniture, and decorations. "Didn't we sweep this room?"

"We were thorough. I don't know how this was missed."

She continued inside toward the back where Maxine insisted there was a secondary storage room. "I think I know." Ellis moved a small bookcase and chairs that were propped in front of the door. "We didn't see it."

McCallister pushed his hand through his hair. "Shit."

Ellis opened the door to a ten-by-eight room with shelves mounted on a wall. "It's empty. No mattress, no backdrop. No camera." She peered around the room and then aimed her index finger ahead. "There. That poster there. And the carpet Maxine mentioned. Both were shown in that photo of Abby Reynolds." She paused a moment. "This is the place."

"Jesus Christ," he muttered as he lowered his head.

Ellis noticed a bottle on a shelf and aimed her flashlight

at it. "I can't say with certainty what this is. It'll have to be tested. But if it's not GHB, I'd be surprised."

"Relatively easy to get hold of if you know where to look. And it's pretty effective." McCallister approached her and eyed the bottle. "The dropper. He must've shoved it down their throats to knock them out."

"That's why the kids felt sick but couldn't remember anything about what happened," Ellis added.

"Stuff's notorious for that, which is why assholes use it," he said. "They must not have remembered being snatched up either. I don't know how he pulled that off."

"Chalked it up to a bad dream, maybe? My God, he could've killed them with this drug. Too much and that's it. You lose consciousness and you're dead. But how had no one ever seen him?" Ellis asked.

"Maxine had keys to the church. He could've copied them to get access. He would've known when the youth activities were scheduled because Maxine volunteered."

"Which means he knew the security code as well." Ellis eyed a narrow door in the corner. "Where do you suppose this goes?" She unlocked the deadbolt and pushed hard until it opened out to the icy night.

McCallister peered outside. "The basketball courts. That's how he got in and out unseen. I don't know how he got the kids away from everyone else, though."

"The bathrooms," she shot back. "He knew when they were alone in the bathrooms. That was what the cameras were for. They'd go in by themselves; he would drug them, I guess, and then bring them here."

"That's a hell of a risk he took. Anyone could've seen him," McCallister said.

"But the only one who did was his own daughter." Ellis let the door fall shut and turned to survey the room. "We'll sweep for prints, but the best evidence we have are the photos on his laptop. I pray to God we can track down whatever websites he sold them to."

McCallister nodded. "We'll need to interview all the parents and the kids involved to get the bigger picture. But we've stopped it, Becca. Maybe not as soon as we wanted, but it's over."

"And the rest? The embezzlement, the affair." Ellis scoffed. "All we did was stumble on a couple of guys skimming off a church."

"Partner." He placed his hand on her shoulder. "Take the win."

27

The church was locked down. The storage room had been secured, and any potential evidence inside was headed down to the station for analysis. Now, as the sun rose, Ellis and McCallister returned to the station. The rest of the team had received word, and all awaited them in the bullpen.

It wasn't the first time Ellis had killed a suspect, but it was the first time she'd done so in front of the suspect's family, including his five-year-old daughter. She was rattled and worked damn hard to not let anyone else see that.

Pelletier was the first to approach. "I heard you two got 'em. Good work."

"Thanks, man," McCallister replied.

"Appreciate it, Bryce." She would tell him, in due time, all that went down, but that time was not now. She turned to Lewis, who was at her desk. "Thank you for your help on this."

"Hey, you guys did the work. I chipped in, but this is all you."

They returned to their desks, knowing Abbott would call

a briefing soon. Ellis looked at her partner. "Townsend's ready to be arraigned today."

"He's still being charged with embezzlement," McCallister confirmed. "For him and for Allen, this was about the money. Unfortunately, Allen was killed for an entirely different reason. Townsend's going to find out that we got the killer. He'll see that as his chance to make a deal. Tell us where the money is, reduce his sentence. Make sure he isn't connected to either of their murders."

"And I have no doubt the DA will offer him one," Ellis said. "Let's talk to Brown and see if he's wrapped up his end of things." They both headed into the corridor.

Brown had arrived in the early hours of this morning as soon as he was notified of what had happened. He went straight to work on the laptop taken from the Rehnquist home. He eyed the detectives as they entered. "Good morning, or is it still night? I have no idea."

"I think it's morning," Ellis replied. "I know you know why we're here."

He pushed back from his desk. "That I do. Let's start with the laptop belonging to Ethan Rehnquist. You wanted to track down whether any video from it was uploaded and, if so, where."

"Yep." She nodded.

"I've had just a few hours to get into this, but I'll tell you what I know as of this moment." He walked to another workstation and entered commands on the keyboard. "After searching the URL history on his laptop, it allowed me to see which websites had been accessed. Our forensics software carves the data to recover files, deleted histories, that sort of thing. I then searched for 'get' and 'post' strings..."

Ellis held up her hands. "Hang on, you're talking over my head. Can you tell us in plain English what you found?"

"Yeah, sure. Sorry, I get carried away sometimes. Here's

the meat of it. Ethan Rehnquist uploaded photos he'd taken of various children in—various positions. They were uploaded to several dark websites, where most were paid for and downloaded."

"Paid for?" McCallister asked.

"I haven't gotten too far into that yet, but it appears Rehnquist was paid for the images. Most likely in bitcoin or similar."

"This wasn't connected to what Allen and Townsend had going on with the mining, was it?" Ellis asked.

"Unlikely. Money isn't money anymore. It's data. And many people who trade in it do so because they're earning it illegally. Not everyone, but it's too easy right now to launder it. Now, crypto mining isn't illegal. But making money off it and not reporting it, or stealing cash and using it to buy equipment? Yeah, that's where the illegal part comes in."

"Can we be assured that whatever Rehnquist was doing wasn't tied to Townsend?" McCallister asked. "That's what we have to know."

Brown regarded them a moment. "The only way to be sure is through the crypto transactions. I'll be able to access Rehnquist's wallet from his laptop. That wallet will contain his receipts and payments in crypto. However, we'll only know which accounts Townsend held if he tells us. I can't find out that information otherwise."

"If he wants a deal, he'll have to give us that information," Ellis said.

"And if he doesn't, we'll tack on charges relating to Rehnquist," McCallister added. "So he'll cooperate on that front."

"Then you'll have your answer," Brown cut in. "He cooperates, the two likely weren't connected."

"Yeah. Okay. We'll let you get back to work." Ellis started away but stopped and turned back. "There was something else we'll need."

"What's that?" Brown asked.

"Once you find all the websites, recover the images, all of that, we'll need to get with the families. That needs to happen as soon as possible."

"Got it," he replied.

ELLIS STIRRED her cup of coffee while she sat across from McCallister at the café. "I don't think I've ever wanted a coffee more than I do at this very moment."

"We've been awake all night. Figured we could use a shot of caffeine," he replied. "You should probably be in with Abbott and Serrano. They're going to want your report soon."

"I have twenty-four hours to make the weapons discharge statement. I get that. I just need some time to slow the adrenaline."

He knitted his brow. "Yeah, drinking coffee maybe wasn't the best solution, then, huh?"

Ellis returned a wry smile. "Maybe not, but it tastes good." She glanced through the window a moment. "You know, according to Maxine, Ethan was hardly involved in the church at all. He didn't go to Sunday service. He didn't go to any of the social events. It was Maxine's thing, not his. Makes me wonder how he even thought to do what he did."

"I'm not sure we'll ever understand why people do what they do. We just have to do our best to try to stop it."

"A never-ending task," she replied. "I wonder how Claire found out. Maxine said Claire had been acting differently toward her. Hesitant. And that final voice message she left indicated Claire wanted to tell Maxine something important. I didn't pick up on it then, but I sure as hell do now."

His grin was closed lipped. "Yeah, hindsight. Go figure?"

THE BRIEFING with Abbott and Serrano was set to happen in a few minutes, so Ellis was finalizing her reports when McCallister called out to her.

"Hey, look who's here."

Ellis stood when she saw Maxine approach. "Hey. Hi, how are you?"

Maxine's eyes appeared swollen and red, as though not another tear could possibly fall from them. "I've been better, Detective."

"What can we do for you?" Ellis glanced back at her partner. "We're still waiting on Forensics to come through before we can move forward."

"That's not why I'm here," she replied.

"Okay." Ellis pulled out her guest chair. "Would you like to sit down?"

"No, I don't want to take up your time. I know how busy you must be." Maxine reached into her coat pocket and retrieved a set of keys. "I was, uh, going through Ethan's laptop bag and I found these."

Ellis eyed her partner a moment before turning back. "Keys. Okay."

Maxine cleared her throat. "These belong to Claire. They're her car keys."

"Are you sure? Her keys were with her at the time of her death," Ellis said gently.

"Right, of course she would've had them. Then they must be Scott's set." She held up the key fob. "The Lexus emblem. Claire drove a Lexus."

"That was how he accessed her car," McCallister said.

Maxine looked at him. "Yeah. He stole his friend's car keys and then murdered his wife. And that was after he molested the children of his community." Her eyes overflowed with tears once more. "I'm sorry. I thought you should have these."

Ellis took them. "Thank you, Maxine. This helps us a lot, actually."

She nodded. "Good. Then at least I did something to help."

"Would you like me to take you home?"

Maxine held Ellis's gaze. "No. I'm okay to drive. Vanessa and I are staying with my mom for a while if you need anything else from me. I don't want to go back to that house."

"I understand. Listen, we'll keep you posted as we know more."

"Sure." Maxine paused a moment as if to gather herself. "Thank you. Goodbye."

Ellis slumped in her chair as she watched Maxine disappear into the hall. "I can't imagine what she's going through."

"Ellis, McCallister?" Abbott marched toward them and thumbed back. "Was that Mrs. Rehnquist?"

She held up the set of keys. "Yep. She found these in her husband's things, which explains how Ethan got into Claire Allen's car to jam the seatbelt. He would've just crawled under the engine to cut the fuel line."

Abbott gestured with his hand. "Well, there you go. You needed definitive proof and now you have it. Listen, Townsend's attorney wants to talk deals. They're downstairs when you're ready."

"Now?" Ellis asked.

"I might have dropped a message to the lawyer that his client may have had ties to Ethan Rehnquist. Sounds to me like he's eager to disprove that. So talk to them. Find out."

"Yes, sir. We'll do that right now." Ellis waited for Abbott to leave and glanced over at McCallister. "Looks like we're finally about to put this case to bed."

IT TOOK ANOTHER DAY, but Ellis and McCallister got what they needed. Brown recovered the images, as many as he could trace, and the families of the young victims were contacted over the course of the next few days.

It was the hardest thing Ellis had ever done. But Serrano wouldn't let them do it on their own. He and Abbott stood behind their detectives and worked with the church and the families involved. No images were ever found that involved Vanessa Rehnquist, the little girl who had been too terrified to speak out about what she had seen her father do.

The congregation was shattered. The church closed its doors, and Ezekiel Townsend was getting a deal to serve a year behind bars and two years' probation for embezzling more than $50,000 from the Grace Community Church. He turned over his crypto accounts, none of which were tied to Ethan Rehnquist.

The team met up at their favorite bar for a few drinks. Ellis bought the first round and raised her glass. "Thank you all for the work you did to help us through this case. Euan and I couldn't have done it without your support. Cheers."

"Cheers," they replied in unison.

Relief at finally bringing justice to Claire Allen over-whelmed her. Hank would say it was all part of the job, but this case was different. She turned to McCallister. "Thanks, Euan. I'm glad you were my partner on this one."

"Ah, you see, I grew on you, didn't I?" He threw back his shot of whiskey. "I always do."

She smiled. "If you mean like a bad rash, then sure."

He returned a puzzled frown. "I still don't get why they all think you're funny."

Another drink and a few more laughs to help bury the true horrors of this investigation and Ellis prepared to head home. Her phone rang while she reached for her coat. "Lieutenant, what can I do for you?" She pressed a finger against her ear to muffle the surrounding chatter. Only McCallister and Pelletier appeared to take notice of her call. "Yeah, okay. Thank you for letting me know. No, I'll tell him if that's okay with you. Thank you, sir. Goodnight." She ended the call and stared at her phone.

"What did Serrano want?" Pelletier asked.

She slowly turned to him with a look of disappointment. "Turns out, he pulled some strings, and the judge is only going to give my brother six months, with the likelihood that he'll be out in four."

"That's a good thing, isn't it?" McCallister asked.

"By anyone else's standards, yes," she began. "But because of Hank, people have helped Carter get out of more trouble than I can recall. He'll never have to face the consequences of his actions. Not fully. So, it's a good thing, I guess, for my dad. He'll be happy he still has some pull, but as far as I'm concerned, Carter skating by on this is only going to do him more harm than good."

Pelletier regarded her. "Sorry, Becca. I know how hard it's been for you dealing with this, but the guy needs help, not prison."

She shrugged and pulled on her coat. "If we hadn't gone down that route many times already, I'd agree with you, Bryce. Nothing I can do, I guess. Hey, I'm going to head out, guys. I'll see you tomorrow." Ellis started toward the door.

McCallister set down his beer and jogged to catch up to her. "Hang on."

She turned to him as she reached the exit. "Yeah?"

He took a deep breath and captured her gaze with his. "I just wanted to say that I admire you, Becca. Everything you've overcome to be here today. You're a hell of a good detective. Don't let anyone tell you any different."

She raised the corners of her lips into a smile. "Don't worry, I haven't yet."

"Good. You're okay to drive?"

"Of course I am. See you tomorrow, Euan." She pushed out the door.

"See you." He returned to the group as Pelletier eyed him. "Hey, Bryce, you good?"

"Yep." He threw back the rest of his drink. "All good here."

Ellis drove out of the parking lot and pressed Hank's contact. "Hey, Dad. We still on for Sunday brunch this weekend?"

"You know it, kid. You hear about Carter?" he asked.

"I did. Guess he got lucky again, huh?"

"I know what you're thinking. But the kid deserves a second chance, Becca."

She closed her eyes. "Okay, Dad. Listen, I'm heading home after a drink with the guys. Just thought I'd check in. You need anything? I can run by if you want."

"No, I'm good. I'll see you in a few days, kiddo. Drive safe."

"Goodnight, Dad." She ended the call and continued her drive home, when her phone rang again. Ellis smiled when she spotted the caller ID and answered. "Well, well, if it isn't my long-lost pal, Piper."

"Hey there, lady. Whatchya up to?"

"Heading home. It's been a long week. What are you doing? Sounds like you're already having some fun, huh?"

"I'm at Bar None Downtown. Thought you might like to join me. It's only 9:30. You aren't going to bed, are you?"

Ellis laughed. "No, but I was planning on a quiet night at home." Another call came in. "Hey, I got another call. How about we meet for dinner tomorrow night and we'll catch up?"

"You sure? I need a wingman," Piper said.

"You? I don't think so. I'll call you tomorrow. Stay safe." She ended the call and answered the other. "Hey, Euan, what's up? Did I forget something at the bar?"

"No, I just thought you might like some company on your drive home."

"What about the guys? Did everyone leave already?" she asked.

"No. I just stepped away for a minute. They hardly noticed. So, you want to talk?"

"About what?" Ellis flicked on her turn signal to merge onto the highway.

"Doesn't matter."

A tender smile drew up on her lips. "Sure, why not? I got ten minutes to kill."

THE END

WE HOPE YOU ENJOYED THIS BOOK

If you could spend a moment to write an honest review on Amazon, no matter how short, we would be extremely grateful. They really do help readers discover new authors.

ABOUT THE AUTHOR

Robin Mahle has published more than 30 crime fiction novels, many, of which, topped the Amazon charts in the US, Canada, and the UK. Also a screenwriter, she has adapted some of her works into teleplays, which have gone on to place in film festivals nationwide. From detectives to federal agents, and from killers to corruption, her page-turning tales grab hold and refuse to let go. Throw in tense action and thrilling twists, and it becomes clear why her readers come back for more. Robin lives in Coastal Virginia with her husband and two children.

www.robinmahle.com

ALSO BY ROBIN MAHLE

Detective Rebecca Ellis Series

No Safe Place

A Frozen Grave

Made in the USA
Monee, IL
28 April 2023

32635421R00189